THE NIGHT DRUMMER

THE NIGHT DRUMMER

A Novel

PAUL NICHOLAS MASON

N O N

CANADA

*Publisher's note: This book is a work of fiction. Names, characters, places and
incidents are either the product of the author's imagination or are used
fictitiously, and any resemblance to actual persons living or dead
is entirely coincidental.*

Library and Archives Canada Cataloguing in Publication

Mason, Paul Nicholas, author
The night drummer / Paul Nicholas Mason.

ISBN 978–1–926942–76–6 (pbk.)

I. Title.

PS8576.A85955N54 2015   C813'.54   C2014–908029–8

Printed and bound in Canada on 100% recycled paper.

Now Or Never Publishing
#313, 1255 Seymour Street
Vancouver, British Columbia
Canada V6B 0H1

nonpublishing.com
Fighting Words.

We acknowledge the support of the Canada Council for the Arts
and the British Columbia Arts Council for our publishing program.

To Muriel and Michael
with Love and Gratitude

Prologue

It's nearly two in the morning, and I'm flat on my back staring at the far wall of the bedroom, my wife Claire soundlessly asleep beside me. It's high summer, mid-July, but the weather is unseasonably cool and we've turned off the air-conditioning and opened the windows, letting in a gentle breeze. Tomorrow, Saturday, we'll be packing the car for a two-day visit to Queensville, the town where I grew up. My old high school is holding a twenty-five year reunion for my graduating class and Claire is coming with me—to make sure I don't get too close to any old girlfriends, she says, but I don't think she's particularly worried. I reach out and gently touch her shoulder as she sleeps.

Earlier in the evening we'd seen a number of cars lined up on the street about a block away, and we'd guessed that one of our neighbours must be having a party. It seems to be breaking up now, and as the host's front door opens I hear music from a powerful sound system. Normally this would anger me—I've become a bit of a middle-aged grump—but the music isn't acid rock or rap, but rather a solo drum, and the rhythm is, if anything, pleasing, at least at this distance. Indeed, the drum lends a certain resonance, a percussive support, to a particularly powerful high school memory.

Here it is.

CHAPTER ONE: GREASE AND MALEVOLENCE

The teacher had just asked that we write her a letter introducing ourselves when the door opened and a male teenager stepped into the classroom. He stood about five foot seven, wore jeans and a plaid shirt, and had shoulder-length black hair. He was thin, but he held himself erect: my mother would say that he had excellent posture. His skin was darker than anyone else's in the room.

"What is your name?" asked Mrs. Evans. Her tone was welcoming, even if the question was a little abrupt.

"I'm Otis," said the boy. "Otis James. The vice-principal said I should come here. I'm sorry I'm late."

"That's fine, Otis," said Mrs. Evans. "You can sit next to Peter. Do you have a pen?"

"No, ma'am," said Otis, taking the seat across the aisle from me.

"I have a spare," I said, and dug it out of my pencil case.

"Thanks," he said and, meeting my eyes, he nodded.

A lazy, insolent voice from the back: "Hey, Tonto. What you doin' off the reservation?"

*

What can I tell you about my high school? The main building—and it was all one building—was large and spread out. The central section, the academic block, went up three storeys, but the wings only went up two: one wing was made up of workshops, and the other of gyms. There were very few trees: the property had once been a farmer's field, and at this point, in the early 1970s, the Board of Education had planted only five small, scraggly evergreens across the front lawn. If you were a visitor you ascended a short flight of long, wide steps to the school's front door, and passed through it en route to the office. But the vast majority of students were bused in, and our buses went around the school to the back parking lot. We disembarked, all 1500 of us, then passed through the large smoking area on our way to our lockers and classrooms.

The school sat on the outskirts of Queensville, a town forty-five minutes northeast of Peterborough, Ontario. Queensville then had a population of about 38,000, and QDSS was the largest of three public high schools. (There was also a Catholic secondary school.) The town was mostly blue-collar, though there was a small stratum of university graduates: professors at the local community college, doctors at the hospital, senior managers at the three factories (furniture, sports equipment and plastics) and, I guess, teachers at the schools. And there was the odd dentist and lawyer and psychologist and chiropractor, too. But if there was something that almost everyone in Queensville had in common, it was the colour of our skin: we were pretty well all white. There may have been a handful of black families and a few Chinese, but Otis was the first native Canadian I had seen in my fourteen years on earth. There were no reservations within an hour's travel of Queensville.

My dad taught communications courses at the college; my mom was a receptionist at a real estate office. We lived in a three-bedroom bungalow in an outer suburb—if a town of less than 40,000 can be said to have real suburbs. My parents had lived there since before my younger brother, Conrad, and I had been born. Our mother had stayed at home with us until Conrad was eight, then done some secretarial training at a business school. When I met Otis, then, I'd lived all my short life in Queensville, with only the odd trip to Peterborough, Kingston and, once, Toronto. I was a small town boy if ever there was one.

In a small town, friends are important: when there's not much in the way of community pools, or arenas, or tennis courts, or soccer fields you have to make your own fun. I wasn't a serious athlete anyway, so I wouldn't have had first call on any of the facilities that were available, and in grade nine my friends and I got together in each other's basements to play cards or darts or just talk. No one I knew had a pool table. In my circles we weren't yet into drinking or smoking dope, which probably made us a bit unusual. Who were my friends? There was Andy, a big, chunky, good-natured fellow who took vocational courses—woodworking, automotive and shop—at QDSS; there was Bruce, a bespectacled electronics whiz who'd built himself an amazing light and sound show in his basement bedroom; there was John, a mild-mannered, kind boy whose father was a Baptist minister. There were a few others, too, but I won't inundate you with names just now. And, sure, there were girls as well, but in grade nine they hadn't become friends in any active sense. We had hopes, all of us, that that might change in grade ten. I'd been skipped a year, back in grade four, so my friends were all about a year older than I was. In those days we didn't socialize much outside our own grade.

Was Queensville District Secondary School typical of small-town Canadian high schools? I honestly don't know. It was a fairly volatile place: people used to tell stories about the old days when such-and-such a teacher would take a strap to kids he didn't like, and when students genuinely feared punishment at the hands of school authorities. That had all but disappeared by the time my friends and I slouched into those halls. The principal was a small, white-haired man who had difficulty getting attention at our rare school assemblies; our teachers spent much of their time and energy trying to keep their classes under control; and the smoking area was a place the staff never visited. I'm exaggerating a little—but not much. There were a few teachers who commanded respect and taught us some important things, but many of them seemed either disinterested or cynical or outright scared.

So who ran the school? If our teachers struggled to maintain order in the classrooms, a slurry of thugs held sway over unsupervised areas. There were places at QDSS—certain halls, the washrooms in the technical wing, the junior boys' changing room and the smoking area—where it just wasn't safe to go alone. Every grade from grade nine up (the school went through grade thirteen in those days) had its hard core of tough kids skilled at menacing those who were weaker than they were. The situation was complicated by the fact that some of these youngsters remained at school even after they'd failed a grade or two, and despite, in some cases, criminal convictions for vandalism or assault. In the fall of grade ten my friends and I knew there were about twenty young men in the school we didn't want to cross. In our own grade, in our own classes, there were three in particular: Ted Staunton, Bill House, and Jake O'Leary.

★

"Hey, Tonto. What you doin' off the reservation?" It was Ted Staunton: two hundred pounds of grease and malevolence.

"Don't speak out of turn, Ted," said Mrs. Evans. She was one of those who did her best. She tried.

Staunton ignored her. "I'm talkin' to you, Tonto," he said, his tone harder.

Otis turned around and looked directly at Staunton. "It's nice to meet you, guy," he said. And his confidence, his refusal to kowtow, meant that he had made an appointment, whether he knew it or not.

Chapter Two: In a Zoo

But I suspect he did know it. Otis was bright: his intelligence wasn't academic, but it was real all the same. He was street-wise without being street-mannered. But I knew nothing of this at the time. At the end of Mrs. Evans's class, only the second English lesson of the fall term, I scanned the room; then, seeing that Staunton had left, asked Otis if he knew anyone at the school yet.

"Not yet," he said. "I only just moved here."

"Where did you move from?"

"From Toronto. My dad wanted to retire somewhere quiet." I must have looked puzzled. "I'm adopted," he added. "My parents are older."

"Oh," I said. And then, as casually as I knew how: "Would you like to meet some people at lunch?"

"Sure," said Otis. "I'd like that." And the two of us went first to his locker, and then to mine, to dump our books and grab our lunches. We both had brought a bagged lunch, though I also had a little money for a small carton of milk from the cafeteria kitchen.

There were no formal divisions in the cafeteria—no tables set aside for certain grades—but there was a very clear understanding about who would sit where. The boys from the vocational stream generally sat in a particular corner, close to the exit; the kids from the academic stream were scattered around the room, though you'd find very little mixing of grades: grade nines would be at certain tables, grade tens at others, and so right through grade twelve. The grade thirteens had a little common room off from the cafeteria, and they generally took their bagged lunches and trays there. There was a small section where kids interested in the arts would usually congregate, and another where courting couples tended to sit. A newcomer might make a mistake on his first day, but he would swiftly pick up on the signals from other kids. Subtlety wasn't a virtue at QDSS.

Big Andy had already established a beachhead when we arrived. He and I had sat together at lunch right through grade nine in spite of the fact that he was in the vocational stream and I in the academic. We'd been friends in public school, thrown together initially because neither of us fit comfortably into other groups, but forming a bond over a shared fondness for a board game called Risk. We'd long since ceased to play, but our friendship had endured, largely, I think, because he was so wonderfully good-natured.

"Otis, this is Big Andy," I said.

"Hi," said Big Andy, munching on a huge sandwich. "I've never met someone called Otis before."

"Hi," said Otis, smiling. "And I've never met a Big Andy before."

"Haw," said Big Andy, laughing. "When they made me, the mold was broke!"

Bruce, the bespectacled electronics whiz, joined us a couple of minutes later, swiftly followed by John, who was shaking his head as he sat down.

"There's a fight in the smoking area," he said.

"First one this year," I said to Otis.

"Second," said John. "There was one at recess, too."

"Who was in it?" asked Bruce.

"I don't know. I didn't stay to look. They were surrounded." John opened a thermos of coffee. "Hi," he said, looking up at Otis. "I'm John."

"John's dad's a preacher," said Big Andy.

"But I'm not," said John, and he extended his hand to Otis, who shook it without apparent surprise. It was an unexpectedly adult gesture, and I made a little mental note that it felt right. I often did that in those days—saw things I liked or didn't like, and tucked the impression away. It pleased me somehow that John and Otis seemed suddenly so much more grown up than I would have expected. So in those few moments Otis met the boys who were, at that time, my closest friends, and he was welcomed without question. Whatever flaws we had, and there were undoubtedly many, we were mostly accepting creatures.

But that wasn't the case in the rest of the school. Otis had attracted some attention as soon as he came into the cafeteria, and we became aware that he was under discussion at a number of tables. Some kids craned their heads around to look at him, while others bent their heads together to talk, occasionally staring in our direction.

"Ignore them," said John. "They've never seen an Indian before."

"I guess not," said Otis. "I feel like I'm in a zoo."

"Have you ever been to powwows?" asked Big Andy, his own curiosity getting the better of him.

Otis laughed. "Sure," he said. "But not many, and not for a long while. My parents are white." He might have expanded on that, as he had with me, but just at that moment two older boys approached the table. I didn't know them by name, but I certainly knew them by sight. They were trouble.

"Hey, Blackfoot," said one of them.

"I'm not Blackfoot," said Otis, calmly. "I'm Ojibwa."

"I don't give a fuck what you think you are," said the boy. "Staunton wants to talk with you."

"Who is Staunton?" asked Otis.

"Come and find out," said the boy.

"I'm right here," said Otis. "Tell him he's welcome to join me."

"Don't be an asshole," said the other boy. "He's up beside the football field, waiting." My heart sank. This was serious, and serious more quickly than I would have anticipated.

Otis considered this. "Tell him I don't have time right now, but I'll see him after school," he said.

"You'd better come right now," said the first boy. His name came to me suddenly: Ricky. Ricky Feldon. One stint in juvie behind him already.

"Yeah, I don't think I will," said Otis. "Tell him to have a sandwich or something. I'll see him after school."

"He's gonna break your fuckin' arm," said Ricky.

"That'll be fun," said Otis evenly.

The two messenger-thugs looked at him for a moment or two, then one of them drew a finger theatrically across his throat. They both turned and left.

There was a silence. "Holy shit," said Bruce. And then, admiringly: "You told them."

"Is Staunton the guy who called me *Tonto*?" asked Otis, turning to me.

"Yeah," I said. "I'm sorry this is happening."

"Don't worry about it," said Otis. "But will you come with me?"

"Yes," I said, and in that instant our friendship was sealed.

★

We were understandably distracted for the rest of lunch, but I did learn a little more about Otis. He was a year older than I was—fifteen to my fourteen—and he wasn't much interested in football (the only sport that really mattered at QDSS). "I did gymnastics at my old school," he told Big Andy, and this struck all of us as fairly exotic. He also let on that he liked music, but said no more about that at the time. Bruce took out a pack of cards, and we played a few hands of euchre, Otis looking at my hand and watching the game unfold. That's what we mostly did at lunch: we played cards. Lots of kids did. It was either that or smoke in the smoking area (which we didn't do), or hang out in the seminar rooms in the library.

Otis eventually took out his academic schedule, and it turned out that he and John had the same class after lunch. "Do you know where the main foyer is?" asked John. "I'll meet you there in five minutes and we'll go up together."

"Thanks, man," said Otis. And then to me: "See you after school?"

"I'll come by your locker," I said.

"I'll come, too," said Big Andy a bit unexpectedly; he hated conflict. "What's your locker number?"

"648," said Otis.

"We'll all be there," said Bruce, speaking for himself and John.

John nodded. "I'll bring donuts," he said wryly.

Otis gave a half smile and left, carting his garbage with him. There was a brief silence among the four of us. "He's gonna get creamed," said Bruce.

"I don't know," I said. "He could be tough."

"Staunton's got fifty pounds on him."

"Some of it's fat," I said.

"Nothin' wrong with fat," said Big Andy.

"Whose side are you on?" I asked.

"I'm on Otis's side," Big Andy said. "I'm just tryin' to be realistic."

"Well," I said, "we can only hope."

"And pray," said John, the preacher's son. And he may have been serious.

Chapter Three: Nice Talking

The five of us met at Otis's locker shortly after the final bell. I was the last to arrive; the prospect of violence always made my stomach upset, and I'd gone by way of a safe washroom next to the history office. Even though we'd said nothing out loud, Big Andy, Bruce, John and I recognized that we were taking a risk in escorting Otis to meet Staunton. Mind you, the die was probably cast the moment I invited him to join us for lunch.

"Have you ever been in a fight?" Big Andy asked Otis.

"This is just a talk, isn't it?" said Otis. It took us a moment to realize he was kidding—that he knew what he was up against.

"Yeah, I've been in fights," said Otis. He didn't elaborate.

We moved down the hall towards the smoking area in silence. More than a few students looked our way, then whispered among themselves: word of a fight spread quickly at QDSS. I was a little surprised at how few people were in the smoking area—the place was usually packed—but the reason became clear when we crossed the parking lot and made our way to the far side of the football field: there was already a crowd of about two hundred there, waiting. Most of them were in grades nine, ten and eleven, but there were a few older kids as well. Boys were in the majority, but there were a surprising number of girls, too: blood lust knows no gender divide.

Staunton was in the middle of the pack, flanked by Bill House and Jake O'Leary. The crucial thing to understand is that these weren't stupid boys; their minds weren't empty. There was, rather, an active malignity about them, a cruelty written on their faces and in the way they held themselves. Staunton radiated malice. He was there to do harm, and he relished the chance. He stepped forward.

"You kept me waiting," he said.

Otis kept moving forward; the rest of us stopped. Some of the crowd flowed around to the sides so that Staunton and Otis were swiftly surrounded. I'm not going to say that all of them were hoping to see Otis trashed and Staunton triumphant—these situations are more complex than that. But I can say, with complete confidence, that all of them wanted to see blood spilled.

"I said, you fucking kept me waiting," said Staunton.

"Well, I'm here now," said Otis calmly. "What do you want to talk about?"

"You going to apologize?" said Staunton.

"Apologize for what?" said Otis.

"Apologize for insulting me," said Staunton.

"When did I insult you?" asked Otis.

"You know fucking well," said Staunton.

There was a pause. "Sure," said Otis, shrugging a little.

"Sure, what?" said Staunton.

"Sure, I apologize for insulting you." Otis again spoke very mildly, but he didn't drop his gaze. He continued looking Staunton right in the eyes.

"That's not good enough," said Staunton.

"What more do you want?" asked Otis.

There was another pause; Staunton's eyes flicked to either side. He needed to raise the ante. "Get down on your knees and kiss the ground," he said.

Otis smiled pleasantly. "No, I don't think so," he said.

"Kiss the fucking ground," said Staunton.

"Nice talking to you," said Otis.

Staunton stepped forward and threw a solid punch. It landed on Otis's left cheek—and it rocked him. He shook his head to clear it. The crowd sighed in satisfaction.

"Come on," said Staunton. "Come on, Blackfoot. Show me some of that warrior shit." He raised his hand and patted his mouth while expelling air, derisively imitating a native war cry.

"Are you happy now?" asked Otis.

"What?" said Staunton. But he didn't wait for an answer. He struck again, landing a solid blow with his left fist this time. And then he moved in for the kill.

What happened next happened too quickly for me to take all of it in. Otis seemed to raise his arms as if in surrender—but then brought the heel of his right hand down on Staunton's nose. Staunton's hands flew up to his face, and Otis followed through with an uppercut to the bigger boy's jaw. Staunton's knees buckled and, as if in slow motion, he sank to the ground. And that was that. The crowd went absolutely silent.

Otis turned to one side and spat some blood on the ground. Then, with Big Andy, Bruce, John and me in tow, he headed back through the parking lot to the boys' washroom in the tech wing—and nobody followed us.

Chapter Four: Something Beautiful

While none of the local thugs followed Otis, word of his encounter with Staunton inevitably spread. When we returned to school next morning everyone knew what had happened. Otis continued to attract looks in the halls and, at lunch, in the cafeteria, but there was a certain rough justice that went to work for him. Everyone knew that Staunton had called him out; everyone knew that Otis had absorbed one hit without responding violently; everyone knew that he'd made short work of Staunton when he had struck back. Taken together these things meant that Otis had earned himself some room—and people were disposed to give it to him.

That room meant that associating with him was now risk-free, even somewhat attractive, and over the course of the next few days several more people shared our table at lunch. Still, on those occasions when we could get together after school, it was the five of us, in various combinations, that did so. On the Friday afternoon that ended the second week of the fall term, Otis and I went over to Bruce's house to see the light and sound show in his basement bedroom.

A number of boys at that time invested in a strobe light or a piece of art that glowed purple or green in the dark. I think the purpose of these things was to enhance the experience of dope-smoking and, perhaps, to improve the odds of seducing young women—though how a flashing light that induced vertigo, or a leering purple death's head, could accomplish either baffles me to this day. But Bruce's light and sound show was something on a different order. He had rigged up a constellation of lights that covered every square inch of his bedroom walls and ceiling, and a system of moveable spotlights on the floor, and he could control their colour, their movement, and the rhythms of their pulsing with three dials on a small handheld box. His party trick was to douse the room lights, put some Pink Floyd or Supertramp on his souped-up stereo, then manipulate the dials to produce an experience that anticipated, on a small scale, the stadium rock concerts of the 1980s.

"That's cool," said Otis when the show was over. "That's really, really cool."

"Thanks," said Bruce, gratified by the strength of Otis's approval.

"You've made something beautiful," said Otis. "I've never seen anything like that."

"It took me a while to put it together," said Bruce. "And I keep improving it."

"Did your dad help you?" asked Otis. Bruce's dad was an electrician.

"He taught me a lot when I was young, but this was all my own project. He just said he had to approve my design before I could build it."

Otis nodded. "You could make a living doing this kind of thing."

"That's the plan," said Bruce. He pulled a box of cookies out from under his bed, and we spent a few minutes snacking and talking about rock music, though we segued pretty quickly into a discussion about attractive girls in our grade. "Man, that Susan Ashe is a looker," Bruce said. "I wouldn't mind getting lost in those jugs."

"She's pretty amazing," agreed Otis. "What do you think, Pete?"

I was interested in another girl altogether, Mary-Lynne Dorset, though I'd not yet said so out loud. She wasn't sexy in the way Susan Ashe was—but, truth to tell, Susan Ashe intimidated me a little. Nevertheless, this was a bonding experience; there were conventions to be observed. "Yeah," I said. "She's got a great bod."

At just that moment Bruce's sister, Millie, knocked on his door and stuck her head round the corner. She was eleven, pigtailed and tomboyish. She was the kind of girl who could catch crawfish and pick up snakes without thinking twice about it. "What do you want?" Bruce asked.

"Mom says it's supper time, so Pete and the Indian boy have to go," she said.

"His name is *Otis*," said Bruce, embarrassed and angry.

"I'm just telling you what Mom said," said Millie as she left.

"Don't worry about it," said Otis. "She doesn't know me. She doesn't mean any harm." Bruce got up off his bed, and Otis and I pulled ourselves out of his beanbag chairs and headed upstairs. We glimpsed Bruce's mother through the kitchen door as we were putting on our shoes.

"Thanks for having us, Mrs. Hutchinson," Otis said. "You've got a really nice home." Mrs. Hutchinson came to the door looking surprised, but she was obviously impressed by Otis's politeness.

"That's all right," she said. "Come again." And she returned to the stove.

"See you on Monday, Bruce," I said, and Otis and I went out the door and onto the street.

"Man, that was something, wasn't it?" said Otis, still remembering Bruce's lights. "He's a talented guy."

My home was closer, and we set out along the side of the road. This road soon ended at a secondary highway, and we had a fifteen-minute walk between subdivisions. "Do you want to hitchhike?" I asked.

"I promised my parents I wouldn't," he said, so we didn't. The early evening was pleasant for walking anyway, if it hadn't been for the cars whizzing by every minute or so.

"What are your parents like?" I asked. At this point neither of us had visited the other's home.

He thought for a bit, though we continued walking. "They're nice people," he said. "They're pretty old, but they're really good to me. I guess they got me out of a bad situation."

"What was that?" I asked.

"I don't remember much. My birth mom was bringing me up, but she wasn't doing such a good job. There were some dangerous people around. So my parents took me as a foster kid when I was four, and then they adopted me a couple of years later."

This was new territory for me. "Was your birth mom doing drugs?" I asked.

"Yeah," said Otis. He didn't volunteer anything else.

Twenty minutes later found us nearly at my home. We usually ate dinner later than other families because my mother didn't get off work until six o'clock. "I'm going to ask if you can stay for dinner," I said.

"It's pretty late to be asking," said Otis. "Maybe you shouldn't this time."

I saw the wisdom of this. My mother could sometimes be persuaded to let me have a friend over for a meal, but she liked some warning.

"I should be getting home anyway," said Otis.

"Do you want to do something tomorrow?" I asked.

"Sure," he said. "What's your number?" And he wrote it down on the top of his right hand. He was the only leftie among my friends.

I came into the house to find my younger brother, Conrad, standing at the living-room window, looking out. "Hey, Kemosabe," he said, "you should have invited the Chief in."

Chapter Five: Action Figures

Grade ten was different in a number of ways from grade nine. Our gym classes were still divided by gender, but a three-week "health unit" was added to the usual mix of team and life sports. For three weeks, thirty-six males were crammed into a tiny classroom to learn about human anatomy and physiology, with a special focus on sexuality. And because everyone had to take gym class, and because there was no academic streaming for the course, there was a mix of advanced learners, average students, and young men who could neither read nor write.

The self-styled tough kids took the seats at the back of the class; the browners—the boys who did well academically—took the seats at the front. I was pretty strong in English and History, but anything remotely science-oriented left me feeling at sea, so I didn't want to put myself where I might attract attention. Otis, Big Andy and I had this one class together, and we elected to sit in a little cluster in the middle of a row on the side of the classroom nearest the radiators.

Mr. Davis, our teacher, was a very earnest young man in his early thirties. He was friendly and well-intentioned—but much more comfortable coaching volleyball than teaching sexual health to a room full of adolescent males. His face, his body language, even his choice of words, betrayed that he wished he were somewhere far, far away. "We're going to begin with basic anatomy, then move into human relations," he announced on the first day. "We'll cover sex drives, masturbation and perversions, then we'll whip through the menstrual cycle and into pregnancy, birth and abortions."

"Are you married, Mr. Davis?" asked Keith Teller, a boy with unruly red hair and a gift for asking loaded questions in an absolutely deadpan voice.

"Yes, Keith," said Mr. Davis. "Why do you ask?"

"So you'll be able to, like, talk about these things from experience?" said Keith. There was a pregnant pause. Even the dullest among us could see a setup.

"Not all of them," said Mr. Davis.

"But, like, some of them?" said Keith.

"Some of them," agreed Mr. Davis.

"Which ones?" asked Keith, pressing his luck.

"Well, just a few of them, really," said Mr. Davis. "I'll tell you when we come to them."

"That's good," said Keith, nodding his head and looking around at the rest of us. "It's good when a teacher has personal knowledge about the stuff he's teaching."

"Yes, thank you, Keith," said Mr. Davis.

A sneering voice from just behind me: "What do you mean by *perversions?*"

Mr. Davis looked uncomfortable. "Well, I guess a better phrase would be dysfunctional sexualities. We're not going to spend much time on them."

"You mean, faggots and stuff?"

"What?" said Mr. Davis. He either hadn't heard the word clearly, or was shocked at its use in his classroom.

"Faggots. Do we have to learn about faggots?" The speaker was Jake O'Leary—a thin, wiry boy with bad skin. He was a pal of Ted Staunton.

This was the 1970s. In the 1980s, Mr. Davis would have thought carefully before making an answer. In the 1990s, he would probably have said that we no longer classify homosexuality as a perversion. In the 2000s, when I write this, he would likely have closed O'Leary down. "Yes, we'll talk about homosexuality," he said.

"I hate faggots," said O'Leary.

"Okay," said Mr. Davis. "Let's begin by taking a look at this filmstrip . . ." And we watched an ancient filmstrip showing first the skeletal structure, and then the muscle groups, of the human body. Mr. Davis gave it up for a bad job when he got to the organs and someone shot a spitball at the illustration of female genitalia. He distributed some handouts and directed us to label body diagrams using a word list provided at the foot of each page. Hippocrates would have wept at the results.

★

At dinner on a Thursday in late September my mother consented to me inviting Otis over for dinner the following day. Conrad, who was initially pleased at the prospect of meeting him, seemed to rapidly lose interest: on Thursday evening he disappeared to the basement to look for something in the storage area. At breakfast on Friday morning, however, he revealed what he had dug up: two large plastic "action figures," Chief Cherokee and Johnny West, that our parents had given us when I was in grade three and he in senior kindergarten. Variations on the G.I. Joes that had been popular two or three years before, they were really dolls for boys. I hadn't seen these things in years.

"Why have you got *them* out?" I asked.

"I just wanted to see them again," said Conrad. "I was thinking maybe they're collectors' items now. Maybe we could get some money for them." This was at least credible: Conrad had already proved himself to be a budding entrepreneur. In grade four he'd made significant pocket change in the school playground by selling two-cent gum for a nickel.

"Well, keep them in your room," I said.

"Why?" asked Conrad.

"Because they're dolls," I said. "I don't want Otis to know that we ever played with dolls."

"They're not dolls," said Conrad. "They're action figures."

"They're dolls," I said.

"Take them off the table, Conrad," said my mother, and that seemed to be the end of it.

The day at school passed unremarkably, and Otis and I took the three-forty bus to the entrance of the subdivision where I lived, which was just a brief walk from Otis's home. We took off our shoes at the front entrance and tucked them into the closet. My mother wasn't home yet, so I made each of us a peanut butter sandwich and, grabbing a couple of glasses of milk, we headed for my room. When I opened the door, however, I was confronted by a sight that stunned me. Conrad had created a dramatic tableau with Chief Cherokee and Johnny West on my bed. He'd trussed the cowboy figure up with string and hung him, head down, from the light fixture. Chief Cherokee, meanwhile, was frozen in a dance of triumph, waving a tomahawk with one hand, and a peace pipe in the other. If this wasn't bad enough—and it was—he'd slathered ketchup all over Johnny West's head so it looked, for all the world, as if he'd been scalped. I was speechless.

I turned to Otis to apologize, and was astonished to find that he was laughing. In fact, he laughed so hard that he had to slide down the door and sit on the floor. "Did your brother do that?" he said at length.

"Yes," I said. "I'm going to kill him. I really am."

"Don't," said Otis, still laughing. "But let's get him back."

A little careful reconnoitering revealed that Conrad was lurking at the bottom of our yard, no doubt waiting for my parents to return before he came back into the house. Otis and I slipped into the kitchen, commandeered the bottle of ketchup that my brother had used, and borrowed a long bread knife from the cutlery drawer. I then slathered the ketchup into my own hair, making sure that some of it dripped down onto an old T-shirt. On Otis's signal, we began yelling at each other and banging saucepans together, before erupting out the back door with me in the lead and Otis in hot pursuit brandishing the bread knife. "Help! Help!" I screamed. "Come back, cowardly paleface!" shouted Otis.

My brother's face moved expressively from bewilderment through sheer terror. He turned to run, then turned back again, caught up in some fleeting sense of fraternal responsibility. At that instant I tackled him and, with Otis's help, put him into a pile of early autumn leaves and buried him. We left him there, shell-shocked and spluttering, and went inside to clean up before my parents arrived home.

So it was a good start to the evening.

Chapter Six: The Weight of the World

Two hours later, with both my parents home and dinner on the table, the world seemed a fairly bright place—in spite of Conrad glaring murderously at me over the brussels sprouts. The sprouts aside, my mother had prepared a boy-friendly meal, and she seemed in a particularly good mood. "And what do your parents do?" she asked Otis.

"My dad's retired," said Otis. "But he used to work for the telephone company in Toronto. And my mom stayed home."

"But surely he's young to be retired?" said my mother. This puzzled me a little; I'd told her about Otis having been adopted by older parents.

"They're in their sixties, Mrs. Ellis," said Otis. "They adopted me when my dad was fifty-four."

"Well, isn't that interesting," said my mother, looking at my dad. "Can you imagine adopting a baby ten years from now, Robert?"

"Hmm," said my father. He seemed preoccupied.

"Actually, I was four when they adopted me," said Otis. "My baby days were over."

"Are your parents Indians, too?" asked my brother.

"No," said Otis, "they're white folks just like you."

"Bad day at the college, Robert?" asked my mother, still looking at my dad.

"No, no. Fine," he said. "Usual stuff. I'm just feeling a bit tired. I may have a nap after dinner."

"I read a book about Indians once," said Conrad, pushing a brussels sprout to the side of his plate.

"Eat your sprouts, Conrad," said my mother. "Does anyone know what happened to the ketchup? The bottle was nearly full yesterday."

And so dinner passed, with mostly light conversation, and with my parents seeming to like Otis, who was polite and friendly and took care to praise the meal without making a big deal about it.

"Whose turn is it to do dishes?" my mom asked after we'd eaten dessert. This was largely a formality; my father was a pretty progressive guy for those days, and he almost always did the clean-up after the meal. On those rare occasions when my brother or I offered—usually because we intended asking for movie money later in the evening—my dad would tell us that he'd do it and that we should go straight to our homework.

But Otis didn't know the conventions. "Peter and I will do it, Mrs. Ellis," he said, and he rose to begin collecting the plates.

"Oh, that's nice of you to offer," said my mother.

I half expected my father to object, but he didn't. "Thank you, boys," he said, and he excused himself shortly afterwards.

My parents and I had pretty good relationships. My mom seemed happy in her work and happy at home, and she was still a pretty woman—slim, dark-haired, and always nicely dressed. She wasn't the kind of mother who baked bread and cookies, but she was good at picking you up when you fell down and looking after cuts and getting up in the middle of the night when you were sick. Before she went to work at the real estate office she'd been great about driving Conrad and me to our friends' homes and taking us to swimming lessons. We never talked much, but she always asked about my day and sometimes told me about the funny things the people in her office did. I think she talked with Conrad more than she talked with me. My dad was a decent guy: he taught Conrad and me to read, and he always made it to our parent/teacher meetings and Christmas pageants. He came away camping with me twice when I was in cub scouts, even though he hated tents and chemical toilets. He didn't play road hockey with us, as some fathers did, but he would help out with our homework and he liked to take us on walks. I counted myself lucky, and I wanted them to like my new friend.

For brothers, Conrad and I got along reasonably well. He was three years behind me—grade seven to my grade ten—and he too had skipped a grade. He was quick-witted, and he could be very funny: it wasn't that he told jokes, but that he often had a witty response to the things other people did or said. Every now and then he got on my nerves, but I probably got on his, too. We weren't really close, not then, but we didn't brawl the way some brothers did. I suspected he'd forgive having been buried in a pile of leaves, even as I'd forgiven his Chief Cherokee tableau—dumb though it was.

"You've got a nice family," said Otis as we were doing the dishes.

"They're okay," I said.

Otis was drying plates with a tea towel that showed a picture of mountains and the slogan, *Beautiful British Columbia.* "Family's important," he said.

"I guess," I said. But I knew, really.

Otis handed me back a plate that wasn't quite clean. I took the dish sponge to it, then rinsed it again under the tap. We only had one sink. The CBC was playing in my parents' bedroom, where my dad was. My mom was reading downstairs in the family room. My brother was probably doing his homework.

"I wish I knew my birth family," Otis said.

"Do you have a brother or sister?" I asked.

"I don't know," he replied. "I wish I did."

★

It took me a little longer to meet Otis's adoptive family. If he and I had lived closer together, we'd probably have been in and out of each other's homes every day. I'd had that kind of friendship with a couple of boys from the same subdivision when I was quite a bit younger. But the fifteen-minute walk between our homes involved crossing a couple of fields—no great challenge during daylight hours, but a bit more intimidating at night. There was another issue, too: his parents apparently expected him to do all sorts of chores, so his time at home was taken up with lawnmowing, weeding and watering the gardens, and painting and even doing minor repairs on their century home. He didn't have as much free time as I had.

A week after his first visit to my house, I received an invitation to his home for dinner on Saturday night. Knowing his parents were older, I went to the trouble of showering and putting on a clean shirt, and Otis and I met halfway, at the first of the two fields, because I didn't yet know exactly where his house was. As we walked, he pointed out different birds and named them, which wasn't something I'd ever known anyone else under the age of forty do. If boys my age went bird-watching, it was usually with pellet guns.

As we drew near to his home, he fell silent, then said, quietly, "My parents are a bit different from yours."

"Well, they're older," I said. "Old people are different."

"They're pretty religious," said Otis. "Especially my mom."

"Oh," I said. This was a bit unexpected. My parents and their friends were very secular, and if anyone in my own circle attended church regularly—apart from John—I didn't know about it. "So they'll probably say grace at dinner?"

"Yes," said Otis. "Do you know what to do?"

"Close my eyes and say *amen*?"

"Yes," Otis said.

"I can do that," I said lightly.

We crossed the newly painted porch, and opened the front door. It was a bright Saturday afternoon, and the front hall was not lit, so it took a moment for my eyes to adjust—but when they did I realized that there was someone waiting for us.

"This is my mom," said Otis. "Mom, this is Peter."

Mrs. James held out her hand, and I moved forward to shake it. She was a tiny woman with white hair, and she looked much older than her sixty years: had I met her on the street, I'd have guessed she was at least seventy. "It's nice to meet you, Mrs. James," I said.

"It's nice to meet you," she said, though, in truth, her expression did not convey pleasure.

"Do you need any help, Mom?" asked Otis.

"Yes, son," she said. "Could you and your friend mop the dining room floor for me?"

"I've already done that, Mom," he said gently.

"When did you do that?" she asked.

"Just before I went to get Peter," he replied.

"Oh," she said, seeming a little flustered. "And have you vac-uumed the living room?"

"Yes, Mom. This morning," said Otis.

"Then you boys can play awhile, and I'll call you when din-ner's ready," she said, and went off towards the kitchen.

"Let's go to my room," said Otis.

Otis's bedroom was upstairs, right next to the master bed-room. It was small and freshly painted, but what struck me most was its starkness. My own room was cluttered with *stuff*: a large chest of drawers, a radio, a desk and chair, books on bookshelves, magazines, two lamps, a globe, and posters on the walls. Otis's room, however, had only his single bed, a small bookshelf with six or seven books (including a bible), a lamp, and a clock. "Where do you do your homework?" I asked.

"At the dining room table," he answered.

I looked around the room. "And what do you do when you're not working?"

Otis laughed. It was a genuine laugh; there was no edge to it. "I read," he said. "And I draw." He knelt down beside his bed, reached under it, and pulled out a drawer on wheels. Inside the drawer were a few clothes, and underneath the clothes were a sketch pad and a set of colouring pencils.

"May I see?" I said.

Otis wordlessly passed me his pad. I opened it, and was amazed by what I found: page after page of beautifully rendered landscapes—forests and lakes and waterfalls. There were human figures, too, here and there, but always at a distance, always far away. I'd had no idea that Otis could draw so beautifully.

"Are these real places?" I asked.

"Sort of," said Otis. "They're memory pictures. I think that's what my old home looks like."

"You should put some of these up on the wall," I said.

★

While we were waiting for dinner, Otis and I talked mostly about school. He was determinedly upbeat and kind in his assessments of people; I was more inclined to judge harshly. But of course we also talked about girls—girls from school, mostly, but I also told him about actresses I lusted after from television: Sally Struthers, Adrienne Barbeau, and the foxy lady from *Mission Impossible*. Otis's family didn't own a television.

Eventually a male voice summoned us to table. When we came down the stairs, our hands washed, I was greeted by Mr. Jones. He would have been of average height, were he not bent over a little. His hair was thin and greying, and he, like his wife, seemed older than he really was—and he was certainly older than her to begin with. "Welcome, Peter," he said. "It's good that you're able to break bread with us."

"It's good to meet you, sir," I said.

We followed him into the dining room, and found that Mrs. James had prepared a chicken and vegetable stew, served with a loaf of pre-sliced white bread. "Your dinner looks wonderful, Mother," said Mr. James. I was briefly puzzled by his calling her *Mother*, but then realized it must be a formal endearment. We sat down.

"Grace," said Mr. James, and I bowed my head and closed my eyes; I'm sure the others did, too. "Lord," said Mr. James, "we thank you that our day's work is mostly done, that there is bread and stew for us to share, and that Peter is able to visit with us this evening. And we ask your blessing on us all, and on all those whom we love."

"Amen," I said, and I raised my head and opened my eyes, only to find that Mrs. James still had her eyes screwed tightly shut. I closed mine again quickly, too.

"And Lord," she said, her voice sounding slightly hysterical, "we pray that you will bring Peter to Jesus even as you have brought Otis out of the darkness of his heathen past. And we pray that you will work your mysterious ways in the lives of all your children, so that they may see the light of your merciful kingdom, and so escape the final judgment and the lake of everlasting fire. Amen, I say, amen."

"Amen," said Mr. James and Otis; I confess that I was too startled to join in. I'd never heard a prayer like that in my life. I opened my eyes, and found that Otis was looking at me. He smiled slightly.

"Would you like some bread, Peter?" said Mr. James. I nodded and took a slice.

"We're glad that Otis has found such a good friend," said Mrs. James, her voice sounding a shade more normal.

"I'm glad he moved here," I said, my tongue untied. "I mean, I'm glad you all moved here."

"We're happy here, aren't we, Mother?" said Mr. James. "It's much quieter than Toronto."

"And I like my school," said Otis.

"There are so many wicked people in this world," said Mrs. James. "We couldn't be sure how Otis would be received. I prayed that he would find a friend."

"Otis is very popular at school," I said. This wasn't altogether true, but I felt it might comfort her.

"So many wicked people," repeated Mrs. James, as if I hadn't spoken at all. "So many wicked, wicked creatures." Her eyes were glistening, and I realized suddenly that she was crying.

"There, there, Mother," said Mr. James gently.

"There are nice people, too, Mom," said Otis.

Mrs. James sobbed once, then breathed in very deeply. "Eat your stew," she said, in a strangled voice. "Eat your stew, and don't worry about me. I just feel the weight of the world's wickedness so powerfully. It bears down on my shoulders 'til I can hardly think straight."

So we ate our stew, which was, frankly, very plain. There was plenty of it, however, and as Otis's mother now fell silent, and as Mr. James drew me out with a few gentle questions, my teenage appetite eventually prevailed, and I gladly accepted a second helping when Mr. James offered it. Apart from the odd snuffle, Mrs. James made no further comment for the rest of the meal.

Chapter Seven: Eyes Peeled

Late September ushered in a kind of anticipatory October-Fest at the school. It was sponsored by the student government, and designed to create school spirit—or so the posters and morning announcements on the intercom proclaimed. What it meant was that classes were cancelled after lunch, and about a quarter of the school population walked off into town. The rest of us remained to take part in activities that were simply meant to be fun: a 1950s style sock hop in one gym; a basketball game between male staff and the senior boys in another; and the opportunity to take a sledge hammer to an old car in the parking lot adjacent to the smoking area.

Otis and I began at the sock hop. The dance committee, which was made up of several upper-grade girls and one young man, Philip, who was also in my health class, had gone to great pains to decorate the gym. They'd hauled in all sorts of 1950s paraphernalia—a juke box, a Coke freezer, an old-style soda fountain—and they'd taped up advertising pages from old magazines.

At that stage in my life I felt hugely self-conscious, so I was reluctant to ask any girl to dance. "Come on," said Otis. "If you ask someone, I will, too."

"Who would I ask?" I said, surveying a sea of female faces—and, unavoidably, breasts and legs and behinds.

"Why don't you ask Mary-Lynne Dorset?" asked Otis.

I jerked my head towards him. "Why her?" I said.

"Oh, I don't know," said Otis. "She's just a nice girl. And she's really good-looking." He paused. "And you like her."

"How do you know?" I said. "I've never told you."

He laughed. "Just ask her," he said. "She won't bite. At least—not on the first date." And he headed off towards Janet Brightman, a heavy but exuberant girl in our own grade. A moment later, and they were dancing to something by the Beach Boys.

Mary-Lynne was standing against the opposite wall, talking to another girl. They seemed absorbed in their conversation, and I felt I didn't want to interrupt them. Except, of course, that I did want to: I wanted Mary-Lynne to myself. But it was difficult to ask one girl to dance when she was talking to another. It was rude, in a way. And it would be embarrassing if Mary-Lynne refused me in front of the other girl, whom I didn't know. Mind you, it would be just as bad if I did know her. So I thought I would wait for the song to end, and then perhaps they would move apart, and I would seize the moment to stride across the dance floor and ask . . . and so, while I was dithering in this way, a boy in grade eleven went up to Mary-Lynne and said something, and she smiled, and a moment later he led her out onto the dance floor, and I felt suddenly useless and sick at heart.

Two dances later, Otis returned. Mary-Lynne was still dancing. "You missed your chance," he said, following my gaze.

"I know," I said miserably. "I hate dances."

"No," said Otis. "You're just angry with yourself." But he stayed with me for the next few minutes, chatting companionably, and just as I was about to say *Let's go*, two giggling grade-nine girls approached us.

"Would you guys like to jive?" one of them said.

"She means, would you like to *dance*," said the other one. "That's what *jive* means. It's like an old-fashioned word. Like, it's not *nasty*, or anything."

"Sure," said Otis. "We'd really like to dance." And we did, and it was nice . . . though I couldn't help but keep my eyes peeled for Mary-Lynne, and wonder where she'd got to when I couldn't see her.

★

About half an hour before the scheduled end of the sock hop, the young men who were on the senior basketball team—and who had attended the dance in uniform—suddenly, and dramatically, left off dancing and moved in a body out the side doors. Word passed that they were heading into the changing room for a strategy session, and then taking the floor of the other gym to play the male staff. Some of the kids let out a sort of desultory cheer as they disappeared, though a good many of the girls looked either disappointed or irritated by this premature end to the dance. Still, we—and they—soon made our way to the gallery overlooking the second gym, and waited for the game to begin.

Otis's first dancing partner, Janet Brightman, came up the stairs at the same time and joined us in the steeply-raked seating. "Oh, man," she said, "I'm really looking forward to this."

"Oh, yeah?" said Otis. "You like basketball?"

"Not really," said Janet. "But some of the senior boys are really cute!" She let out a great cackle.

"I don't know," said Otis. "They don't do it for me."

Janet laughed again. "You're funny," she said. "Are all Indians this funny?"

"Every one of them," said Otis. "We're a confederacy of comedians." Janet cackled again. At that moment Big Andy and John came up the stairs and, seeing us, headed in our direction.

"Geez, that guy's fat," said Janet, not immediately realizing Andy was a friend of ours.

She was no sylph herself, so her comment surprised me a little. "He's a good guy," I said defensively.

"Didn't say he wasn't," said Janet cheerfully. "Hey, guy, you're really fat," she said to Andy.

"So are you," said Big Andy, equally cheerful.

"Let's be fat together," she said, and Andy obligingly sat down next to her.

"Big Andy's not fat," said John, sitting down just behind us. "He's an endomorph." All the grade-ten gym classes had been learning about body types.

"Naw, he's fat," said Janet.

"More of me to love," said Big Andy, jostling her in a friendly sort of way.

"Don't you wish," said Janet. "You'd squash me. It would be like lying under a truck."

"Yeah, a big truck," said Big Andy. "And you should see my stick shift." Janet howled with laughter—and so their rather unorthodox courtship began.

The seats were almost full when the male staff team came running out onto the floor. First in line were the three phys ed teachers: Mr. Davis and one of the other two were still reasonably young and well-conditioned, but the third guy was older and overweight. He looked like the kind of man who'd been a football star in high school, played second- or third-string in college, and rapidly gone to seed in his first decade teaching. Still, these three fellows had at least played basketball, which couldn't be said of many of their colleagues. The crowd cheered a little when they appeared, but quickly began a mostly good-natured cat-calling as the team began to practice—attempting foul shots and layups and simply passing the ball. With the exception of the gym teachers, a middle-aged math teacher and, surprisingly, a little drama teacher, Matthew Dunn, they were all pretty hopeless.

"They're going to get skunked," said Big Andy.

"You're a skunk," said Janet.

"Yeah?" said Big Andy. "You should see my tail."

"Oh, God," said John. "Big Andy's feeling his oats."

"Well, he's not going to feel mine," said Janet.

"I bet I will," said Big Andy, making as if to paw her breasts. Janet shrieked happily.

"I'm going to sit between you two," said Otis, half-rising.

"No, stay there," said Janet, pushing him down. "I wanna be a Janet sandwich."

At that moment, happily, the senior boys team erupted from their dressing room, and we felt obliged to give them a proper cheer. They ran around their half of the gym in a rather self-conscious, self-important circle, then their captain broke off and, scooping basketballs out of a big bin, began passing to his teammates as they went by, each subsequently heading towards the basket for a layup. I didn't know it then, but our basketball team was, by American standards anyway, absolutely pathetic: if they'd faced a team from south of the border they'd have been humiliated.

"They're pretty good," said Otis generously.

"What's wrong with Porter?" said John.

Our attention was drawn to a tall, rough-looking boy with several days' growth on his chin and long, unkempt brown hair. He was running with the rest, but every now and then he seemed to stagger. When he called for the ball, his voice was unnaturally harsh, and he fumbled it as soon as he got it, shouting out a profanity as he headed into a corner.

"He's drunk," howled Janet. "Porter's drunk! What an *idiot!*" But there was a kind of admiration in her voice.

"He can't be," said Big Andy, suddenly serious. Big Andy didn't like alcohol; his father was a drinker—and a mean drunk.

"He is," said Janet. And he was. Porter didn't play in the first shift, but two minutes into the game he was subbed on and it swiftly became clear that something was very wrong. He tripped Mr. Dunn, the first teacher who came near him with the ball, and immediately began arguing loudly with the referee.

"Oh, come on!" he said. "I was nowhere near him!"

"Oh-oh," said John.

"I'm giving you a warning," said the ref, and two of Porter's teammates promptly pulled him away. Mr. Dunn failed to sink his baskets, however, and Porter celebrated by doing a derisive little dance in front of him.

"Spaz-out!" he yelled. "Spazzy freakin' spaz-out!"

The teachers seemed uncertain how to respond. Had they been coaching and refereeing, they would no doubt have acted, but as players on the court they clearly felt their hands were tied. The ref, meanwhile, was someone from outside the school. He seemed unsure how much authority he could exercise.

Play resumed. Twenty or thirty seconds on, Porter pulled something out of his back pocket, came up behind the little drama teacher, reached over his shoulders—and pulled back hard, his hands on either side of Mr. Dunn's neck. The teacher's head jerked back, and an instant later he was on his knees with his hands clawing at his neck.

"Holy shit," said John. We all rose to our feet. Porter had just done his best to strangle a teacher.

"You're off! Out!" shouted the ref, and Porter left the court without argument. Mr. Dunn's teammates gathered round him and the crowd gave him a round of applause when, eventually, he got back on his feet and was escorted to the staff changing room. But the game wasn't called, and Porter would be back at school the following week, absolutely unchastened.

"Jesus, that wasn't very nice," said Janet. "That was pretty weird. You know?"

★

What interest I'd had in the game flagged after this incident and, indeed, everyone seemed subdued. We knew something had just gone very wrong—that a significant violation had occurred—even if we couldn't articulate it more clearly than to say that Porter was an idiot.

The senior boys won the game by a narrow margin, and they celebrated in a way that seemed forced—noisy and disproportionately triumphal; I found myself wishing that the teachers had been able to put it away. They were gracious in defeat. They lined up for the traditional handshake, then headed for the showers. As soon as they'd left, however, a member of the student team moved to the centre of the court and faced the gallery. "Students rule!" he shouted, pumping his fist in the air in a rough approximation of the black power salute: "Teachers suck!" Pockets of kids in the stand let out a raucous cry of support in response, but most of us were silent; it was too much. It was over the top.

"Well, that's pretty dumb," said John.

Jake O'Leary and a boy I didn't recognize were already descending the steps, and O'Leary overheard. "What's the problem, faggot?" he said.

John ignored him.

"You cheering for the chickenshit teachers?" said O'Leary.

"I wasn't cheering for anyone," said John.

"He's a faggot," said O'Leary to his friend.

"Just move along, Jake," said Otis. "You're blocking the stairs."

"You a faggot, too, Blackfoot?" said Jake.

Janet Brightman suddenly spoke up fiercely: "No, he's doing *me*, Jake, which is more than you could ever do."

O'Leary looked at her for an instant, then continued on his way, his friend in tow.

There was an uncomfortable pause. "Um, thank you," said Otis to Janet. "But you didn't have to do that, you know."

"I know," said Janet. "But I hate him. He diddled his little cousin. He's a creep." She took Big Andy's left hand in her right. "Come on, big guy. Show me where your locker is."

★

Otis, John, and I left the gym and emerged blinking into the sunlight. It was another very bright day. We were at one end of the parking lot and we could see, at the other end, adjacent to the smoking area, a group of students gathered around an old car.

"Do you want to see what's going on?" asked Otis.

"*I* don't," said John. "I'm going to walk into town. Why don't you come with me?"

"I can't," said Otis. "I can't miss my bus."

"Me neither," I said. "It leaves in about half an hour."

"Okay," said John. "I'll see if I can find Bruce. See you guys later." And he left. Otis and I watched him go, then turned and walked towards the smoking area. As we drew closer, we could see there were only about fifteen or sixteen kids circling the car. This suggested that most students had simply lost interest in the festivities, or had already left campus.

The head of the student council, a good-natured young man called Chuck, was selling chances to hit the car with a sledgehammer. "Three swings for a buck!" he was saying. "All money goes to charity!"

"I don't think this is such a great idea," I said.

"Maybe not," said Otis. "They should be wearing safety glasses, anyway."

We watched as first one boy, then another, took three swings each. The car was surprisingly resistant to their attacks; they were able to crack the glass of the windows, but not smash through.

The second boy focused on the headlights, and he was more successful there; after taking his third swing, he raised his arms in a V
for victory.

"That's right," said Chuck, "Take your rage out legally—and
raise money for the Red Cross! Be bad and feel good!"

Otis nudged me. Porter, the drunk basketball player, had just
come out of the school, and was staggering towards the student
council head, who had his back to him. "Look behind you!"
called Otis.

"What?" said Chuck, but it was too late—Porter grabbed the
sledgehammer from him and began to attack the car. Three, four,
five, six hits—and the more he lashed out, the more frenzied he
became. He screamed profanities as he flailed away, and as the
windows at last smashed, people moved farther from the car to
escape the flying glass.

"Hey, are you going to pay?" asked Chuck. Porter ignored
him. Eleven, twelve, thirteen hits . . . but now he was losing steam.
On the seventeenth he missed the car altogether, and the force of
the blow caused him to spin around, stagger, and fall.

"I think we should go," said Otis. "Let's check out the
library." So we went, and much of the rest of the crowd left too,
leaving Chuck to pry the sledgehammer from Porter's tired grasp.

"Do you think he's an alcoholic?" I asked Otis.

"I think he's got a lot of problems," said Otis.

★

We made our way to the library, a large, high-ceilinged room
presided over by a tall spinster called Miss Leggat. Miss Leggat
could be a bit intimidating—but then she had to be. She conceived of the library as a place to find books and get some work
done, and that understanding was profoundly at odds with the
view of most students, who saw the place as a social venue. This
meant, then, that Miss Leggat prowled her library like a tigress,
ready to spring on her prey—unruly teenagers—without a second's warning. Because Miss Leggat was tough but fair-minded,
she enjoyed the respect of most students. Inevitably, though, there

were some who loathed her. I was still a little wary of her in grade ten, but as the years passed I grew quite fond of her.

On this day, Miss Leggat was in a foul mood. She'd already had to expel a good many students who'd expected to use the library for socializing, and her patience had worn perilously thin. "Are you here to find books?" she barked as we came through the door.

I hesitated—which was a fatal mistake.

"Aha!" she roared. "You can turn right around, you two, and head off somewhere else! This is a *library*, not a damn social club."

"We're looking for books for a school project," said Otis quickly.

"Oh? What's the project on?" asked Miss Leggat, smiling dangerously.

"It's on science stuff," said Otis, improvising.

"What science stuff?" asked Miss Leggat? "Physics *stuff*? Biology *stuff*? Chemistry *stuff*? Geology? Meteorology? Astrophysics? Metaphysics?" She paused, and cocked her head.

"Yes, that one," said Otis. "Metaphysics."

"*Metaphysics* isn't a science," said Miss Leggat. "It's a branch of theology. Out. *Out!*"

So Otis and I turned around again and left, me with my face burning, Otis smiling a little. "Boy, she's a character, eh?" he said.

"I guess," I said. "I wish she hadn't been so public about it."

"Nah, she was right," said Otis. "She's just doing her job."

We wandered idly through the halls. Queensville District was a big high school. If you set out to explore it all—from the tech wing to the gyms, from the academic stream classrooms to the front foyer—it took some time. Usually, of course, it was crowded, but on this afternoon there were very few people about. Several kids were playing cards in the cafeteria, but we didn't know them so we didn't stop. We passed by the band room and looked in the window: the music teacher was listening to a senior girl play the clarinet. A couple more students were looking through music scores in the back. We poked our heads into the little black box theatre. Having had a length of fishing line wrapped around his neck an hour before, the drama teacher wasn't there, but there were two senior students painting scenery: the male was tall and had very long hair; the female was a petite brunette.

"Are you guys looking for Mr. Dunn?" the girl asked. She was very pretty.

"No, we were just curious," I replied.

"You're welcome to come in," she said.

"Sure, guys," said the boy. "Grab a paintbrush."

"We can't right now," I said. "Our bus comes in fifteen minutes."

"Come back another time," said the girl.

"Maybe we will," said Otis. "I like to paint."

"There's always work to do," said the guy. I remembered that his name was Colin.

We left, closing the door quietly. "They're nice people," said Otis.

"The guy's name is Colin," I said. "He looks like a hippie."

"Hippies aren't so bad," said Otis.

"I wonder if he was high," I said. "Hippies are usually high. On grass and stuff."

"I can't see *him* strangling anyone," said Otis. I took his point. Booze seemed to do worse things to people.

We had further evidence of that when we passed into the athletics area. A group of four cheerleaders had apparently just finished a practice, and they were talking excitedly outside one of the girls' changing rooms.

"Does she want to?" one of them said. She was a grade-eleven student. So were the others. They were all dressed in very short blue dresses with white tops.

"Who cares? She's got to," said another, a lithe blonde. "We all did it."

"I didn't do *that*," said the first.

"Maybe you just don't remember," said the second. The other two howled with laughter. Then they saw us. There was a pause. "Hey, guys," said the blonde.

"Hi," I said warily.

"Do you want to see something neat?" she said. One of the two who had laughed so hard whispered something in the other's ear.

"No way. They're in like grade ten," said the first. "It's *humiliating*."

"It's perfect. They're nobodies," said the blonde, as though we weren't there.

"Thanks," said Otis, turning to go.

"No, don't go," said the blonde. And then to me: "You stay, anyway. What's your name? Paul?"

"Peter," I said. She'd grabbed me by the arm. I allowed myself to be pulled.

"Let's go, Pete," said Otis.

"Don't listen to him," said the blonde. "Come. Come with me." She continued pulling me back towards the changing room.

"I'm not having anything to do with this," said the first cheerleader.

"You don't have to," said the blonde. "Open the door, guys." One of the other two, laughing, opened the door to the changing room, while the other came between Otis and me and helped to push me through—not that I was resisting hard. Even as I was moving, however, I was conscious of the smell of alcohol: both girls had obviously been drinking. An instant later, and for the first time in my life, I found myself in a girls' changing room—and there, lying on the floor, was a girl from my own grade, Wenda. There was a liquor bottle beside her, and she was naked—"bare naked" as we used to say in public school—with her eyes closed, her arms over her head and her legs spread. The cheerleaders let go of me and stood shrieking with laughter as I took in the scene. As I looked down at the naked girl, she stirred suddenly, opened her eyes, then began to throw up.

"Okay, that's enough," said the girl who had been pushing me, and she took me by the arm and pulled me back towards the door. Even as we began to move, however, that door opened and in came one of the female phys-ed teachers, a lovely woman whom I'd long admired from afar.

"What on earth?" she said—then, taking in the whole scene: "Get him out of here! Rhonda, get Wenda up. Oh my God." But by this time I was out the door. The girl who had hustled me out began sobbing, then took off down the hall, wailing.

Otis was leaning with his back against the wall, his arms folded. He pushed himself away, and fell into step beside me as I walked. He didn't say anything, but I knew he knew what had happened. We went and waited for our bus.

Chapter Eight: Holy Ghost Power

That was Thursday afternoon. I spent Thursday night expecting a call from the principal to my parents. The next morning I took the bus to school with a heavy heart, sure that the summons would come during the brief homeroom period or, at latest, during period one. It never came. It slowly dawned on me, over the afternoon, that the school administration didn't know how to deal with the issue, and that my culpability was probably somewhat less than that of the cheerleaders anyway. That took away much of my fear, but it still left me feeling a bit sick. I knew that I should have listened to my own conscience, which had told me something was wrong; and I knew too that my conscience had found a voice through Otis. And I felt lousy over what I had seen—lousy that I'd felt aroused, as I had, by something that I knew was wrong.

I saw the lithe blonde cheerleader at lunch, and she glared at me as though I'd done something awful to her. Wenda was supposed to be in my geography class in period five, but she didn't appear. I wondered if she'd be able to show her face at school again—or if she'd have any memory of what had happened.

At the end of the day I ran into Bruce in the foyer. We'd played cards together at lunch, but there had been plenty of other people there so I hadn't spoken of the previous afternoon's events. We went into the cafeteria to grab a soft drink each, and sat down together at one of the tables. I filled him in, more or less.

He listened carefully. "Wow," he said, when I'd finished.

"Pretty awful, eh?" I said.

"Did Otis go in, too?" asked Bruce. I hadn't made that part clear.

"No," I said. "He told me not to."

Bruce digested this. "What are you going to do?" he asked.

"About what?" I said. "I mean, what can I do?"

"I don't know," said Bruce. But I sensed he was holding something back.

We sat in silence a while. Otis came in, perhaps looking for me, and headed over. He sat down beside us. "I told Bruce about yesterday," I said. Otis nodded.

"What do you think Pete should do?" asked Bruce.

Otis looked at me. "I wasn't in there," he said. "Pete knows what he should do."

I felt a wave of nausea—then pushed it away. "There's nothing I can do," I said angrily, and I got up and left.

★

Otis called me the next morning, Saturday. We had, without addressing the matter directly, put it behind us on the bus ride Friday afternoon. Otis had talked about birds. I had listened. I'd felt better.

"My mother wants to know if you'd like to come to church with us tomorrow," he said, his tone neutral.

"To church!" I said. "I don't know. What do you think?"

"It's your decision," said Otis. "You might find it interesting. Or you might hate it."

As it happens, I was curious. There was in me even at that age a taste for the theatrical, and I intuited that any church that commanded the allegiance of Otis's mother would be livelier than the polite United Church services my family attended at Christmas and, once or twice, Easter. "Sure, I'll come," I said. "If my parents say it's okay. I'll call you back."

My mother seemed surprised. "You want to go to church?" she said. "Why?"

"I'm just curious," I said.

"He's probably got something awful on his conscience," my brother Conrad said. I shot him a glare.

"You'll have to dress up nicely," my mother said.

"A feather headdress," said Conrad. "That's what you need. And buckskin moccasins. And a huge crucifix."

"You're hilarious," I said.

"Well, I don't have any problem with it," said my mother. "And I'm sure your dad won't mind."

"Great," I said. "Could I have some money for the collection?"

"I'll give you fifty cents," she said. "Remind me tomorrow morning."

I called Otis. "I can come."

"Okay," said Otis, his tone still neutral. "We'll pick you up at ten o'clock tomorrow morning."

"Mom's giving me fifty cents for the collection," I said. "Will that be enough?"

"You don't need to worry about that," said Otis.

★

The Jameses' old Dodge Dart pulled into our driveway promptly at ten the next morning. Otis's dad was driving; his mom was sitting in the front passenger seat, and Otis, of course, was in the back. I slid in beside him. My brother was standing in the living room window: he solemnly made the sign of the cross.

"Is your family Catholic?" asked Mr. James.

"No, sir," I said. "He just thinks he's being funny. My family doesn't really go to church." Mrs. James made a noise as though she were sucking her teeth.

"That's all right, son," said Mr. James gently, as if I had just revealed my family's involvement in some terrible crime.

"The Lord finds a way," said Mrs. James, clutching her white handbag.

"I've brought a soccer ball," said Otis. "We can kick it around with some of the other guys after church."

"Great," I said.

Mrs. James cleared her throat. "I've got a surprise for you, boys," she said. "We're not going to church this morning."

"You didn't tell them, Rita?" said Mr. James, glancing sideways at his wife.

Mrs. James ignored him. "We're going to be with our church people, but we're joining them at the swimming pool. There's a baptism today."

I looked over at Otis in some surprise. His eyes met mine, but his face remained carefully placid. I realized suddenly that, whatever he privately thought of his mother's eccentricities, he was a loyal son. "Who's getting baptized, Mom?" he asked.

"The Connor boy," said Mrs. James. "The older one. Frankie."

Otis nodded. "Okay," he said.

Mrs. James turned in her seat and looked directly at me. "Frankie's announced that he's ready," she said, "but anyone can come forward. Anyone who hears the calling of the Holy Ghost can declare himself and be cleansed." She could hardly have been more direct.

I felt profoundly uneasy. I'd been hoping for a little drama, certainly, but it hadn't occurred to me that I might find myself a major player. Neither the thought of being called by a Holy Ghost, nor the prospect of a public cleansing, appealed to me at all. "What does a Holy Ghost sound like?" I asked.

Mrs. James laughed mirthlessly, though that hysterical note I'd heard when she prayed over dinner was back again. "Oh, if He calls, you'd know—wouldn't he, Father?" (The *Father* directed to Mr. James.) "If the Holy Ghost calls, there'd be no question who was doing the calling."

"It would be an inner call, son," said Mr. James. "It would be the most beautiful voice you'd ever heard in your life, whispering in your ear."

"Oh, yes," said Mrs. James, and the catch in her voice told me she was crying again. "You'd know if He called, all right."

I looked over at Otis again. He couldn't meet my eyes this time. He stared down at his feet.

★

We pulled into the parking lot of the Queensville Municipal Swimming Pool at twenty after ten. There were already about fifteen or so cars there, and another one drove in right behind us. A short, balding, rotund gentleman was just moving towards the front entrance of the building in the company of a tiny woman his own age; they were both carrying bibles. "There's Pastor Rod," said Mrs. James, and she got out of the car more quickly than I'd have imagined possible. "Pastor Rod," she called shrilly.

Pastor Rod turned at the sound of her voice and smiled a wide smile, though it seemed to me a little artificial. "Well, hello, Sister Rita," he said.

"Pastor Rod, we've brought—" but I didn't hear the rest of what Mrs. James had to say, because she was moving towards the pastor and because she dropped her voice suddenly. Otis, Mr. James, and I closed our car doors and moved more slowly towards the main building. As we walked, Mr. James was greeted by one of the other men milling around the front entrance, and he stopped to shake hands and exchange a word or two.

"I'm sorry," said Otis. "I didn't expect that." We stopped. Otis scuffed at the ground with his right foot.

"The baptism?" I said.

"Well, that too, I guess. But I meant that I didn't think my mom would . . ." he paused. "Come on quite so strong."

"That's okay," I said. "I don't have to go in the water, do I?"

"No," said Otis. "No one has to go in."

"Have you gone in?" I asked.

"I've been baptized," he said. "Not here. At my old church. We all went up north one weekend and I was baptized in a lake. It was a while ago."

Mrs. James' voice was suddenly lifted again: "Come on over here, Peter." I looked up to see that she and the pastor were both looking expectantly towards me. Otis and I advanced, and Pastor Rod held out his hand.

"Welcome, Brother," he said. "I understand this is your first visit to a church."

"Well, not quite my first," I began—but Mrs. James spoke up first.

"It's his first visit to a real, Bible-believing church," she said. "At first I thought it was a shame he wouldn't see our own gathering place, but then I saw he couldn't do better than a real baptism—especially when it's a young man like himself answering the call."

"There's plenty of time for him to see the church," said Pastor Rod. He was still holding my hand, which I found powerfully uncomfortable. "You look like a young warrior, son. Do you feel like a warrior?"

"I don't know," I said. "Sometimes, I guess."

"He means a warrior for Christ," said Mrs. James.

"A warrior for Christ," repeated Pastor Rod, putting his second hand over mine, so that my hand was held between two of his. "Well, we'll see. The Lord will see. The Lord always recognizes his own. Let's go in, shall we?" So we entered the building together, with the pastor greeting people and shaking hands left and right on his way in.

There was a mass of people in the foyer, and for a moment things were a little confused, as though they weren't quite sure where to go or what to do. "Where's Brother Ted?" asked the pastor, raising his voice.

"Here I am, Pastor," said a middle-aged gentleman with a goatee standing in front of an interior set of glass doors I knew led to the pool. The electric lights were apparently off in the pool area, though we could see a little by natural light.

"Are the doors unlocked, Brother?" asked Pastor Rod.

"They surely are," said the middle-aged fellow. "The Missionary just asked if he could have a couple of quiet moments to pray, so I've been giving him that. He's got Frankie in there with him, too."

"You reckon they've had enough time now?" asked the pastor.

"Yes, sir," said Brother Ted. "They've had about five minutes now."

"That's enough time to open a channel to the Lord," said Pastor Rod. "Open up, Brother Ted. But we should all take our shoes off before we go in, to respect the rules of the pool."

There was a stir as we all removed our shoes, some of the women putting an arm on their husbands' shoulders to do so. Not having to meet people's eyes meant that I could look around freely for a moment, and I saw that it was a fairly mixed group so far as age went. Many were middle-aged, certainly, but there were a few grey-haired folk as well, and, more interestingly, there were eight or nine teens apart from Otis and me, as well as fourteen or fifteen children younger than twelve. Very importantly, some of the teenage girls were quite attractive. *Very* attractive. And the fact that they were got up in colourful dresses made them seem almost exotic. Standard dress for boys and girls alike at QDSS was jeans and a shirt—though some of the more daring girls had taken to wearing mini-skirts. That certainly wasn't the case in this crowd. In any event, I took in all these things in the short time it took for most of us to remove our shoes, at which point we began filing into the pool area, with Brother Ted holding the door open for us.

"Oh, it's humid," said a middle-aged mother in a blue dress, fanning herself with her hand as we were engulfed in a warm, chlorine-scented miasma. Indoor pools smell the same the world over.

"We'll be washing our hair tonight," said another lady, and many of the women laughed. Not for the first time, I was struck at how people will laugh at things that really aren't that funny. Even some of the teenage girls laughed, showing their teeth and looking around at one another for moral support.

"Where are them lights?" said a male voice behind us. Daylight was coming through high windows on two of the walls, enough that we could clearly see the water, but a moment later the electric lights flickered on and we could see very well indeed. The Missionary and a young man I took to be Frankie—he attended one of the other high schools in town—were on the other side of the pool from us as we came in. Frankie, a chubby young man, was dressed in shorts and a T-shirt, and kneeling in front of the Missionary. The Missionary was a man of medium height, but very lean and very intense. He had his eyes closed and his hand on Frankie's head, and he didn't look up as we approached.

"Brother Aaron's deep in prayer," murmured Pastor Ted's wife to her husband.

"In deep," he replied. "In deep."

The congregation, for so we were, clustered around the Missionary and the boy, arranging ourselves in a horseshoe configuration and leaving them only enough room to get to the side of the pool without hindrance. The Missionary continued praying, his eyes closed, his lips moving silently; Frankie, for his part, stayed kneeling with his eyes closed, but I noticed he was quivering a little from holding himself erect. Not only was he on the chubby side, but he also had a troubled complexion; I guessed it would be very painful for him to feel the close-up scrutiny of so many eyes.

Aside from some shuffling of feet, and the odd cough, we were a quiet and respectful gathering. Several people bowed their heads in prayer, but most of us kept our eyes open and focused on the two central figures. Poor Frankie looked awkward and disheveled in his shorts and logo-free T-shirt, but Brother Aaron managed to look dapper in much the same outfit. Leanness covers a multitude of fashion sins.

At length, the Missionary's eyes opened. He took a moment to settle back into an awareness of his surroundings, then took his hand off Frankie's head and looked around. "Pastor Rod?" he said.

"Here I am, Brother Aaron," said the pastor. Frankie opened his eyes at the sound of Pastor Rod's voice.

"You can get up now, son," said Brother Aaron. Frankie did so, awkwardly. I thought I could already glimpse his middle-aged self, big-bellied and triple-jowled, rising laboriously to his feet from a beach towel or picnic blanket.

"Pastor Rod," said Brother Aaron, "it gives me great joy to have this opportunity to meet with your congregation and minister to them. I want to thank you for that."

"You're very welcome, Brother," said Pastor Rod, beaming.

"And I want to thank you for giving me the privilege of baptizing this fine young man," said Brother Aaron. "Some of you folks may not know this," he added, taking in the rest of us, "but bringing a soul before Christ, and washing him clean, is one of the greatest gifts of ministry, and your pastor is a generous man to share this gift with me."

"It's a pleasure and a privilege to have you here, Brother," said Pastor Rod.

"Amen!" said Brother Ted, off to one side.

"I'm here to bring you all a message," said Brother Aaron, "and then to baptize Frankie. And I'm going to keep the message short, because you've got a pastor who's a fine preacher, and because it's hot in here for you people in your fine suits and your pretty dresses, and because a baptism shouldn't be cluttered up with too much other stuff. It's a special occasion. A very special occasion."

"Hallelujah!" said Brother Ted.

"Praise God," said someone else. Mrs. James looked meaningfully at me and nodded slightly, as if to reinforce the point.

Brother Aaron turned to Frankie. "Frankie, you've come before us today with all your sins weighing heavy on your conscience. There's the sin of pride. That's in all of us, and it's offensive to God. There's the sin of greed: eating too much. You've been eating too much, son, and polluting the temple of your body with your cookies and your chips and your ice cream and things like that. There's the sin of sloth, and I don't reckon I need to say much more about that. You obviously haven't had to do much hard work in your life. But the thing I mean to talk about, and to bring you all a message about, is the sin of lust. Because that's the sin that's most destructive to a young man in the prime of his life. That's the sin that's blackening your soul right now, and making you unwholesome and unworthy in the eyes of the Lord."

I'd not previously felt much of anything for Frankie, whom I didn't know and who I figured had let himself in for this. Yes, I had suspected his acne might make him leery of close scrutiny, but even that recognition had been more intellectual than sympathetic. It wasn't until this instant, when I saw the alarm in his eyes at Brother Aaron's words, that I felt a stab of fellow feeling. I realized, suddenly, that he'd had no idea what he was getting into.

Brother Aaron again addressed himself to the whole group. "I don't need to tell any of the grown men or the boys about teenage male lust," he said. "I don't need to talk about the wicked, evil movies that are playing in their heads all the time. And it's likely that Frankie's movies are much worse than any of the movies that the older fellows would remember, because Frankie is growing up in a highly sex-u-a-lized culture. He's seen the depraved pictures in the pornographic magazines. He's seen the sick stag movies and the nasty playing cards. He thinks he knows all he needs to know about the bodies of you ladies and your beautiful daughters."

Frankie gave a strangulated cry, and his eyes rolled from side to side in his head like an animal wondering where it could bolt. Brother Aaron appeared not to notice.

"But he doesn't know *squat* about women, does he, ladies? He doesn't know even the smallest thing. Because with all his obsessing about the *breasts* and the *be*hinds and the other parts I'm not even going to mention, he misses the most important part of all about a woman, and that's her *soul*. Her *eternal* soul." Brother Aaron nodded to the crowd, and his nodding eventually took over his whole body and he began to rock back and forth.

"The unredeemed Frankie, the Frankie who stands before you now, might want to despoil your bodies, and do *unspeakable* things to your daughters, but if you've been baptized, *if* you've been *baptized*, he cannot despoil your eternal soul. No, he can't. And after he's been baptized—and I'm about to take him into the cleansing waters—his desire to do sick and filthy things will be moderated, if not extinguished, by his recognition that he is liable before the throne of Almighty God for his every lustful thought."

It seemed to me that every woman in the congregation was now eyeing Frankie with a distaste that bordered on revulsion. Even *I* didn't like him much—and I knew that everything Brother Aaron had said about him was true about me, too. Frankie himself looked just plain terrified, as if he were standing naked before a field of angry fathers to whose innocent daughters he'd just done those unspeakable things.

"Come, Frankie," said Brother Aaron. "Let me take you into these waters and ask the Holy Ghost to wash you clean." He held out his hand and led a traumatized Frankie to the swimming pool ladder. "You'll have to go down backwards, son," he said, when Frankie tried to go down facing out.

Frankie turned around, then took a step or two down the ladder. He stopped suddenly. "It's cold," he said. "The water's cold."

"It sure beats the fiery furnace of hell!" cried Brother Aaron, and he gave Frankie an encouraging push. So shaken was Frankie, however, that his hands lost their grip on the ladder and he fell backwards into the pool. He slipped under the surface, but, this being the shallow end, he quickly emerged splashing and snorting.

Brother Aaron didn't miss a beat. He didn't bother with the ladder, but threw himself into the pool after Frankie. "Are you ready to be saved, boy!" he shouted. He grabbed the unfortunate teenager, hauled him off his feet, and plunged him backwards under the water again, submerging him long enough to cry out, "Come, Holy Ghost—come and redeem this wicked boy!" When Frankie once again popped up into the air, looking, if it were possible, even more wretched, Brother Aaron spread wide his arms, raised his head towards the ceiling, and bellowed out, "Holy Ghost power! Holy Ghost power!" At which point a little boy standing near me burst into tears and wet himself, the urine coursing down his leg and forming a puddle on the swimming pool deck.

★

The little boy's distress created a kind of brief intermission. Several of the women attended to him, and Brother Ted disappeared into the men's changing room in search of paper towels. Frankie, meanwhile, made his way to the side of the pool, and heaved himself up the ladder. I'm sure he wondered what sort of reception he might get, but Pastor Rod impressed me by stepping forward and hugging the poor fellow. "Welcome to the Kingdom, Brother Frankie," he said. That kind act seemed to soften people's hearts, and several of the other men came forward in their turn, shook Frankie's hand, and said helpful things like, "Way to go, boy," and "You're saved, son," and "The devil can't get you now." But the excitement was not quite over.

Brother Aaron had remained in the water. I don't know what he did immediately after our attention was distracted by the little boy crying, but by the time I looked his way again he was standing stock still in the shallow end, his arms in the air, his hands open, and his eyes cast heavenward. I noticed him at roughly the same moment as Otis' mother. "Look to the Missionary!" she said suddenly. And the rest of the congregation returned their attention to him, too.

Whether Brother Aaron heard Mrs. James, or whether he sensed our collective attention, I don't know, but a moment later he dropped his eyes from the ceiling and turned them on us. "Yes, that's one for the Kingdom," he said hoarsely. "That's one washed clean by the blood of the Lamb. But I know there are others in this place who are ready to be made whole. I sense there's another young man here among us whose heart is yearning to be free." And with these words, Brother Aaron's eyes stopped scanning the crowd and fixed on me. *Me.*

"He means you," whispered Mrs. James excitedly. "The Holy Ghost has told him you're in need of saving, too. Go on in, boy. Heed the call!"

I felt a potent mixture of terror and despair. The last thing on earth I wanted was to jump in that pool and be half-drowned by the holy madman who was now beckoning to me with a hand that looked like a cramped claw. The last thing I wanted was to have my sins enumerated publicly before strangers whose first knowledge of me would be that I too had filthy movies playing in my head. Every fibre in my being urged me to run, get out, disappear—and never come within hailing distance of any Missionary, Pastor or Lay Brother again, ever. And yet to resist—to defy the Missionary—was more than I had it in me to do.

In that instant then—in the instant before I surrendered and climbed into the pool—I felt a stirring at my side, and Otis took a step forward. "You're right, Brother Aaron," he cried. "I hear the call. The Holy Ghost is calling my name, too! I have backslid, and I need to be washed clean!" And my friend, my brother, my own personal savior, took a running jump and landed, fully dressed, in the pool beside the Missionary.

And so my friend saved me from something I feared, and gave me the room to find my own way. And while it may seem a small thing—a punctuation point to a strange story—I'd never felt such gratitude before, and I feel it still.

Chapter Nine: A Scientific Discussion

"Hey, Bateman," said Jake O'Leary. "Does your mom wear army boots, or what?"

It was the final Thursday of our gym class's health unit, and Mr. Davis had decided he could no longer postpone a discussion of "sexual perversions." Philip Bateman, a small and delicate boy in the front row of the class, was the one male on the school dance committee. He was known to have a large collection of show tune records, and he had a good eye for designing posters and setting up displays.

"Male homosexuality may come about when a boy has an overly strong mother figure," Mr. Davis had just told us. "We don't understand the mechanism by which it happens, but some scientists believe that a male child's sense of sexual roles may be disorientated if the female parent is stronger than the male parent. It may lead him to be passive in his relationships when he should be asserting himself." He made a note on the overhead transparency projected onto the screen at the front of the classroom.

We had a stenciled handout in front of us, and some of us followed Mr. Davis's lead in writing "overly strong female parent" under the heading "causes of homosexuality in males." This was the context out of which O'Leary's comment had sprung.

"Don't speak out of turn, Jake," said Mr. Davis.

"I'm just asking," said O'Leary. "It's just a question." Philip stared down at his desk. He was accustomed to taunts in the hallways and on the school bus, but an open gibe in a classroom was something new.

"Hold your questions for later," said Mr. Davis. He took a deep breath. "This may explain the development of the passive homosexual. We don't yet know how the more aggressive male homosexual is formed. Some scientists think—"

"I'm just trying to understand how this thing works," said O'Leary, "and I thought maybe Bateman could help us out."

"That isn't an appropriate question for you to ask," said Mr. Davis, flushing a little.

"Why not?" said O'Leary.

Otis, one seat ahead of me, turned round and looked directly at O'Leary. "You seem really interested in homosexuals, Jake," he said mildly.

"Are you saying Bateman is a faggot?" said O'Leary, looking sideways around the room for approval. Some boys laughed at his daring.

"No," said Otis pleasantly. "You're the one who seems really interested in the subject."

"I just wanna know who the faggots are," said O'Leary.

"This is not the place—" Mr. Davis began.

"Why? Are you looking for a date?" said Otis.

"What did you say?" said O'Leary, leaning forward.

"'Cause I don't know why you'd ask so many questions otherwise," said Otis. "What does that mean, Mr. Davis—when someone wants to believe that other people have the problem he's got himself? I think there's a word for it."

"*Projection*," said Brendan Ross, a tall boy with glasses. He was the son of an engineer at the local plastics factory. "It's a Freudian term."

"Shut the fuck up," said O'Leary, looking meaningfully at Brendan.

"I'm just telling him the word," said Brendan.

"Hey," said Mr. Davis. "Hey! You will not use that word in my classroom, Jake!" His face was now red with fury, and he advanced a few steps towards O'Leary, his fists clenched at his sides.

"Okay," said O'Leary. "But I'm not going to just sit here and take it when someone suggests I'm a fag."

"That's exactly what you did to Philip," said Otis.

"Bateman *is* a fag," said O'Leary.

"Jake!" shouted Mr. Davis. He was losing it.

"Okay," said O'Leary. "Okay."

There was a moment when it seemed that Mr. Davis might take some kind of strong action, and we boys watched him with interest. He had certainly been provoked to the point where a couple of his colleagues would have erupted—though more, I think, would simply have told Jake to go down to "the office" (and a couple of the women would have burst into tears). The vice-principal's office got a lot of traffic in those days, even if trips there didn't seem to cause any significant change in anyone's behaviour. But Mr. Davis collected himself; he breathed deeply for a moment or two, looked down at his notes, and then made an unexpected decision. "Let's talk about this," he said. "Let's talk about attitudes. I want to discuss what you feel about homosexuality, and why. But I want you to discuss it without using any nasty or obscene words. I want to have a . . . scientific discussion."

We digested this. "It's sick," said a boy called Brad Harvey. "Sick and weird."

"A *scientific* discussion," said Mr. Davis.

"Yeah, but we've got to be able to call it what it is," said Harvey.

"I'm asking you to try to use more neutral language," said Mr. Davis.

"It's *disgusting*," said another boy. I didn't know his name, and was a little surprised by the tone of his voice. It was at odds with his generally mild disposition.

"Again," said Mr. Davis, "I want less angry language. I'm looking for a . . . a *tone* that lets us discuss something contentious without getting all worked up."

"They should be put on an island somewhere," said O'Leary. "With barbed wire around it. And machine gun towers."

"Why?" said Otis.

"What?" said O'Leary.

"Why?" said Otis again. "What's the point?"

"It keeps the sickness away from the rest of us," said O'Leary. "Or do you want it here?"

"There are worse things," said Otis, slowly. "There are more dangerous things." He paused a moment, struggling to find words to express something that would not be popular in this group.

"There's a lot of hate in the world. There are far worse things than loving someone who's the same sex as you are."

"You and Bateman will make a great fucking couple," said O'Leary. And that did get him sent to the office.

Chapter Ten: A Dinner Party

And so the year unfolded, with its tiny triumphs and tiny tragedies, its new friendships and old quarrels, its minor adventures and passing regrets. For the most part my own close relationships remained unchanged: Andy, Bruce and John were still the chief figures in my social circle, but they were joined by Otis, with whom I grew closer to the point that I saw more of him, outside school, than anyone else. And, yes, there were others, too—including at least a couple of young women. Janet Brightman was a special if somewhat volatile gal pal to Andy, and so she often joined us for lunch; and by the end of the year I had begun to make shy and tentative overtures towards Mary-Lynne, though I did not, that academic year, find the courage to ask her out. Don't ask me why now, because I couldn't begin to understand, let alone explain.

The day after our 1973 summer holidays began, my father solicited my help in planting a tree in our backyard. Otis was free, on this occasion, and already had experience with tree-planting on his family's property, so he came over to help. He surveyed the hole we'd dug for a moment, then fetched a shovel and jumped in. "What are you doing, Otis?" my dad asked.

"I'm just making the hole a little bigger, Mr. Ellis," said Otis.

"Don't you think it's big enough?" said my father, a little surprised.

"No, sir," said Otis, and he gestured at the tree that had been delivered a couple of hours before. "Look at the size of the root ball. The hole has to be big enough that the root ball fits with room to spare. Then when you've set it in, you backfill around the roots with earth."

"Oh. All right," said my father. He was full of good intentions, but he was not the most practical of men.

"Maybe you should get the hose, Pete," said Otis, digging away industriously. "We'll need to water the tree in."

I fetched the hose, and eventually took a shift in the hole which, an hour later, was a good deal bigger than it had been. And when, a little later still, we slid the blue spruce into position, it was clear that Otis had been absolutely right: the root ball would have been squished without more space to settle into. My father took Otis on a little tour of our other proposed planting sites while I watered the base of the tree. I felt the tiniest niggle of jealousy as I watched them move around the yard, but the feeling was mostly overshadowed by gratitude for the work my friend had put in: he'd spared me a great deal of extra effort. Besides, I found it difficult to get angry with Otis; if there was any malice in his soul, I had yet to see it, and he had already proved his friendship with his swimming pool re-baptism, and with a hundred other smaller but still meaningful kindnesses.

My father was very grateful for Otis's help. That night, over dinner—which Otis was not able to attend—he said: "Peter, I like your friend. He's a good lad." And to my mother he added, "He was very helpful with the tree-planting today, Jessica. The boy knows what he's doing."

My mother nodded, apparently preoccupied with something else, but Conrad spoke up: "Did you give him some tobacco, Dad?"

"No," said my father. "Why would I give him tobacco?"

"That's the way these injuns work," said my brother. "If you don't give them tobacco or a string of beads they scalp you in the middle of the night."

"Yes, very funny, Conrad," said my father.

"You're an idiot," I said. "You know that? An idiot."

"Don't get me wrong," said Conrad. "I like injuns, and everything. But I don't think it's safe to have them wandering around the backyard."

"Which reminds me," said my father. "You need to set up the sprinklers this evening."

"I did it yesterday!" my brother protested. "It's Peter's turn."

"Peter helped me plant the tree," my father replied. "And you're getting on my nerves."

However this may sound to an outsider, it was in fact fairly good-natured. My brother was no racist, and my father would have challenged him forcefully if he'd thought he was serious. Tone counts for a lot.

"If you don't finish what's on your plates," my mother said, suddenly remembering her maternal responsibilities, "I'm sending you both up north to plant trees for the whole summer."

★

But Otis could not always be the hero, and there was one occasion when he embarrassed himself terribly and I felt bad for him. About a week after the tree-planting, Otis came for dinner on the same evening my parents were entertaining a professor friend of my dad's, Professor Pierce-Eliot, who taught at Queen's University. My mother had made a chicken curry, and it came with all sorts of extras—rice, of course, but also shredded coconut, peanuts, sultanas, sliced banana and chutney. The professor and his wife, Edwina, were well-traveled, and I guess my parents thought they'd appreciate something cosmopolitan (though our 1970s understanding of what constituted worldly sophistication was perhaps a little different than it might be now).

Conrad had been sequestered in his bedroom, picking away at the guitar he'd received for his most recent birthday, and Otis and I had been throwing a baseball back and forth in the yard, when we were called to dinner. We washed our hands vigorously—a ritual on which my father placed huge emphasis—and I ran a comb through my hair in deference to the lofty status of our parents' friends, and then we presented ourselves at table.

"Curry!" said Conrad. We'd already met our grown-up guests so he saw no need for further formalities. "Your people invented curry, didn't they, Otis?"

"You know they didn't, Conrad," said my father, with some exasperation. "Curry was developed by different Indians altogether."

"I guess those were *real* Indians, then," said Conrad, looking slyly at Otis.

"We invented popcorn," said Otis mildly. He was very patient with my brother. The notion of having a younger sibling seemed to appeal to him.

Our guests made a few nice remarks about the bounty of the table as we sat down, and then my mother began to serve. While she did so, the professor, a tall, heavy man with a large white beard, described his most recent trip to Thailand, where he'd apparently delivered a paper of some kind. We youngsters sat listening quietly for a while, but eventually Otis was moved to speak. "Couldn't you have just mailed the paper?" he asked.

Professor Pierce-Eliot paused a moment, and looked suspiciously at Otis. "What do you mean?" he said.

"Well, it's a long way to go to just deliver a paper, isn't it?" said Otis. "And it must have been expensive to fly there. Couldn't you have just taken it down to the Post Office and mailed it?"

Mrs. Edwina Pierce-Eliot gave a high, whinnying laugh. "Oh, he thinks you were there as a sort of delivery man, Hugh!" she said. And then, to Otis: "No, dear. Hugh means he gave a talk—a public lecture. 'Delivered a paper' is an expression from the world of academe." She laughed again, and my mother and the professor joined in. Conrad didn't laugh, but he looked gleefully at Otis. I could see he was contemplating a crack about smoke signals, but there were limits, even for him.

"Well," said my father, "it's an understandable mistake. And the academic world is full of specialized language of that sort, Otis." He turned to his guests. "Otis is a first-class gardener," he said. "He's been showing me how to plant trees properly."

"That's a fine thing," said Professor Pierce-Eliot magnanimously. And this tidbit of information launched him into a description of a tree-planting campaign somewhere in Africa—a description that lasted the next several minutes.

I don't think Otis had eaten curry before, but he tucked into it eagerly enough, though I noticed he took two tablespoons of yogurt, at my father's gentle suggestion, to moderate the heat of the spices. (My mother had a generous hand.) Conrad and I were by now accustomed to our mother's curries, and we ate a little more slowly than we usually did, taking care to spread the curry sauce over large quantities of rice. The adult conversation gathered steam, with my father drawing out his guest on things he and Edwina had seen and done in a variety of exotic locales. It would take me another couple of years to recognize that my dad wasn't necessarily as interested in certain topics as he sometimes seemed, and that he encouraged talkers to hold forth in part because he took pleasure in their eccentricities of speech and idiosyncrasies of character.

In any event, the professor eventually got around to the subject of Buddhism, and Otis was again prompted to enter the conversation. "I did a project on Buddhism last term," he said. "In my world religions class."

"Did you?" said Professor Pierce-Eliot, using a tone of voice that told me he was patronizing Otis. "Well, that's very interesting."

But Otis didn't recognize the tone. "It was," he said enthusiastically. And he launched into the story of the life of the Buddha, telling it with some dramatic verve. He was just hitting his stride when the professor cleared his throat noisily and interrupted.

"I'm a leading authority on the subject of Buddhism," he said. "As a matter of fact, that was the subject of the paper I delivered in Thailand."

There was a pause. The professor was apparently struggling to contain his irritation, though why he should feel irritated was beyond me; Edwina seemed to take her cue from her husband and looked at Otis as if he'd just passed wind noisily. My mother looked vaguely cross—and I realized, suddenly, that she didn't much like him. My father was just leaning forward to try, I think, to rescue Otis and put the conversation on another track, when the expression on my friend's face suddenly changed dramatically.

"What's wrong, Otis?" I asked.

"I think I'm going to be—" he began, and then he ducked, mercifully, and vomited under the table. It was not a happy end to my mother's dinner, and it did not dispose her to like him any better.

Chapter Eleven: Spitting Venom

In the previous three summers I'd played box lacrosse, and I played again that summer, the summer of 1973, though I'd already resolved it would be my last year. It was a game about which I felt some ambivalence; I wasn't reckoned much of an athlete at school, where the big sport was football, but I was, to my surprise, reasonably skilful with a lacrosse stick. What put me off was the fact that the older you got, the rougher the game became, and in this year it became rough enough to be frightening sometimes. There were always St. John's Ambulance volunteers on hand in the arenas, and they were often summoned out when the rudimentary first aid skills of our coaches were not up to the injuries we sustained.

My coach in this my final season was, I now realize, a psychopath: the genuine article. A white-haired chain-smoker in his early sixties, Mr. Tonelli relished violence, and he encouraged the natural viciousness of a couple of boys on the team. One of them, Liam, he openly hailed as our enforcer. When the rest of us were running laps or doing ball drills, he'd have Liam working with his coaching assistant, Keefer, who taught him how to use his elbows and the butt end of his stick. Keefer, a smaller, weasel-faced fellow in his twenties, was a featherweight boxer at a dingy gym in south Queensville: he spent the last quarter-hour of every practice teaching Liam the finer points of throwing a bare-knuckle punch, so that if and when gloves were dropped our guy had the skills to knock out his adversaries quickly. Liam thrived on the attention. A big boy, with big hands, he knew what his job was, and he did it brutally.

Otis came to one of my games in the middle of June. He sat in the stands and watched us play a more skilful team from Peterborough. They had a very fast centre who found the corner of our net three times in the first fifteen minutes. Coach Tonelli yelled abuse at our goalie whenever this centre scored, but after the third goal he went behind Liam and spent a couple of minutes quietly spitting venom into his ear, stabbing towards the opposing player with his finger as he did so. The next time Peterborough's first line went over the boards, Tonelli called our team captain off and sent Liam in for him.

It soon became obvious that Liam's job was to make the centre's life miserable: he stuck to him like a limpet, often placing the head of his stick on the boy's kidneys and, I was sure, pressing hard. Once or twice when he was confident the referees weren't looking, Liam slashed or poked at the other player, clearly trying to provoke him. The boy was nimble and fast, so on two occasions he was able to take a pass and simply outrun Liam, but eventually he had to slow down again, and when he did our enforcer was on him, cross-checking if he came anywhere near our goal, and slashing at his legs when the action was elsewhere. The inevitable, engineered crisis came a couple of shifts later when the other boy took a pass and tried to go around our defenders. If he'd had just a little more room he might have succeeded in breaking free, but Liam—ignoring the player's stick and concentrating on his body—hooked him around the waist and hip-checked him into the boards. That much was almost excusable, if against the spirit of the game, but Liam followed it up by kneeing the other boy in the face as tried to get up. "Nice one," muttered our coach—but the whistles blew.

"Whasthematter, Ref? Whasthematter!" Tonelli yelled, as Liam made a gesture of incredulity at the referees. "This ain't some weird pansy-fest! Nothin' wrong with that check!" But the refs weren't buying it, and they sent Liam off with a five-minute penalty. One of the other Peterborough players said something to our man as he was heading towards the penalty box, and for a moment it looked as though a fight might break out, but their coach spoke sharply to his player and nothing further happened. Peterborough's assistant coach helped their centre to his feet, checked his eyes, and took him back behind the boards to recover.

But the game went downhill from there. The Peterborough team was tough as well as skilful, and they began playing a much rougher game. Our own forwards were taken into the boards with much greater force, and elbows were deployed more viciously in the corners. When Liam had served his penalty and returned to the game, he found that he was now a target himself. No single player was assigned to him, but it was striking how often one opponent after another made contact—an elbow here, a cross-check there—and Liam didn't handle it well. He kept trying to focus on the Peterborough marksman, who had also returned, but he had to keep one eye open for drive-by clips, and this rendered him much less effective: the centre scored twice in the second period, and earned his second hat trick in the first minute of the third period. And that's when things got ugly.

As the centre was returning to his side of the box after briefly celebrating his goal with his two wingers, Liam broke into a trot behind him. The refs were focused on recovering the ball, which our goalkeeper had fished out of his net and flung towards the other end in disgust, so they did not see Liam raise his stick and slash at the other player's head. The centre dropped to his knees, a shout went up from the small crowd in the stands and from the Peterborough benches, and suddenly gloves were dropped all over the arena. "Over the boards—go on! Fight like men, you bastards!" said our coach, and we vaulted up and over, each of us rushing to engage a player from the other team.

It took well over ten minutes for the refs to get things under control again—ten minutes during which Liam did some damage to a second Peterborough player before going down himself, and ten minutes during which many of us, willingly or not, found ourselves punching away at or wrestling with someone against whom we had absolutely nothing personally. Things got bad enough that a policeman on duty in the arena had to come out and help the refs pull people apart, and I wasn't surprised when the game was simply called with the points awarded to Peterborough. St. John's Ambulance workers went to work on some of the players, and those who weren't injured were ordered to their respective dressing rooms.

Our coach seemed surprisingly satisfied, for all that we'd just lost the game. "That's showing them, boys—yeah, that's showing them," he said. "Queensville don't get pushed around, hey? No, sir. No fucken way." He clapped Liam on the back, and had encouraging words for a couple of other boys who'd apparently distinguished themselves with their fists. It was strange: much as I disliked the man, I felt an odd kind of glow at his praise for the team as a unit. And yet . . . things didn't feel quite right.

Once changed, and a shower reserved for getting home, I left the dressing room, bought a can of pop at a vending machine, then went off to find Otis. He was waiting for me in the foyer of the arena, nursing a Styrofoam cup of coffee and watching people come and go. "Do you want a chocolate bar?" he asked, producing one from his pocket.

"No, thanks," I replied, brandishing my canned drink. "I just need a pop right now." We headed for the exit, emerging from the hot arena into a warm July evening. "What did you think?" I asked him.

Otis took a moment or two to compose his answer. "You played well," he said.

"Thanks," I said. "Did you see that check I put on number four?"

"That was a good one," he replied. "Are the games always like that?"

"Usually," I admitted. He nodded, and didn't comment. "Too much?" I said, already knowing the answer.

"A lot of anger out there," he said.

As we rounded the corner of the arena, heading towards the parking lot where my father would eventually pick us up, we passed Keefer, who'd preceded me out of the changing room to have a cigarette. He was talking with another man who had occasionally joined him behind the bench—though what his status was I didn't know. "Nice game, Pete," he said.

"Thanks, Keefer," I replied, and moved on with Otis—but Keefer had something more to say.

"Who's the half-breed?" he called after us.

Otis turned: "I'm no half-breed, guy," he said. "I'm the real thing."

"Watch he don't scalp ya," Keefer yelled to me, and his friend laughed raucously.

"Jerks," I said, under my breath, embarrassed.

"Don't worry about it," said Otis. "They don't know any better." But he was silent as we made our way back to my house.

Chapter Twelve: Shaken, Not Stirred

Early the next week I turned fifteen, and my parents agreed that I could have a few friends over, and that they'd pay for a trip to the movies. The latest James Bond movie, *Live or Let Die*, had just been released, and I invited Otis, Bruce and Big Andy to see it with me (John was at some sort of church camp, so he couldn't come). My dad dropped us off near the movie theatre, and we walked down King Street enjoying each other's company, but conscious too, I'm sure, that we were all guys—that there weren't any girls with us. Certainly, this thought was preying on my mind more and more.

I bought our four tickets at the box office, then joined my friends in the line that formed along the street waiting to get in. In those days the Odeon hadn't a lobby to speak of, so people were forced to queue outside. In the summer this wasn't much of a hardship, but in the winter it could be pretty grim. Because this was summer, however, we had the consolation of watching girls in miniskirts parade by, and we began to do just that—though we tried not to be too obvious about it. Joining my friends had involved cutting in ahead of several other people who had queued up in the interim, however, and it soon became clear that one of them was agitated about it. He was a plump boy of about my own age, and I recognized him from school, though I didn't know his name. He was immediately behind us in the line, and on his own. At first he didn't say anything; he just flapped his arms and sighed—but at length he spoke. "Hey, you butted in," he said.

"I didn't really," I said, a bit embarrassed. "My friends were holding my place while I got our tickets." I fanned them out to show I was telling the truth.

"Yeah, but that's butting in," said the boy. He didn't look directly at me; he peered at me sideways.

"That's not butting in," said Big Andy, with a snort. "We couldn't get in without the tickets. Lemme have mine, Pete," he added, reaching for it.

But the boy wasn't going to be calmed so easily. "It is so butting in," he said. "You should have been behind me, and now you're ahead of me. It's not right. You'll get a better seat than me. It's going to be crowded in the theatre."

I was a little more unsettled by this than I probably appeared, because I had had kids butt in ahead of me in movie lines, and in other places, too, and I'd resented it—but this seemed different to me, and I really wanted to persuade the other boy that I wasn't that kind of person. "Look," I said, "they were holding the place for me. They were. I asked them to." I felt a mounting sense of frustration.

"No!" said the boy, and he began rubbing one of his wrists against the front of his shirt. "It's not right. It doesn't matter. Everyone should play by the same rules! Everyone should line up right!"

"Oh, for Christ's sake—" said Bruce, looking thoroughly irritated, but at that point Otis spoke up.

"Hey, guys," he said, addressing Bruce, Big Andy and me, "why don't we just let our friend slide ahead of us?" There was a pause while the rest of us thought about this, then, shrugging our shoulders, we stepped aside, and the plump boy moved ahead. As he did, his mood changed; he stopped looking agitated, and the hand that had been rubbing against his chest dropped to his side. "Feel better?" said Otis, but he said it without either rancor or sarcasm: it was just a question.

"Yeah," said the boy. "'Cause it's right."

"Okay, then. Good," said Otis.

"Yeah," said the boy. "I got here by bus," he added, apropos of nothing.

"We came by rocket ship," said Big Andy helpfully.

"I took the Bayridge 'A'," said the boy, ignoring Big Andy. "It comes every half hour between 9AM and 5PM on Saturdays. Then it comes every hour. The driver's name is Mr. Nash. He's married."

Big Andy, Bruce and I exchanged glances. It was suddenly clear this young man was a little odd, a little off-balance. It occurred to me he was probably in the Occupational Stream at school—a group of kids whom we thoughtlessly called *Okkers.*

"Is he a nice guy?" asked Otis, apparently referring to the bus-driving Mr. Nash.

"Yeah," said the boy. "He calls out the names of the stops. Dwight. Glenbourne. Davis. Sycamore. Maple. Earl. Crosbie. Hunter. Jessop. Glenn Pitt. King. I get off at King. Then he goes to the depot. He stays there for fifteen minutes."

"So he gets a little break?" said Otis.

"Yeah. He drinks a coffee and has a smoke. A Camel."

"Good," said Otis. "Hey, my name's Otis," he added. "And this is Pete, and Bruce and Big Andy."

"Hi," I said. Bruce and Big Andy also offered a greeting— though without much enthusiasm.

"I'm Chris Madchen," said the plump fellow. "I live in Bayridge. I live at 42 Power Street. It's a red-brick house. I have a mom and dad and a sister and a dog. The dog's name is Kaiser."

"Great," said Otis. "Are you excited to see the movie, Chris?"

"Yeah," said Chris. "I like James Bond. He's English. He drinks vodka martinis. Shaken, not stirred. He's a spy." He scratched his nose by brushing it several times in quick succession with the back of his right hand, all the while screwing up his face. Then he turned away from us, facing the front of the line. It was as though we'd ceased to exist.

'Well," said Bruce. "That was informative."

Otis winked. "Takes all kinds, Bruce," he said. And at that moment the line started to shuffle forward.

★

We enjoyed the movie, though Bruce and Big Andy got into an argument over whether Roger Moore was as good a James Bond as George Lazenby or Sean Connery. Truth to tell, I didn't have an opinion either way. My approach to movies was just to sit back and let them wash over me: I enjoyed pretty well anything with colourful characters and beautiful women and exotic locations, and I was as ready to embrace Roger Moore as James Bond as I'd been to accept either Connery or Lazenby. Besides, Paul McCartney's song "Live and Let Die" had deeply impressed me, and I found myself singing it under my breath, and banging out the percussion with imaginary drum sticks.

My dad was waiting for us in the car near the theatre, so we were able to jump in and leave right away. As we were driving down King Street we saw Chris walking along the sidewalk. He was talking to himself, and gesticulating wildly. "There's Chris the Bayridge Bus Guy," said Big Andy.

"Do you know him from school?" my dad asked, briefly taking his eyes off the road and registering the strange progress of the young man to his right.

"He goes to our school, but we don't really know him," said Big Andy.

"He freaked out when Pete got ahead of him in line," said Bruce, laughing at the memory.

"Well, well," said my dad, his tone telegraphing that he'd moved on to something else in his mind. "Pete's mom has made two big pizzas," he added, "and my instructions are to pick up two giant bottles of root beer on the way home."

"Is there a cake?" asked Big Andy.

"There's a chocolate cake—and there's ice cream," said my dad. It was a good birthday.

Chapter Thirteen: A Trip to the Beach

Halfway through July my father announced that we would take our annual camping trip to Picton that weekend—news that Conrad and I greeted with mixed feelings. On the one hand, we very much enjoyed the Picton beach: it was long and wonderfully sandy and the water was usually clear and warm. On the other hand, we were no longer as keen as we'd once been to share a tent with our parents, mostly because we liked to stay awake quite late, and our mom was a great believer in putting the lights out at nine o'clock and getting a good night's sleep. She seemed to believe that a few hours in the fresh air would exhaust us in the same way it exhausted her.

"We're taking two tents this year," my father added, and my spirits rose.

"Have you bought another one?" asked Conrad.

"No," said Dad. "I've borrowed one from Jim." (Jim was a colleague of his at the college.)

"It's another four-man tent," my mom said, "so you boys can each bring a friend, if you'd like."

This was great news, and I instantly resolved to invite Otis, while Conrad declared that he'd bring Robin, a friend of his since grade one.

"Are you sure you want to bring Otis?" asked my mother, focusing on me. "What about Bruce? Or John? John missed your birthday party, didn't he? It would be nice to have him."

"John's still at camp," I said, "and Bruce is at his uncle's cottage." And this was true—but it was also true that I most wanted Otis's company. "Don't you like Otis, Mom?" I asked.

"I'm sure he's a very nice boy," she replied. But her expression, and her choice of words, told me she wasn't fond of him, and I had no idea why.

Both Otis and Robin accepted gladly, and their respective parents gave their consent, but vacation plans often go awry. Otis presented himself on a brilliant Saturday morning at eight-thirty as directed, but Robin's parents called to say he'd come down with a nasty case of poison ivy, and they thought that he should not go. Conrad was bitterly disappointed, and I was sorry, too—not least because I feared this meant he would attach himself to Otis and me for forty-eight hours. But there was no help for it, and the five of us piled into the packed station wagon, and hunkered down for the two hour trip to Picton, the windows cracked open and my parents' eight-track player blaring Jim Croce and Roberta Flack (of whom my mother was particularly fond).

On arrival, and after paying for our weekend pass, the first order of business was to put up the tents. One weekend camping trip a year didn't exactly make us experts in this department, but we managed. At this, as with planting trees (and anything else of a practical nature), it soon developed that Otis had greater skill than his hosts—or, in any event, greater skill than me and my father—so he and Conrad did much of the planning work, and Dad and I pitched in as best we could once the tents were laid out with their various pegs and poles in roughly the right places. While we were occupied in this way, my mom put a table cloth on one of the picnic tables and unpacked a lunch of sandwiches, potato chips, sliced carrots, cucumber circles and cookies. We'd bought some firewood at the park office, but she and my dad had decided to hold off lighting a fire until dinnertime.

Otis's excitement at the prospect of seeing Lake Ontario was palpable: he was usually quite composed, but during lunch he kept turning his head and looking towards the sandy hill just beyond which, we'd told him, lay the beach. He wasn't so distracted that he left any food on his plate, or forgot to say thank you for the meal, but he twisted around often enough that my father teased him gently: "It'll still be there when you're finished, Otis," he said.

"Yes, sir," said Otis. "I know."

"Haven't you been to the beach before?" asked my mother, with a trace of exasperation.

"No, Mrs. Ellis," said Otis solemnly.

"Oh," said my mother, startled. That Otis should be so deprived had clearly not occurred to her.

"But I can swim," Otis added. "My parents made me take my Star 6 at the Y."

"Well, that's good," said my dad. "I'm kicking myself that I didn't think to ask."

"That's okay," said Otis. "My parents would never have let me come if I couldn't swim."

"Oh, we could have strapped a life-belt on you," said my mother.

"We don't have a life-belt," Conrad pointed out.

"Well, we would have got one if we'd needed it," said my mother crossly. "Finish your cucumbers, Conrad."

"I hate cucumbers," said Conrad. "They give me gas."

"Don't talk that way during a meal," said our mother.

"But when am I supposed—"

"Listen to your mother," said my dad sternly. He looked worn, I noticed. There was a weariness about him I hadn't noticed before.

At last the meal was finished and cleaned up after, and my father signaled that we were free to go over the hill and see the water. "But don't go in until your mother or I are there," he added.

"We can all swim, Dad," said Conrad sulkily. He was clearly feeling rebellious.

"I don't care," said our father. "Stay out of the water 'til there's an adult there. We're responsible for you."

So we grabbed our towels and headed towards the water, Conrad and I scrambling up the sandy hill with the same degree of anticipation we'd have felt seven or eight years before, and Otis almost beside himself with excitement. And suddenly, there it was: a beautiful white sand beach stretching a long, long way to left and right (and with lots of space between families and couples), and Lake Ontario glittering in the sun and looking for all the world like the ocean.

"It's beautiful!" said Otis, stopping to drink it all in.

"Last one there's a rotten egg!" shouted Conrad, taking off even as he spoke, and relying on surprise, and Otis's enraptured state, to give him the edge. So we raced to the water's edge, and splashed around a bit up to our ankles, and kept an eye out for the sight of one or another parent coming over the crest of the hill, at which point we were ready to wade farther out and plunge into the waves which, while modest, held out the promise of body-surfing and duck dives and splashing wars. But neither parent came. We waited five minutes, ten, fifteen, twenty—and neither Mom nor Dad appeared.

"I'm going back to hurry them up," I said at length, and I started back towards our side of the sandy hill.

"Maybe you shouldn't, Pete," Otis said.

"Why?" I asked, a bit surprised.

"I don't know," he said. "Maybe they just need a bit of privacy."

"They're probably fighting about something," said Conrad.

"Fighting?" I said, surprised by the suggestion. "Why would they be fighting?"

"I don't know." Conrad shrugged, and looked out at the lake. Something about the way he held himself struck me as strange, but I didn't push—not with Otis there.

"Let's just lie on the beach," Otis suggested. "We can store up some heat while we wait. That way the water will feel even better."

"Okay," I said, noting that a good many people were simply stretched out on their towels enjoying the sun. It had always seemed a fairly daft thing to do, but I was willing to give it a try.

We spread out our towels a couple of yards from the water's edge, then racked out on them. Conrad watched us. "You gonna join us, Conrad?" asked Otis.

Conrad thought for a moment. "No," he said. "I'm going swimming."

"Don't be an ass, Con," I said. "Dad will hit the roof."

"I don't care," said Conrad, and he turned and waded out into the lake. The water was quickly over his shins, then up to his thighs, and at the point where his swimsuit almost disappeared from view he dove into a wave, re-emerging thirty seconds later even farther away from the shore.

"My dad's going to be so mad," I said.

"Is Conrad a good swimmer?" asked Otis.

"Yeah," I said. "He's stronger than he looks."

"Good," said Otis. We lay on our backs and looked up at a brilliant blue sky, with only the odd wisp of cloud miles above our heads. It was warm, and my stomach was full, and I began to feel sleepy.

"Where did you live before you lived in Toronto?" I asked, suddenly remembering the pictures Otis had shown me in his bedroom.

My friend was silent for a moment. "I was born in Toronto— or I moved there really soon after," he said. "But I think my birth mother's people may have come from north Ontario."

"Really far north?" I asked.

"I don't know," said Otis. "I wish I did. I just think it was somewhere with lots of lakes."

"Why do you think that?" I asked, turning my head to look at him.

He shrugged. "I just do."

"And you've never been to a beach before," I said, running my fingers through the sand. It wasn't as though I had spent a lot of time at beaches myself, but this particular beach was an important part of my childhood. Sometimes, in years gone by, we'd travelled there with one or more other families, and those were some of the happiest memories of my life.

"Not that I remember," said Otis. And there was silence between us for a couple of minutes as we both stared up at the sky. I found it was possible to induce a weirdly pleasant dizziness if I stared hard enough and simultaneously imagined myself falling.

"Where's Conrad?" Otis asked, sitting up suddenly.

I sat up, too, and looked out at the water. We could see a few heads bobbing in the waves here and there, and a few smaller children playing close to shore, but I could not immediately pick my brother out. "He's probably swimming underwater," I said.

We waited a moment longer. "Not for this long," said Otis, scrambling to his feet.

"Maybe he got out while we were talking," I said, but I had a sick feeling in the pit of my stomach, and it spread rapidly as I stood up and surveyed the beach. I knew that Conrad was perfectly capable of playing a trick on us, but I also suspected that he would be much more interested in enjoying the water. Conrad liked to swim: in past years he'd had to be ordered out of the water at mealtimes.

We raced into the water, looking towards the spot where we'd last seen Conrad a few minutes earlier—but there was nothing to be seen on the trajectory he'd seemed to be following. "Conrad!" I shouted. "Con, where are you?"

A few faces turned towards us from some distance away, but none of them was Conrad's. "Oh, Jesus," I said. "What should we do?"

We stood there, the two of us, up to our thighs in the water, looking desperately from side to side, and in that instant, as I began to register the enormity of what must have happened, Otis suddenly pointed towards something in the water and shouted something inarticulate. He then dove into an incoming wave, resurfaced on the other side, and began swimming furiously towards whatever he'd seen—though I still couldn't make out anything. I followed anyway, wanting to do something—anything—rather than stay still and think.

Otis was several lengths ahead of me, and he reached whatever it was before I had taken more than a few strokes. He grabbed something, then turned on his back and began swimming backwards towards the beach. I arrived a moment later and realized, instantly, that the something was indeed my brother, white-faced and silent, and I swam behind him and lifted his legs as Otis continued pulling his head. In this way we quickly reached an area where we could again stand, and the two of us wrestled his body up out of the water and onto the beach.

"Get him on his side," I said, remembering fragments of the life-saving techniques we'd learned in our swimming lessons, but Otis was already tilting Conrad's head and opening his mouth—and a moment later he began administering mouth-to-mouth resuscitation—something he'd presumably learned to do, as had we, on plastic models. I was dimly aware of a flurry of activity around us as someone else, then two other people, arrived, and almost immediately there was a confusion of concerned voices offering advice of one kind or another. All the while, however, Otis kept breathing air into my brother's lungs, until, in a blessed moment, Conrad's body heaved, and water started coming out of his mouth—at which point Otis, with help from two other people, rolled him onto his side and rubbed his back while Conrad threw up. And at that moment my father arrived.

If I draw something of a curtain over the next few minutes it's because there's much I simply don't recall. At moments of crisis, certainly, events can have a vivid clarity, but in their aftermath, emotions rush in and beshroud and distort an orderly remembering. Conrad and I had usually gotten along reasonably well, but I wouldn't have said there'd been a special closeness between us. In the previous two minutes, however, I'd faced what it would mean to lose him, to have him vanish from my life, and the thought left me shattered. I think I wept.

My father's distress was easily as great as my own, but he managed to project an outward calm. He held Conrad for a while, rocking him slightly, as Otis recounted what we knew, then he thanked the other people who had come to help. Quite a crowd had now gathered, but onlookers gradually drifted away when it was clear Conrad was all right, and after a few moments it was just the four of us.

"I'm sorry, Dad," said Conrad, still cradled in our father's arms. He looked small—very small—and his face was still white. I suppose he was literally back from the dead.

"Don't worry, son. It's all right," said my dad.

"Where's Mom?" I asked, suddenly feeling that she should be there, too.

"She's getting a cup of coffee from the refreshment stand," said my father. "Let's go and find her."

So we got up, my father with his arm around Conrad's shoulders, and made our way up and over the sandy hill, and down towards our camping site, to find my mom sitting at the picnic table nursing a cup of coffee and smoking a cigarette—something I'd never seen her do before. She realized something was wrong immediately she saw us, and she came running. "What is it—what happened?" she asked, and we told her as she fussed over Conrad and insisted that he lie down on his sleeping bag in our tent. She stayed in there, talking to him, while my father, Otis, and I began lighting a fire: having one suddenly seemed like a good idea.

We were just putting a saucepan of water on the fire to make some tea when my mother came out of the tent and marched over to Otis and me. "How could you have let him go in the water?" she said, her face contorted with anger.

"We told him he shouldn't," I said, feeling a profound sense of injustice.

"You're older: you should have stopped him. You should *both* have stopped him," she said. "If he had died, *you* would have been responsible."

"Jessica!" said my father. "Come on. That's not fair. You know that's not fair."

"I know nothing of the kind," said my mother. "What I know is that I nearly lost my baby."

"It doesn't help to blame the other boys," said my father. "Conrad has a mind of his own. We both know that."

The look my mother gave my father told me something bigger than this was wrong between them.

Chapter Fourteen: A Little Sweetness

We seemed to put the beach episode behind us, though I was conscious, as the rest of the summer unfolded, of a growing estrangement between my parents. It never manifested itself in angry words—at least, not in my hearing—but it could be felt in the silences between them at the dinner table or in the living room. When we sat down together to eat, my father might ask Conrad or me something, and we would respond, but if my mother joined the conversation it would be to ask something different altogether, or to make an observation that could not be linked with what we had been talking about before. It was subtle enough, at times, that I could almost forget about it for a few hours, but there were other occasions when I felt it as almost a tangible darkness in our home.

The beginning of the new school year, then, came as a relief in the sense that it required I direct attention and energy elsewhere. And, indeed, the prospect of seeing my friends regularly, rather than every now and then, was very appealing. I had spent as much time as I could with Otis over the summer, and I had seen Big Andy three or four times, and Bruce twice, but John had stayed at church camp longer than he'd done in the past, and while playing lacrosse sated whatever blood lust flowed through my veins, I had other needs too, and they were beginning to assert themselves with growing urgency in my dreams and daydreams. I missed the company of young women.

In the first day of my first History class of grade eleven, I was excited to find that Mary-Lynne Dorset was sitting right in front of me, and I made a silent promise that I would do something—anything—to put myself decisively on her radar. On this day she was wearing a long, dark blue dress with black stockings and white shoes. To my eyes it was very elegant—like something out of the 1930s—particularly when set beside the crop tops and flared jeans a number of the other girls were wearing. (Though my attraction to her did not preclude my admiring the taut bellies of the girls in crop tops.)

An opportunity presented itself just as we were gathering our books at the end of class. As Mary-Lynne was standing up, she dropped her pen, and I immediately stooped to pick it up. A quicker thinking or more romantically experienced young man might have found a better line than, "Here, you dropped your pen," but her smile gave me some hope.

"Oh, thank you, Peter," she said. She was several inches shorter than my own five foot ten, and a critical onlooker might have said she had a few extra pounds on her—by which I mean that she wasn't fashion-model thin—but to my eyes she was beautiful.

"You're welcome," I said, absurdly grateful that she had remembered my name.

"Did you have a good summer?" she asked, holding her books to her breasts.

"Yeah. It was okay," I said, and then, in a moment of staggering idiocy added, "Can I carry your books?"

"What class are you going to next?" Mary-Lynne asked, smiling still.

"Geography," I said. "I have Geography next."

"Oh, that's too bad," said Mary-Lynne. "I have French next—on the third floor." My face must have fallen. "Maybe we can talk later?" she said kindly.

"Sure. Of course," I said. And as she was leaving the room I wondered if there were as many ways to say *idiot* in French as there are in English.

John was in my Geography class, and greeting him after the summer prevented me from absolutely immersing myself in self-loathing. "Hey, how was camp?" I asked.

"It was great," he replied. His face and arms were nicely tanned, and he exuded an air of robust good health.

"You did some swimming," I observed.

"Swimming and canoeing and hiking and soccer—you name it," said John. "And it was fun being a C.I.T."

"What's a C.I.T.?" I asked. Never having been to camp myself, I didn't know the lingo.

"A counselor-in-training," said John. "I had to help look after a cabin of younger boys, and get the chapel ready for services."

"That sounds like a fag thing to do," said Jake O'Leary, pushing past us. He didn't wait for a response, but threw his books down on a spare desk and eased into it. We ignored him. None of his friends was on the horizon.

"Have you seen Big Andy and Otis?" I asked. I had ridden the same school bus as Otis, but I hadn't seen our large friend.

"Big Andy's locker is near mine," said John. "He's lost a bit of weight this summer." At that moment the teacher came in, and we found seats across from each other about half way up the class—and at the opposite end of the room from O'Leary.

★

I had Science in fourth period—the period before lunch—and none of my closest friends was in that class, so I went from there to my locker, and from my locker to the cafeteria, alone. My mother had packed me a lunch, just as she had in the previous ten years, and my dad had doubled my supplementary money, so I could afford both a carton of milk and a cup of coffee, if I wanted one. I bought a milk right away, then went to the table my friends and I had staked out in grade ten. Big Andy was already there, and Bruce arrived a moment later, and we spent a couple of minutes catching up as we took out our lunches. Just as we began to eat, Otis arrived—but he wasn't alone.

Walking a step or two behind Otis, and smiling hesitantly, was a girl called Edith I knew from a couple of my classes in grade ten. She was a nice girl, no question about that, and attractively busty, but she also had a very big nose. That sounds like a lousy thing to say, but that was the truth of it. She'd been razzed about it in grade nine and even grade ten, and I suspect that some kids had been merciless in elementary school.

"Hey, guys," said Otis. "You're lookin' like a pro wrestler, Big Andy, all bulked up. How you doin', Bruce?"

"He's been working out," said Bruce, referring to Big Andy.

"Nah," said Big Andy. "My dad made me do some work around the house this summer. We built a deck." He flexed his right bicep. "I've been carrying wood and hammering nails."

"Good stuff," said Otis. "Guys, this is Edith. We're in the same English class."

"Hi, Edith," I said. She smiled a little more broadly, and gave a funny sort of wave—even though she was only a few feet away. I tried hard to focus on her eyes.

"You gonna sit down?" said Bruce, shuffling along a little. His gesture indicated Edith as well as Otis, and the two of them seated themselves. At that very moment Andy's friend, Janet, appeared carrying a tray loaded with French fries and coffee, and with— and here my heart rate increased dramatically—Mary-Lynne Dorset in tow.

"Shove over, Big Andy, you big lug," said Janet, elbowing him cheerfully in the face.

"French fries!" said Big Andy.

"Yeah, it's good to see you, too—asshole," she said. "And look who I found," she added, reaching back and pulling Mary-Lynne towards me. "The girl Pete's too chickenshit to ask out."

Mary-Lynne blushed, and I suspect I turned red, too. "I'm not too chickenshit—" I began.

"Oh my God," said Janet, clearing a space by hip-checking Big Andy in one direction, and shoving me in another, "your mother's probably still changing your diapers. Siddown, Mary-Lynne," she added. "You're not in any danger of *his* hands going where they shouldn't. Hey, Edith. Look out for that redskin. He's got a tomahawk in his pants."

And so I shoved over, and Janet and Mary-Lynne sat down, and our little corner of the cafeteria went from being a male island to an awkwardly good-humoured coed circle, the magic wrought mostly by one loud girl's boldness and mildly foul big mouth. Nor was she finished yet. "What's that you're eating, Edith?"

"It's a cheese sandwich," said Edith.

"No wonder you've got such big boobs," said Janet. "I wish I had big boobs. Don't you look at my boobs, Andy!"

"I've seen 'em," said Big Andy gleefully.

"Liar," said Janet, "it was way too dark. Hey. Hey!" she said, turning to me. "I caught you checking out Edith's boobies. You keep your eyes on Mary-Lynne when I've been nice enough to bring her over!" And then to Mary-Lynne: "No, really, don't worry about him. If he got a boner he'd think it was a hernia. He hasn't got a clue."

Bruce laughed—though as much from embarrassment on my behalf, I think, as anything else. "Don't you laugh, Bruce Hutchinson," said Janet warningly. "You're the only guy at the table without a chickie-poo, so even poor Petey here is ahead of you."

"How do you know I don't have a chickie-poo somewhere else?" asked Bruce, leaning in just a little. He wasn't intimidated.

"Blow-up dolls don't count, Sunshine," said Janet cheerfully.

But there was a part of me that was somewhere else altogether: I was coming to grips with the fact that Janet had brought Mary-Lynne to the table knowing of my interest in her, and with Mary-Lynne's tacit acceptance of it—for here she was! Surely that's what her presence meant. And the warmth of her thigh against mine, and the fact she wasn't withdrawing, suggested that she wanted to be where she was, that my company was to some degree welcome—even desirable.

I looked up from my sandwich to see that Otis was grinning at me. He winked.

★

Living in a rural subdivision has its advantages, but the absence of public transportation (except for school buses) makes dating a little complicated when you're too young to have your driver's license. At fifteen, I was too young—but Otis had just qualified for his, and so my first date with Mary-Lynne was in the company of Otis and Edith. It happened on the second Saturday of September: Otis and Edith arrived in the Jameses' aging Dodge

Dart, and we set off to pick up Mary-Lynne, whose address, 62 Copperfield, I had written on a small strip of paper and lodged in my wallet.

"Did you have any trouble borrowing the car?" I asked, settling into the backseat. Edith was up front sitting next to Otis.

"I had to earn it," said Otis cheerfully.

"What did you do?"

"I cleaned out the eaves trough. It's a messy job," said Otis.

"My dad does ours after the leaves have all come down," said Edith, looking sideways at Otis. Yes, she did have a big nose—but she also had nice hair, I noticed, and she had that attractive bust, and her perfume was sweet-smelling.

"I'll do it again in October," said Otis. "My mom likes to see water rushing out of the downspouts."

"Were they okay about us seeing *Jesus Christ Superstar?*" I asked.

"Yes," said Otis. His tone told me nothing, but I wondered if he had trimmed the information he gave them, just a little. It would be true to say we were seeing a film about Jesus, certainly, but I doubted that Mrs. James would feel good about the music. But it turned out I'd misjudged both Otis and Mrs. James. "Our pastor talked about the movie in church," said Otis, "and he said he cried when he saw it, so my parents said it must be okay."

"Are your parents very religious?" Edith asked Otis.

"Yes," said Otis again, nodding seriously. "Church is pretty big in my family. What about yours?"

"We don't really go," said Edith. "Maybe at Christmas."

"That's the same with Pete's family," said Otis. "And I think visiting my church has scared him away for the next ten years." He laughed easily. "What street does Mary-Lynne live on, Pete?"

★

When we arrived at Mary-Lynne's, I swiftly realized I had a little ritual to undergo. Again, more experience might have made me better prepared for it, but the nervousness created by anticipating it might also have frozen me up. In any event, when we pulled into the driveway at 62 Copperfield, I climbed out and went to the front door—and Mr. Dorset answered when I knocked. "Come in, young man," he said. "Your friends won't mind waiting a minute, will they." It wasn't a question.

"So, your name's Peter," he said.

"Yes, sir," I said. "Peter Ellis."

"Well, it's nice to meet you, Peter," he said, offering me his hand. At six feet, he was a couple of inches taller than I was, and his hand was large and strong. I had misjudged the contact, so I wasn't able to return his handshake as firmly as I'd have liked. Mary-Lynne was nowhere in sight.

"What do your parents do, Peter?" he asked, folding his arms and looking at me.

"My dad teaches communications at the college, and my mother's a secretary, sir," I said. "She works in a real estate office." I had no idea what Mr. Dorset did for a living, and nothing in his manner or bearing gave me any clues.

"A college professor, eh?" said Mr. Dorset. "So he's an educated man." Again, it wasn't really a question.

"Yes, sir," I said.

"Are you going to college, son?"

"I think I'll go to university, sir," I said. This much was taken for granted in my family: Conrad and I would both go to university.

Mr. Dorset nodded, and looked at me in silence for a moment. I felt a terrible pressure to fill the gap. "I'm thinking about law," I said.

"What kind of law?" asked Mr. Dorset.

Until that instant I hadn't realized there were different kinds of law, so Mr. Dorset's question struck me as very strange. "The kind that involves going to court," I said. "I'd like to go after criminals."

"Criminal law," said Mr. Dorset, looking at me very closely. "You'd like to be a crown prosecutor. Well, let's hope you have nerves of steel." We heard light footsteps descending a flight of stairs. "I want Mary-Lynne back at ten," he said. "And that's inside the door—not sitting out in the car. Do you hear me?"

"Yes, sir," I said. At that moment Mary-Lynne came into sight: she looked demurely beautiful in a new pair of jeans and a white sweater. "Hi," I said—relieved, grateful and delighted to see her.

"Hi, Peter," she said. "Good night, Daddy." She kissed him on the cheek.

"Good night, Princess," said Mr. Dorset. "Good night, Peter. Have fun, both of you." I opened the door, and allowed Mary-Lynne to step past me. "Ten o'clock," he said.

"Yes, sir," I repeated, and followed his daughter towards the car, conscious that I had been evaluated and grudgingly passed. When I opened the car door for her, I risked a glance towards the living-room window, and there, framed between two slightly parted curtains, was a woman I took to be Mrs. Dorset. They'd both had a good look at me.

★

So it was back to the Odeon, and back to the line-up out-side, and, astonishingly, there we bumped into Chris the Bayridge Bus Guy, relatively close to the entrance. I had glimpsed him briefly at school, but his classes were all in a corridor set aside for occupational students.

"Hi, Chris," said Otis, pausing a moment as we made our way down the line.

"Hi," said Chris. "You can't butt in."

"No, that's okay," said Otis. "I just wanted to say hi."

"You're with girls this time," said Chris. He didn't look directly at either Edith or Mary-Lynne, but he'd clearly noticed them.

"That's right," said Otis.

"I took the Bayridge 'A' bus to get here," said Chris. "The new bus driver is Sam. He has a beard. Mr. Nash doesn't drive on Saturday and Sundays now. He's got seniority. Your girls smell nice."

"Yes, they do," said Otis, patting him on the back. "Hope you enjoy the show, Chris." He was conscious, as was I, that people who had bought their tickets after us would be getting into line ahead of us. It looked as though it might be a full house.

"Yeah," said Chris. "It's directed by Norman Jewison. He's Canadian. He went to the University of Toronto. He directed *In the Heat of the Night* and *Fiddler on the Roof*. He's famous."

"Great," said Otis. "I think it's gonna be good." We walked down the rest of the line and joined the queue.

"We met Chris the last time we were here," I told Mary-Lynne. "He goes to our school, but he's in the occupational program."

"I thought there was something a little different about him," said Mary-Lynne. "Is he on his own?"

"I think so," I said.

"It's brave to come to the movies alone," said Mary-Lynne. I breathed in her perfume and the warmth of her body, and I felt something approaching joy that I was there with her.

★

When the movie came to an end, most people stayed silent in their seats for a moment or two. It was the first time I'd known that to happen: usually audience members made a rush for the exits. In this, we were with the majority; the film had moved us.

"That was great," said Edith, at last breaking the silence. "What did you think?" she asked Otis.

"I really liked it," he replied. He stood up, and the rest of us rose to our feet, too, and joined the slow exodus. As we moved, my hand brushed against Mary-Lynne's, and she reached out and took it. And so, at the age of fifteen, and for the first time in my life, I found myself holding hands with a girl I really cared about.

We made our way out of the theatre, past the concession stands, and through the small lobby that opened out onto the street. En route I found myself nodding at a couple of people I knew from school, but did not speak with anyone. My heart was singing, and I feared that speaking might disrupt the music.

But a disruption of some kind was inevitable. It was nearly nine o'clock as we emerged into a warm and humid night, and the main street of downtown Queensville was busy. There was a long line-up for the second show, and we had to pass alongside it as we made our way back to where the car was parked. About halfway down the line Ricky Feldon was queued with a couple of young men I didn't recognize. Feldon himself was wearing a pair of Doc Martens, which were still a rarity in Canada at that time. The other two wore what were popularly known as "shit-kicker" boots.

Feldon didn't speak to us as we passed, but I saw his eyes light first on Otis, then on Edith, before flicking casually over Mary-Lynne and me. But his eyes returned to Edith, and he smirked and dug one of his friends in the ribs before leaning forward and speaking to him.

We passed by, and had probably travelled about ten yards or so, when suddenly we heard a chorus of fake dog barks behind us. It was, I guessed, a gesture of contempt for Edith, and through her at Otis. Neither of them turned round, but I saw that Otis's back had stiffened, and I assumed that he had heard and understood the insult. Mary-Lynne did glance back, but she said nothing. Our eyes met briefly, and hers were puzzled.

None of us made any reference to the incident as we drove away from the downtown. Instead, we talked about the movie. Mary-Lynne was surprised the director had chosen a black actor to play Judas; Otis noted that the film had not ended with the resurrection; Edith thought the song "I Don't Know How to Love Him" was really beautiful. As with the James Bond movie, I found I really didn't have much to say. I'd enjoyed it, and I wanted to stay in it somehow—so long as I could keep Mary-Lynne with me. Her hand had crept back into mine after we climbed into the backseat, and it felt like the best thing in the world.

Otis drove us to a Dairy Queen before we took the girls home, and he and I bought ice cream cones for ourselves and our dates. We ate them in a booth at the restaurant, and the conversation shifted to the summer just past. I learned that Mary-Lynne had spent Monday, Wednesday and Friday mornings babysitting two small boys. "I have to start saving money for university," she said.

"Do you have to save all of it?" I asked.

"No. I'm allowed to spend half on clothes and books and things," she said, "but the rest of it—zip!—it's sealed up in a savings account. How about you, Peter? Did you work?"

"Not really," I said, suddenly feeling inadequate. "I just turned fifteen, so I couldn't get a real job. I mowed some lawns and dug a couple of big flower beds for neighbours—things like that. I'll work at something regular next summer."

"You also played lacrosse," said Otis, and we talked about lacrosse for a while. "Did you work, Edith?" he asked at length.

"I had to look after my little sister all summer," she said, taking some wet wipes out of her purse and cleaning the stickiness off her hands. She offered the package round, and we all took one.

"Is she still a baby?" asked Mary-Lynne.

"No, but she's got a medical problem," said Edith. "Someone has to be with her all the time, and both my parents work." There was clearly a bigger story there, but Edith didn't volunteer it, and a certain delicacy prevented us from plying her with questions. Instead, Otis told us about the work he'd done on his parents' house. Because it was a century home, it needed a lot of upkeep, and his father's health apparently prevented him from doing as much as he used to.

And then, at nine-thirty, Mary-Lynne looked at me significantly, and I said I had to have her back by ten, and Edith said she should probably be in by then, too—so we left the restaurant, and drove back toward Copperfield. When we were still a couple of blocks away, Mary-Lynne tugged at my hand. "No need to come to the door, Peter," she said, and she kissed me on the cheek. When we arrived at her home I climbed out and opened the car door for her, and stood there while she walked up the driveway and opened her front door—at which point she turned and waved, and blew me another kiss.

★

To my surprise, Otis dropped off Edith next. Their leave-taking was friendly—not romantic. Yes, he walked her to the door, but they simply exchanged a hug and a good-night. I had moved into the front seat, and just for a moment I thought he had pushed the incident from his mind. As we drove off, however, I could see his anger had been burning just below the surface. "Are you okay?" I asked.

"I'm pissed-off," he replied. "Not quite sure what to do about it right now."

"It was a lousy thing to do," I said.

Otis nodded.

"Sick bastards," I said.

"Yup," Otis said. "Lot of them out there." We passed the next couple of minutes in silence, then Otis flicked on the radio. It was a request program on the local commercial station, and the hour was late enough on a Saturday night that the requests were guaranteed to be for hard rock bands—Led Zeppelin, the Who, Deep Purple, Alice Cooper. I noticed that Otis wasn't driving to either of our homes, which was fine with me: we listened to most of "Smoke on the Water," then suddenly Otis pulled off the road into a small strip mall with a payphone on the corner. "Be right back," he said—and he left the radio on.

Puzzled, I watched him go into the glass cubicle and drop a coin into the pay slot. A moment later "Smoke on the Water" ended and the DJ came back on. A female caller requested Nazareth's "Bad Bad Boy," and she was followed by a voice I recognized. It was Otis. "Hi, it's Ricky Feldon calling," he said. "Could I send out a song to all the guys at QDSS?"

"What can we send out to all the guys at QDSS, Ricky?" asked the DJ smoothly.

"Um, I'm thinking something by Donny Osmond," said Otis. "Maybe 'Puppy Love?'"

It's difficult to convey now what a professed fondness for Donny Osmond would do to a guy's reputation back in 1973. At a time when the greatest insult you could throw at a boy was that he was a faggot, a homosexual, liking Donny Osmond was tantamount to waving a pink flag and wearing toenail polish. As Otis returned to the car, we both knew his call was going to be the talk of the school come Monday. But my friend was not smiling. The expression on his face was grim.

Chapter Fifteen: Brothers and Sisters

There followed the happiest six months I could remember. The world felt right in a way it hadn't since I was very small. While I was far from being the brightest kid in my grade, I was strong in a couple of subjects, and had no difficulty with the others. The one course I'd always dreaded in past years, math, I'd been allowed to drop, and this left me the psychological space to relax. On the home front, meanwhile, my parents trundled along well enough: they lived largely separate lives, each seeking out private space before and after our family dinners, but at least they weren't warring openly. My friendships with Otis and John and Bruce and Big Andy—and now with Edith and Janet—were richly sustaining. But the chief source of my happiness was Mary-Lynne: her sweetness, her warmth and gentleness, made me whole, and I was a better person for her presence in my life.

My parents liked her. "Why don't you invite Mary-Lynne to dinner?" my mom would say at least once a week. And my dad always greeted her warmly, and drew her out in conversation, and quietly slipped me an extra few dollars every Friday night—"so you and the girlfriend can do something special." Conrad, for his part, pretended to be indifferent to her, but he never missed a meal when he knew she was going to be there, refrained from making his usual wisecracks when she was around, and I caught him looking at her every now and then with something between wonderment and pained longing. And I couldn't blame him.

"You're nicer now that you're dating Mary-Lynne," he said to me once.

I thought about that for a moment, then just nodded. He was right. I was nicer.

One modest story illustrates the kind of person she was. Mary-Lynne was a talented seamstress, and she made some of her own clothes. Her mother, who had taught her this skill, was zealous when it came to getting rid of clothing that had ceased to fit: she would regularly go through Mary-Lynne's closet, and take anything she judged to be too short or too tight to the St. Vincent de Paul thrift shop. One morning in November, Mary-Lynne saw a girl in grade nine wearing a dress that she herself had made two years before, and that her mother had taken away in one of her periodic purges. Now, some girls might have revealed that the dress was one of their own hand-me-downs, but Mary-Lynne raided her own closet again, found the belt she had bought to go with the dress, and discreetly gave it to the young woman, saying simply that it was now too small for her, and she thought it might match the girl's new outfit perfectly. And she didn't volunteer this story; I drew it out when I saw the belt in her locker.

My relations with Mary-Lynne's parents weren't as warm as Mary-Lynne's were with mine. They attended a church rather like the one Otis's parents went to, and I think Mr. Dorset saw me in much the same way the Missionary had seen poor Frankie—as lustful to the exclusion of every finer sentiment. I wasn't. Yes, I lusted after Mary-Lynne, and was disappointed we never got beyond what my contemporaries called second base, but I loved his daughter with all my heart and soul, and would have died for her, had she but asked.

★

I don't pretend to know how the world works—whether there's any order at all behind the randomness and casual cruelty that it so often displays. On bad days I suspect we're accidental alignments of molecules in a hostile universe. On good days, and I have them, I believe the very existence of people like Mary-Lynne and Otis (and a whole host of others) reveals that a God of Love created us and intends that we see each other as brothers and sisters. In any event, in the early evening of November 5, 1973, Mary-Lynne was killed when the car her dad was driving was forced off the road by a driver who'd had five beers with his supper. Mr. Dorset's car hit a limestone outcropping. He suffered a serious whiplash . . . but Mary-Lynne died on the way to the hospital. And when I heard the news—when my dad knocked on my bedroom door, came in and sat on the bed, his face ashen—my response was to slide out of my study chair, fall on my knees, and howl—howl for the loveliness and beauty and grace that had just gone out of the world.

My parents were good—they really were. Conrad was good: he burst into tears when he saw my face, gave me a long, fierce hug, and for weeks and weeks afterward he'd make me a cup of tea in the evening and bring it to my room. But it was Otis who, eventually, found the words and the way to assuage the most corrosive sadness I had ever known, and who helped me begin to crawl out of the abyss I felt I'd been cast into.

But first there was the funeral to endure. I went with my parents and Conrad, but all my friends were there. Otis and Edith came together in the Jameses' Dodge Dart; Bruce rode on the back of John's new motorcycle; Big Andy and Janet caught a bus (the church was in town). And a couple of other boys from school I didn't know well were there, too: a tall, wild-haired fellow called Stephen, and a short, intense young man called Dent, they both wore sunglasses. There were female friends of Mary-Lynne as well: Megan, a petite fireball of mixed Japanese and Irish ancestry; and Patti, a gentle and soft-spoken young woman who also attended Mary-Lynne's church.

In the front row, of course, were the Dorsets. Mr. Dorset was in a neck brace, but the main change in him hadn't been wrought by the whiplash: if my father's face had been ashen when he told me the news, Mr. Dorset's was tinged with blue and his posture suggested he'd aged thirty years in a handful of days. Mrs. Dorset was veiled, but she sobbed through the service—although, God knows, she wasn't the only one. Mary-Lynne's younger sister, Tammy, looked as though she'd been sedated: the only sign of life she exhibited was an occasional fluttering of the hands.

The service was fine, in its way, until the homily, when the pastor, a blonde young man in a stylish black suit, somehow found a way to tie Mary-Lynne's death to the threat posed by international communism. He went on for several minutes in this vein,

saying things that had no discernible connection to the real life of
the young woman I'd loved and loved still. At first I was simply
bewildered, and then my bewilderment turned to anger and I
clenched my fists, but just when I found myself ready to stand up
and shout out my fury, my mother gently put her hand on my
back and began to rub, and her gentle touch brought me to tears
instead.

The Dorsets were too far gone in their grief to acknowledge
that I had any special share in the communal sense of loss. After
the service, Mr. Dorset shook my hand as though I were just
another mourner. Tammy's eyes were empty. Mrs. Dorset was
unable to talk to anyone: she was led away to the car that would
take her to the graveyard.

There was a gathering after the burial, but it was only for
church members and family. I didn't blame the Dorsets then. I
don't blame them now. But I still wish they'd found it in their
power to recognize that I loved Mary-Lynne, too.

★

Queensville wasn't a beautiful city in the 1970s, but it had
some beautiful places. One of them was a spot not far from the
city centre where, in the early 1800s, an aristocratic Englishman
by the name of Cyril Ransome had owned a big house and gardens. Shortly before his death in 1822 a fire had claimed the
house; he decided not to rebuild, but he deeded the property to
the city on condition it maintain his gardens as a public park. On
a bitterly cold afternoon in late January, when I was in the deep-
est and darkest rat-hole of despair, Otis borrowed his parents' car
and drove me to Ransome Gardens. The sun was still out, though
it was beginning its descent. It was a very cold day. I didn't want
to be there. I didn't want to be anywhere.

The gardens were surrounded by a fine old stone wall, and
entered through a wrought metal gate. We went through the gate,
our boots crunching in the snow, and followed a winding path-
way through the trees, coming eventually to a bench overlooking
a circular pond. Of course the pond was frozen over now, and the

fountain in its centre turned off until April or May, but there's something calming about water, even when it's frozen, and we sat down together on the bench.

We were silent for a while, then Otis turned to me and said, "She was a lovely girl."

"Yes, she was," I said.

"You have to let her go, Pete."

"I don't want to."

"I know," he replied. "But if you don't, you'll go crazy."

"Maybe I have gone a little crazy," I said.

"She wouldn't want that," he said.

I bit my lip. It was still afternoon, but this was January and the light was failing early. The shadows began to lengthen as we sat there.

"Do you ever talk to her?" Otis asked.

"Do you mean now?" I said. "Now that she's dead?"

"Yes."

"No," I said. The idea seemed absurd.

"Maybe you should," said Otis, looking fixedly at the pond.

"That really would be crazy," I said.

"It depends what you say to her."

I thought about that for a moment—thought about what I'd say to Mary-Lynne if only I could. And suddenly the idea didn't seem so mad. And if I was going to do it, doing it with Otis as witness and comforter seemed almost sane. "I miss you, Mary-Lynne," I said out loud.

There was a silence in the garden. We were far from the road, and the stone walls blocked out most of the traffic noise.

"I don't know what I'm going to do without you," I said. Otis remained silent beside me, but he put his left hand lightly on my right shoulder.

"I love you forever," I said, my voice breaking. Otis gripped my shoulder.

At that moment—at that very instant—a ring of Christmas lights came on around the pond. They were blue, and against the white snow they looked almost magical. And the shock of having those lights flick on somehow short-circuited my descent into self-pity. Of course it wasn't an answer to my declaration of love—how could it be?—and yet . . . and yet . . . it did answer somehow. There's darkness, yes, but there's also light.

"Let's come back again in the spring," Otis said quietly. We rose and retraced our steps, discovering, as we walked, that there were blue Christmas lights in many of the trees along the path.

I wouldn't feel truly happy again for a long time, but the beauty of those blue orbs in the winter garden allowed me to see the possibility of happiness, and that glimpse would sustain me, and light my way, in the days, weeks and months that followed.

Chapter Sixteen: Katherine

So January turned into February, and Valentine's Day was grim, but the month wore on. Towards the end of February I was in the library, studying in a seminar room, when I was approached by one of the other young men who'd been at Mary-Lynne's funeral. He was tall and wild-haired, and his accent and manner of speech were vaguely American.

"Mind if I sit down?" he said. He wore blue jeans and old cowboy boots, but his shirt was new and nicely pressed.

"Go ahead," I said.

"I'm Stephen," he said, easing himself into a chair across the table from me.

"I know," I said. I'd seen him around. He'd always struck me as a bit crazy, but not dangerous.

"I sort of knew Mary-Lynne," he said. "Back in elementary school."

I nodded.

"She was a great gal," he said. "She did something nice for me once."

"She never told me," I said.

"Well, she wouldn't," said Stephen. "But I never forgot." He gave a sudden loud snort, startling me a little.

I wasn't sure what to say. Should I ask him what it was? Did he want to tell me?

Stephen leaned forward. "She really loved you," he said. That came too close. I looked down at the floor, tears beginning to prickle in my eyes. I didn't want him to see that. "So if there's anything you ever need," said Stephen. "Just come and talk to me." He snorted again, and stood up.

"Need?" I said, looking up at him in some astonishment. I had no idea what he could have in mind.

"Yeah," said Stephen. "See you around." He left the seminar room. I noticed his friend Dent leaning against one of the study carrels waiting for him, and they walked off together. The strangeness of the conversation stayed with me for the rest of the day.

★

But, in truth, it was a strange winter at QDSS. There was something in the *zeitgeist*—something unsettled and disturbed and out of joint. At the beginning of March, perhaps a week away from the March break, I was walking from my English class to my locker which was, that year, in the technical wing. This was my one spare of the day, and the next class had just started, so the traffic in the halls had largely disappeared. I was about halfway through the school's main lobby when I saw a group of four grade-nine girls erupt out of the bathroom. At least two of them were laughing, and they all looked excited. "Jesus Christ," said one of them, "that'll fucken teach her!" "Shut it," said one of the others, gesturing towards me. They passed me, silent now, with furtive looks and stifled giggles.

I thought very little of it. They were three years younger than I was; they were in grade nine; none of them was particularly pretty. I continued on my way, put my English books in my locker, took out my bagged lunch (the meal followed my spare), and headed towards the cafeteria to buy a cup of coffee and see if anyone might want to play euchre. John was there, and the two of us spent some time talking about his motorcycle, and he asked me, delicately, how I was doing around Mary-Lynne's death, and then lots of other people began filtering into the cafeteria, and Bruce and Otis and Edith joined John and me at our table.

Several minutes later Big Andy and Janet arrived—and Janet was clearly distressed. "Holy fuck!" she declared, putting her books on the table. She hadn't gone through the lunch line yet.

"What's the matter?" I said.

"You haven't heard?" she said.

"No." I glanced around the table. Clearly no one else there had heard anything out of the ordinary either.

"I've just come from the girl's bathroom," she said. "Blood fucking everywhere—all over the floor. Blood and—no, I'm not going to tell you while you're eating."

"Shall I get some fries?" said Big Andy.

"No, I don't want to eat, Andy," said Janet. "Christ. I don't think I'll eat for a week. Get me a coffee."

"Okay," said Big Andy, and off he went.

"What do you mean, blood?" I asked. "Was there anyone there?"

"No," said Janet shortly. "Just a teacher. She told me to go somewhere else."

As Janet didn't appear disposed to say anything else, other conversations resumed, but my own thoughts were, of course, troubled: I wondered if I should do anything there and then. After a couple of uneasy moments I glanced sideways and realized Janet was crying. Otis and Edith saw her tears at the same time.

"Oh, Janet," said Edith, "what's wrong, honey?" She rummaged in her purse, found a little pack of Kleenex, and passed a couple across the table. Janet took them, and blew her nose loudly.

"Someone beat up this girl," said Janet. "And they beat her so bad she lost her baby." She began sobbing. I felt sick.

A moment later, a hush descended on the cafeteria. The principal and vice-principal had just entered, and there were a couple of police officers with them. The two school officials split up and began walking down the aisles of the cafeteria, scanning the tables, clearly looking for someone—or for a group. Whoever they were seeking was not there, however, and after about three minutes they and the police officers left, leaving behind a great hum of conversation. And by this time, not surprisingly, news of the blood in the girls' bathroom had spread.

★

By the next morning, the full story was out—or, at least, a version of it. It seems that a grade-nine girl, Katherine, had become pregnant, and was just beginning to show. A group of girls in the same grade apparently decided this was proof of sluttiness on her part, and they conspired to trap her in the lobby bathroom and beat the hell out of her. And they beat her so badly, it was said, that Katherine aborted right there, on the bathroom floor. My mother would eventually raise doubts about this, saying it would take more time, but Janet said she had seen what she had seen, and I believed her.

A school assembly was called—our teachers escorting us from our first-period classes to the cafeteria en masse—and when the little white-haired principal came to the microphone there was, for once, silence. "This is the kind of assembly no principal ever wants to call," he said, "but I have no choice. By now you will all have heard that an assault took place yesterday, in our school. I want to assure you of two things: first, that no one outside this community was involved; and second, that the four perpetrators were questioned by police yesterday evening, and that charges will be laid later today." There was a bit more, of course—the vice-principal eventually came to the mic and talked about how QDSS was basically a safe place, and that no one should ever have to worry about physical abuse—but the official word was significantly less detailed than the rumour mill. Remarkably, too, there was absolutely no mention of the girl who had been attacked. Her name wasn't spoken, and nothing was said about how she was.

Lunch that day was a more somber affair than usual—at least at our table. Janet was still emotionally volatile. "I can't believe they didn't say a fucking thing about Katherine," she said.

"Does anyone know how she is?" asked John.

"How the fuck do *you* think she is, John?" asked Janet. "She just had her kid kicked out of her."

"I know, Janet," said John. "Hey, *I* didn't do it."

"Do you know her, Janet?" asked Otis. "I mean, personally."

"No," said Janet. "But that doesn't mean I don't care."

"I know," said Otis. Later that day, after school, I was heading out to the bus when I ran into Otis and Edith going against the tide.

"Aren't you going home?" I asked.

"No," said Otis. "We're going to the hospital, to visit Katherine. Edith called, and they're allowing visitors." He paused, and looked at me quizzically. "Do you want to come, too?"

I understood his hesitation; I still wasn't myself. Anything that reminded me of Mary-Lynne made me tear up. A graphic reminder of how cruel life could be was, perhaps, the last thing I needed, but.... "Sure. I'll come," I said.

Otis didn't have his parents' car, so we set ourselves to walk to the hospital, hoping one of our teachers, or a friend, might spot us and give us a lift at least part way there. And that's what happened. About five minutes into our walk a hearse passed us—then pulled over. When we came level with the passenger window it was rolled down, and there in the passenger seat was Dent, with the wild-haired Stephen at the wheel. "You guys like a ride?" asked Dent. He and Stephen were both wearing sunglasses.

"Uh, thank you," Otis said, after glancing quickly at Edith and me. The three of us piled into the back seat, doing our best to ignore the utter strangeness of hitching a ride in a hearse. I did my best to push away the memory of the last time I'd seen one.

"It's a 1959 Cadillac Eureka Combination Coach," said Stephen, looking at us in his rearview mirror, from which dangled a Playboy Bunny logo. "I just bought it. Put in the backseat myself."

"It's different," said Otis.

"Yeah. Great car," said Stephen. "Where you guys going?"

"To the hospital," I said.

Stephen again looked at us in his rearview mirror. "Family?"

"Katherine," I said. "The girl who was beaten up."

Stephen nodded. "That was some weird shit," said Dent.

"No need to go out of your way," said Otis. "Even just a few blocks from here makes a difference."

"No, we'll take you," said Stephen. And he gave another of his strangulated snorts.

★

Katherine was out of intensive care, and had been placed in a single room. We thought she would probably have family there, but she was alone—a small, pale figure in a hospital bed. When we entered, Edith in the lead, she looked at us with big, frightened eyes.

"Hi, Katherine," said Edith. "You don't know us, but we're from QDSS."

"You're Edith," said the girl. "And you're Otis, the Indian guy. But I don't know your name," she said, looking at me.

"I'm Peter," I said. "Hi." I didn't know what else to say.

"Why are you here?" she asked, taking us all in.

"We figured you might like some company," said Otis. "We just thought we'd say hello and tell you lots of people are thinking about you."

That Otis and Edith had planned this visit the night before came clear to me when Edith drew a couple of items out of her purse. "We brought you a stuffed animal," she said, and she handed Katherine a teddy bear. For an instant I thought this was a crazy idea, but Katherine took the creature and hugged it to her thin chest.

"Thank you," she said. "I've only got one stuffed animal, and he's at home." She kissed its head—and that gesture testified eloquently to how young she really was.

"And we got you some books," said Otis. Edith passed the girl a package of secondhand books tied up with string—*Little House on the Prairie*, *Anne of Green Gables*, and a Nancy Drew title.

Katherine took them, and looked at them dubiously. "Thank you," she said. "I don't really read, but they might be good sometime. I really like my teddy bear." She kissed it again.

"Do you mind if we sit down?" asked Edith. There were two chairs in the room, though one of them had a pair of slippers on it.

"Go ahead," said Katherine. "Just move the slippers. They're my mom's. Put them on the floor, or something."

"Is your mom somewhere in the hospital?" Otis asked.

"No, she's at work," said Katherine. "She was here before she went, and she left them there for when she comes back."

"Is your dad around somewhere?" I asked. Otis looked at me in a way that suggested this wasn't a good line of enquiry, but, in that instant, I couldn't see why.

"I don't know who my dad is," said Katherine, and I understood.

So we stayed awhile, and we talked about this and that, with Edith taking the lead when it came to school gossip—a funny thing Miss Leggat (the librarian) had said recently when she was really angry—and all the while Katherine hugged her teddy bear, her big eyes looking gradually more relaxed. I felt a desperate desire to give her something myself, though she probably thought the books and the bear were as much from me as from Otis and Edith, and, having a little money in my pocket, I went down the hall and bought her a tube of butterscotch lifesavers from a machine. She accepted these with real gratitude, and gave me a smile I found almost heartbreaking.

A few moments later a nurse came in and told us it was time to go, and Katherine looked stricken suddenly. "Will you come back and see me again?" she asked.

"Yes," said Otis, responding before either Edith or I could speak. "If you'd like us to."

"I would," said Katherine. We said our good-byes, a little awkwardly, but just before we left, Otis bent down and kissed her on the forehead. Katherine's response was touching: she threw her arms round his neck and hugged him close, and, not for the first time, I marveled at my friend's brave decency.

As we were walking down the stairs that would take us out of the building, Edith suddenly burst into tears. "She's just a baby herself!" she said. And she was right.

Chapter Seventeen: The Museum

In the early spring of 1974, my father encouraged me to begin looking for summer employment. I had a secondhand typewriter, and I typed up my first resume—a pretty pathetic document that gave my work experience (grass-cutting), my academic level (entering grade twelve in the fall), and my hobbies (playing lacrosse and reading). This seemed pretty thin, even to me, but it was at least truthful. My mother, for her part, showed me where to find job listings in the newspaper, and so it was that I began mailing application letters and resumes to restaurants and construction companies and the public library.

I found out about the job I eventually landed, however, by a different route. My dad had a colleague whose neighbour, a Mr. David Spurr, had recently opened a private museum, and he suggested I give the gentleman a call, providing a business card to assist in doing so. The business card read, very simply:

Mr. David Spurr, Proprietor
The James Alfred Spurr Memorial Museum

—and there followed a mailing address and telephone number. So on a bright Saturday morning in early April I shooed my younger brother away from the kitchen (where the phone was located) and made my call.

The voice at the other end was deep and richly resonant. "David Spurr, here," it said. I conjured up a picture of the actor Orson Welles in the then famous commercial for Paul Masson wines.

"Mr. Spurr?" I said. "My name is Peter Ellis, and I'm interested in applying for the position of tour guide at your museum."

"At the James Alfred Spurr Memorial Museum," said David Spurr, giving the place its full title. "Have you a resume I might peruse?"

This was the first time I'd heard (rather than read) the word *peruse*, and I found I needed to suppress the desire to laugh—but I sensed that would go down very badly. "Yes, sir," I said.

"Why don't you bring it down to the museum later today," said Mr. Spurr. "We're not officially open until the summer, but I'll be there between one and three. Can you make it at two-thirty?"

"Yes, sir," I said again, confident one of my parents would drive me. And after thanking him and saying good-bye (and then telling Conrad he was an ass for making faces at me while I was on the phone), I went to my room and worried over what I should wear to my first real job interview.

★

The James Alfred Spurr Memorial Museum was housed in a low, modern building just outside the downtown core of Queensville. It looked nothing like a museum from the outside: anyone viewing the façade might imagine it contained a lawyer's office or insurance broker, an impression powerfully reinforced by the smoky brown front window. To one side a single storey secondhand bookstore; to the other a bit of an alleyway (leading to parking behind the building), and then the oldest and most old-fashioned pharmacy in town, Angus Lynch Chemist.

My father had dropped me off fifteen minutes early so he could accomplish a few errands before picking me up, so I went next door to the bookstore to pass the time. My impression as I came through the door was of mild mustiness, but that olfactory response was swiftly overtaken by my awe at confronting books by the thousands in shelves reaching from floor to ceiling. Subject areas were demarcated by hand-lettered signs—fiction, travel, theology, gardening, romance—and perched behind an old desk was a little elf of a man in his early forties. "Well, hello," he said.

"Hi," I replied, looking around me still.

"Are you looking for anything in particular?" he asked.

"No," I replied, "just browsing." And I nodded to him and moved to the fiction section, my eyes skimming over the titles and noting the variable condition of the books themselves.

"Let me know if I can help you," said the elf-man, "and help yourself to a cookie if you'd like one." There was a plastic tray of chocolate chip cookies in front of him, and he was munching away himself.

"Thanks," I replied, and I spent about ten minutes looking at books and checking my watch obsessively. Because I'd exchanged a few words with the owner (as I guessed him to be), and because I enjoyed reading anyway, I decided I should buy something. I counted the change in my pocket, and discovered I had eighty cents. "Do any of your books cost less than a dollar?" I asked.

"They might," replied the elf-man, looking at me from under lowered eyebrows. "Do you have a particular title or author in mind?"

"I'd like something funny," I said, feeling a bit gormless. I couldn't think of a particular title or author in that instant.

"*Lucky Jim* is the funniest book written in the twentieth century," said the elf-man. He rose and, brushing the crumbs from his sweater, went directly to the fiction bookshelf and pulled down a paperback. He handed it to me.

I hefted it speculatively for a moment, registering that it had a spritely cover and that it wasn't covered in mould. "How much is it?" I asked. He reached for the book, opened it, and showed me that $1.25 was penciled on the top right hand corner of the title page. "Oh," I said disappointedly, "that's more than I have."

"Well, I'm willin' to do a deal," he said, affecting a cowboy accent. "How much do you have, pah'dner?"

"Just eighty cents," I replied, wincing a little at my poverty.

"You'll drive me out of house and home," he said looking injured, but there was a smile in his voice. "Eighty cents it is." We completed the transaction without going through the cash register, and he offered me his hand to shake. And so, cheerfully complicit in a minor commercial fraud, I left the store, took a breath of the cool spring air, and pushed open the door to the museum.

I would spend many hours in the museum that summer and in the two summers that followed, and its two rooms—originally designed as a waiting room and office—would become very familiar to me. On this, the first occasion that I saw it, I was stunned at how small it was—and at the largeness of Mr. Spurr. When I came in he was standing at an old-style writing desk, going through a stack of papers. He looked up, took me in with a glance, and gestured towards a chair facing him. "Sit down, Mr. Ellis," he said, his tone brooking no argument.

My future employer was a good six foot, but his girth was even more impressive: his waist must have been at least fifty inches. For all that, however, my impression wasn't so much of fatness as of power. Mr. Spurr had presence, authority; one didn't want to disagree with him. I sat where he indicated.

"This museum is dedicated to the memory of my grandfather," said Mr. Spurr, not looking at me. "He was a formidable man. One way or another he was associated with some of the greatest intellectual breakthroughs of the modern era." He paused, and shot me a glance. "Are you familiar with the names Charles Darwin, Alfred Russel Wallace, Sigmund Freud, and Albert Einstein?"

"Yes, sir," I said. "A little bit. Not all of them."

"Which ones?" asked Mr. Spurr.

I tried frantically to remember the list. "Um, Einstein and, and, Freud, and . . ."

"Wallace?" prompted Mr. Spurr, raising his eyebrows.

"No, sir," I said. "Darwin. I learned about Charles Darwin in biology class."

"I'm glad to hear it," said Mr. Spurr. "Perhaps public education is not a complete failure after all. But you know nothing of Alfred Russel Wallace?"

"No, sir," I said.

"You will," said Mr. Spurr. "For the moment, let me simply tell you that my grandfather corresponded with all these men, and that he was able, in every instance, to offer them insights that helped them significantly with their work."

He clearly expected a response to this, and I did my best to supply the correct one. "That's amazing, sir," I said. And then, seeing that this wasn't quite enough: "Maybe he should be famous, too."

"I intend that he become so," said Mr. Spurr, becoming the first man to deploy a subjunctive clause in my presence. "This museum is dedicated precisely to that goal."

"Yes, sir," I said.

"You will begin at $2.25 an hour," said Mr. Spurr, "a full twenty-five cents above the minimum wage. You will wear a pressed white shirt and black dress pants with a blazer. You will also wear polished black dress shoes. Do you own these items?"

"Some of them, sir," I said.

"I am prepared to assist financially with the purchase of any items you do not have," said Mr. Spurr. "Buy them sometime before the summer begins and present me with the receipts. Do you have any questions?"

"Yes," I said, surprised, though pleasantly, that I'd been given the job so quickly. "Am I the only employee?"

"I anticipate hiring one more young man," said Mr. Spurr. "Have you a friend you'd like to recommend?"

"Yes, sir," I said. "I have." It occurred to me how wonderful it would be if Otis could work here, too.

"What is his name?" asked Mr. Spurr.

"Otis James," I said. "He goes to my school."

"Otis?" said Mr. Spurr, raising one eyebrow. "Is he a black young man?"

"No, sir," I said. "He's Indian—Ojibwa." I worried that might sink my friend's chances. "But he has white parents."

Mr. Spurr thought a moment, then simply nodded his head. "You vouch for this young man?"

"Yes, sir," I said. "He's a great guy. Very—very dependable."

"All right. Tell him to come and see me. But tell him to leave his feather headdress at home." Mr. Spurr gave a dry chuckle.

I sighed inwardly. "Yes, sir," I said. And two days later Otis had the job.

Chapter Eighteen: New Beginnings

Otis and I duly reported to work as soon as school ended for the summer. We had outfitted ourselves as Mr. Spurr directed, and our parents were gratified when he reimbursed them in full for our purchases. "That's a very good sign," said my father. "He's not a man who nickels-and-dimes."

The museum was open five days a week, from Tuesday through Saturday. We opened the doors at ten o'clock in the morning and closed them at five in the afternoon. The idea was that we should go to lunch separately, making sure that one of us was always there, but we decided early on that we would bring lunch in and eat together—though often one or the other of us would go out to buy a couple of cold soft drinks.

The museum was dominated by a huge oil painting of James Alfred Spurr. In the portrait he was probably about fifty-five, generous of paunch, and sporting a large white beard and moustache. He glared out at the viewer with one hand in his waistcoat, and the other resting on the silver handle of a walnut walking stick. Unfortunately, this was the most visually dramatic artifact in the museum. The other exhibits consisted largely of framed letters from various nineteenth- and early twentieth-century luminaries thanking him for this or that piece of correspondence, each of which had apparently contained some vital piece of information or stunning insight that allowed said luminaries to move their work forward. There were a few other things: the fountain pen with which Spurr wrote his letters; a brass letter opener; a snuff box; a handful of early editions of books or articles written by Darwin, et al; and a photograph of Spurr's home in Port Hope, Ontario—but the whole collection could be viewed comfortably in five to ten minutes.

There was a flurry of activity in the first few days of the season, as local history buffs made their visits. People forked over fifty cents when they entered, admired the portrait, glanced at the framed letters, went hopefully into the second room where we displayed the other artifacts, and returned to the front desk asking, with evident disappointment, "Is that it?" We acknowledged that it was; they looked puzzled; then, as often as not, they shrugged, and went out the door. A reporter and a photographer from the local newspaper came late on the second day, and, by pre-arrangement, Mr. David Spurr was there to meet them. The photographer took a picture of the current Mr. Spurr in front of the portrait of his glowering ancestor, then left, leaving the reporter, a fellow of about twenty, to ask some questions.

"So what's this all about?" he asked Mr. Spurr, producing a notebook from the back pocket of his jeans.

Mr. Spurr glared at him. "What precisely do you mean?"

"I mean, why the fuss over this old guy?" asked the reporter, flicking the hair out of his eyes. "So he wrote some letters. Is that really such a big deal? I mean, big enough to get him a museum?"

I hadn't known Mr. Spurr long at this point, but even I could see he wasn't pleased with the tone of the question—let alone its content. "Do you have a university degree?" he asked silkily.

"I went to the college," replied the journalist. He clearly meant the community college where my father taught, a place geared towards vocational training rather than academic enquiry.

Mr. Spurr smiled like a crocodile. "Oh?" he said. "So you weren't actually required to read books or learn history or anything of that sort?"

"I learned some things," said the journalist defensively. His fingers played with a little plastic cylinder intended to hold film but containing, I was pretty sure, a stash of marijuana.

"Do you know who Charles Darwin was?" asked Mr. Spurr.

"Yeah," said the reporter. "He was the guy who said we came from monkeys."

"Well, some of us are closer than others," said Mr. Spurr. "Try not to scrape your knuckles as you leave."

"Scrape my knuckles?" said the young man, imagining, perhaps, that he was in danger of getting into a fist fight.

"On the floor," said Mr. Spurr. "Good day to you."

★

Remarkably, the story accompanying the photo in the next day's newspaper was neutral. The article did manage to convey that the collection was small, but it didn't call the manager an arrogant bastard or suggest that fifty cents would be better spent on a tube of candy or a soft drink (and I confess there would be days when both Otis and I thought this). But while the publicity, such as it was, led to a few more curious visitors, in the weeks that followed we would rarely entertain more than six or seven guests a day—and at just fifty cents a head we realized very quickly that the museum was a money-losing venture. Mr. Spurr seemed quite unfazed, however. He would regularly drop by just before five and collect the day's proceeds.

But starting work was not the only significant event of late June. For one reason or another my birthday celebrations outside the family had been pushed back a week, but my parents told me I could again take some friends to the movies on the last Saturday evening in June, then bring them all back for cake and ice cream. John had gone off to church camp as soon as the summer began, but Otis and Edith, Big Andy and Janet, and Bruce all accepted the invitation, and Mr. James kindly said that Otis could take the car. So my dad drove Big Andy, Janet and me, and Otis drove himself, Edith and Bruce, and at six-thirty we all converged at the Odeon once again, I with a fistful of dollars to buy six tickets to *Blazing Saddles*.

Against all odds we once again ran into Chris the Bayridge Bus Guy, though this time Otis and I found him at the snack bar.

"Chris!" said Otis. "We always run into you at the movies, man!"

"Yeah," said Chris. "My parents give me the money for the ticket and for popcorn and a drink. I get 7Up because it doesn't have the caffeine." He scratched his nose in the characteristic way he had, brushing it several times in quick succession with the back of his right hand, all the while screwing up his face. "Where are your girlfriends?" he added, looking from Otis to me, then back to Otis.

"Edith is in the theatre," said Otis, "and Peter's friend had a car accident."

"Is she dead?" asked Chris, not quite looking at me, but directing the question my way.

"Yes," I said. I suddenly felt Mary-Lynne almost as a physical presence. I felt her warmth at my shoulder, and smelled her perfume.

"Kaiser died, too," said Chris. "He got hit by a car. The car didn't stop. It was a green Impala SS 427. I didn't get the plate. The police said they couldn't do anything." And right there, in the middle of the small theatre lobby, Chris began to sob.

"Hey, Chris," said Otis. "Hey, Chris—don't cry, man." He put his arm on Chris's shoulder, but Chris shook it off.

"He was a good dog!" Chris sobbed. "He loved me! Nobody loves me like that dog! He slept on my bed. He jumped all over me when I came home." He put his head in his hands and began to rock back and forth. Everyone in the lobby was looking at us.

"Chris," said Otis. "Are you alone here tonight?"

"Yes," Chris sobbed. "I don't come with anyone. My parents give me the money."

"Come sit with us," said Otis. "Okay? Let's get your popcorn and 7Up, and we'll get our stuff, and you can come and join us. We're celebrating Peter's birthday. It's a kind of party."

"A birthday party?" said Chris, and he stopped sobbing.

"Yeah," said Otis. "A birthday party. Come join the birthday party."

"Okay," said Chris. "I'll come to the birthday party."

So we made our purchases, and Chris came and sat with us in the theatre. After the movie it just seemed natural that he accompany us to my house for cake and ice cream. And after the cake and ice cream, Otis and Edith drove him home. And while Mary-Lynne's absence was like a hole in my heart, in a weird sort of way Chris plugged a small part of that hole.

Chapter Nineteen: The Walking Stick

Fall found us back at school again, now in grade twelve—and if that wasn't change enough, Conrad was now in grade nine. When, on the first day, we walked to the bus together, he was quieter than usual. Then: "Is there any kind of initiation no one's told us about?" he asked.

Just for an instant, I played with the idea of telling him horrendous stories about greasy poles and mud baths and public speeches—but I decided against it. "No," I said, "there used to be a grade-nine initiation day, but things got out of hand a few years ago, and now they're not allowed." And this was true: a few kids had been really traumatized.

"So there isn't even a secret one?" Conrad asked.

"Nope," I said. "If there was, I'd know about it."

"Well, that's lousy," said Conrad, showing I'd misread him completely.

"What do you mean, that's lousy?" I asked. "Do you want to have people yelling at you, and making you run through obstacle courses and eat raw hot dogs?"

"Sure," said Conrad, all bluff and bravado. "It's a good way of bonding with other guys, going through that sort of thing. I'd be up for it."

"You're an ass," I said.

"You're what comes out of an ass," said Conrad cheerfully, and so we went merrily to school.

On a Tuesday morning, in late September, I was in English class with John and Edith and Otis and thirty others, when the intercom crackled to life and one of the secretaries asked our teacher to send Otis to the office.

"Oh, you're in trouble now, Otis," said John. "They've found out about the you-know-what."

"They won't get the truth out of me," said Otis. "I'll take one for the team."

"Don't be long, if you can help it," said Mr. Watt, a stocky, rosy-cheeked young teacher who was said to be a former provincial kayaking champion. "This stuff is important."

But Otis didn't come back—and he wasn't the kind of guy who would deliberately prolong an absence to miss class. When the period was over, I gathered up his books, and Edith headed off to the office to see what was up. I chatted with John for a moment or two, but left when I saw his eye wandering towards Megan, an Irish-Japanese girl he'd taken an interest in. He was too polite to tell me to get lost, but I could see my place was elsewhere, and I followed Edith down to the office.

When I arrived, I found Edith in earnest conversation with a secretary behind the counter. She was a tall and sharp-featured lady, and she looked annoyed, so just for a moment I thought Otis might indeed be in trouble—but when Edith turned towards me I saw there were tears in her eyes. "What's wrong, Edith?" I asked.

"Otis's dad is dead," she said. "The vice-principal has taken him to the hospital to be with his mom. Do you have any money?"

"Money?" I said stupidly. "I think I have a couple of dollars. Why do you need money?"

"I want to take a cab to the hospital, but I only have a dollar fifty," she said.

I thought for a moment. "John could take you!" I said. "He has an extra helmet." We ran upstairs together, found John in the hall talking with Megan, and told him the problem. "I don't have it here today," he said, shaking his head. "The strap's broken and I left it on the kitchen table at home. I'm really sorry."

"How about a cab?" said Megan, but just as we were all digging into our pockets to see if we had enough money among us, Stephen and Dent came down the hall. I remembered his offer of seven months back—and his kindness in taking us to the hospital before—and I called out to him. "Stephen," I said, "Otis's dad has just died. Could you drive some of us to the hospital?"

Stephen didn't miss a beat. "Let's go," he said. "My hearse is out back."

"You're not going anywhere," said a gravelly voice behind us, and we turned to see the large Biology teacher, Mr. Harcourt, pointing at Stephen. "You've got a lab next period, boy. You can go wherever you're going at lunch, if it's important."

"The guy's dad is dead," said Stephen.

"Nothing you can do to change that," said Mr. Harcourt.

"Fuck off," said Stephen, and he and Dent turned and ran towards the back exit, with Edith right behind them. John shrugged apologetically at Mr. Harcourt—"Otis is our friend," he said—then he and I took off, too.

★

Mr. James had died of a heart attack: Otis told me he'd already had one heart attack and was taking medicine for angina. Apparently the men in the family tended to go before their seventieth birthdays. "He knew he was living on borrowed time," said Otis. The funeral was held at the Jameses' home church—a small grey building on the outskirts of town. My father came with me, for moral support, and we were welcomed by the short and balding Pastor Rod. "Welcome, brothers," he said, shaking each of our hands in turn, gripping our right hands with both of his.

The church was full. Focused though I was on Otis's grief, I was relieved not to see the Missionary anywhere—clearly he was spreading joy somewhere else on this occasion. Otis and Mrs. James were in the front row, accompanied by Edith, to Otis's left, and a woman I didn't recognize, but who, I learned later, was Mr. James's sister, on Mrs. James's right. The women were all crying softly, even before the service began; my friend sat stoically among them, but he too would weep later on.

All of Otis's school friends were there, scattered throughout the church: John and Megan had taken seats about halfway up the centre aisle; Bruce was there with his mom; Big Andy and Janet were at the back. Stephen and Dent were there, too, I saw—both wearing their trademark sunglasses, and looking vaguely mafia-like in their jackets and ties (though the fact they were also wearing jeans subverted the image a little). Even Mr. Spurr was there, impeccably dressed and carrying what I later discovered was a gentleman's walnut walking stick. My dad and I found seats a couple of pews behind Otis; I wanted to be close to my friend without encroaching on family space.

A door opened from a vesting room at the front of the church, and a group of men and women in choir robes shuffled out. They took their places on a bench facing us, and a moment later Pastor Rod's rotund wife seated herself at an electric piano and launched them—and us—into a hymn. While we were singing, the pastor himself advanced from the back of the church to the front. "I want to say a warm welcome to you all in the name of Jesus!" he said. "I know that Brother Harry is grateful to see you all here supporting his family. Family and friends were real important to him in this world, and I reckon they're important in heaven, too—and you can be sure that's where Brother Harry is right now."

"Amen!" cried Brother Ted, the goateed gentleman I'd met, after a fashion, at the swimming-pool baptism. Mrs. James sobbed aloud, but shook her head in assent.

And so the service unfolded, with words and music and tears. For me the most challenging few moments came when Otis himself rose to speak. He went up to the front, faced us, and spoke from his heart. "My dad wasn't my biological father," he said, "but he was the best dad I could ever have asked for. He and my mom took me in when I was four years old, and raised me as if I was theirs from the beginning. My dad taught me to drive, and he taught me the different kinds of birds, and he showed me how to fix things, too. I love him, and I'm going to miss him." And then he broke down—the first time I'd ever seen him cry. And that sight, and the still raw memory of Mary-Lynne, brought me to tears, too, and I had to bite down on a wad of Kleenex to keep from sobbing aloud, while my own dad alternately gripped and patted my shoulder.

I've encountered some stupid clergy over the years, and I've told some rude jokes at the expense of church people, too, but at this time and in this place the round and ruddy-cheeked Pastor Rod conducted himself and the service with dignity and grace. When he spoke of Otis's dad, he spoke with affection and as someone who really knew him. When he spoke directly to Otis and to Mrs. James, he was gentle and warm and kind. And when he spoke to us, as a congregation, he found the right words to reach even those who did not share his own faith. I don't know what that small church was able to pay him, but he earned his keep that day; and I know, too, that in the months that followed he was good about visiting Mrs. James and listening to her and praying with her.

★

At the reception in the Jameses' home—after the funeral and the burial—I paid my respects to Mrs. James, then went looking for Otis. He was sitting on a straight-backed chair in the corner of the dining room, Edith at his side, overlooking a table covered in salads and casseroles and fruit pies. There were all sorts of people milling about, many of them eating, but in this moment anyway Otis occupied a little pool of peace, supported only by Edith, who was holding his hand. "Hey, buddy. It's good to see you," he said, and to my surprise he rose and embraced me.

"I was at the funeral, too," I said, though why I felt the need to say so is beyond me.

"I know. I saw you," he replied. "Mom and I really appreciate you being there."

"He was a good guy, your dad," I said.

"Yes, he was," said Otis. Edith stroked the back of his hand.

"Are you and your mom going to be okay?" I asked. My dad had spent a little time the previous evening explaining how insurance and pensions worked. It's a measure of my staggering naïveté that I had no idea.

"You mean, how are we going to pay the bills?" he said. "I don't know yet. Pastor Rod has a guy from the church looking at my dad's papers and bank books. If I have to get a part-time job, that's okay." That possibility hadn't occurred to me, but it didn't surprise me that Otis had already considered it.

At that moment Mr. Spurr came up, holding his walking stick in both hands and pressed against his stomach so he could wend his way through the crowd. "Otis, my boy," he said ponderously, "I'm so sorry for your loss."

"Thank you, sir," said Otis. "It's good of you to come."

"I only met your father on one occasion," said Mr. Spurr, "but he struck me then as one of nature's gentlemen."

"Thank you, sir," said Otis again. "He was." And then, hoping to break the formality, perhaps: "Hey, I really like your walking stick."

Mr. Spurr glanced down at the walking stick, looked back up at Otis, then extended the stick to him. "A small present," he said. "It once belonged to James Alfred Spurr himself."

Otis did not take the stick. "I couldn't accept it, sir," he said. "But thank you. It's really kind of you."

But Mr. Spurr insisted. "I have two others," he said, "and I want you to have this one." He pushed it to within an inch of Otis's hands.

Otis took the stick. "Thank you," he said. "That's just about the nicest gift anyone has ever given me."

Mr. Spurr nodded, half smiled; then, with a curt "I'll take my leave," turned and headed back through the crowd, a man not fully moored in his time and place, but with a moral compass in his waistcoat pocket.

Chapter Twenty: Rescue Operation

The gift of a walking stick meant more to Otis than Mr. Spurr could possibly have realized—and I should probably emphasize that this wasn't a cane, a medical appliance, so much as a nineteenth-century fashion accessory. If Otis's ethnicity and long black hair had made him stand out at QDSS before now, the addition of a gentleman's black walnut walking stick confirmed his status as the most eccentric character in the school. He was careful never to wave it around inside, rather tucking it under his arm or holding it at his side while he was in the building, but once he got outside he wielded it in the way its maker had surely intended—as a pointer, as a conversational exclamation mark, and as a means of eloquent self-expression. Some young men sucked on cigarettes; Otis shook his stick.

But the possession of a gentleman's walking stick did not make Otis and his mother immune to the pressures of the marketplace. Indeed, Mr. James did have a pension, but that pension was cut in half upon his death, and if the whole provided an adequate living for three, half was not quite enough for two. My friend found work in a convenience store, Becker's, near the school, from four to seven in the evening Monday through Friday. Fifteen hours a week wasn't much, but it bought his clothes and school supplies, and he also began saving for college.

My brother Conrad settled into grade nine very quickly. He had never played lacrosse, but he was a fine soccer player, and he made the school's fifteen-and-under squad. This meant he often took the second bus home, while even in grade twelve I usually took the first. To my parents' astonishment, I had conceived an interest in maps, and I would spend hour after hour in my room, poring over atlases, and then challenging myself to draw freehand maps of the various continents. My goal became to be able to draw, from memory, accurate maps of the whole world, complete with borders, capital cities, and natural and cultural heritage sites. My father encouraged this, but it seemed to worry my mother. One day she suggested I might like to see a counselor of some kind, and afterwards I overheard an argument between her and my dad. "He needs help handling his grief," she said. "This *is* the way he's handling it," my father replied.

On a Saturday evening in late November, Conrad secured our mother's permission to go to a party at a friend's house. As it happens, my father was in Kingston that weekend, doing some research for the graduate program he was finishing at Queen's. My mother said she was going to play bridge with some old friends, and I was perfectly happy staying home with my atlases and drawing pads. At around eleven o'clock, however, as I was thinking of making myself a Kraft pizza, the telephone rang.

The voice on the other end was male and agitated. "Hey, man, is that Mr. Ellis?" it said.

"No," I answered. "He's not here. Can I help?"

"Fuck," said the voice at the other end. "Okay. Are you, like, Conrad's brother?"

"Yes, I am," I said.

"Maybe you should come get him," the voice said. Behind him I could hear shouting, banging and the sound of breaking glass.

"Where is he?" I asked. The voice gave me a house number on Highway 6, which I wrote down, but he hung up when I asked his name, the phone taking a long time to find its cradle. And suddenly I had a problem, because my father had the car in Kingston (and I had only my learner's permit anyway), my mother was at a friend's home for which she'd forgotten to leave a number, and I hadn't enough money for a taxi. As I was standing by the phone, wondering what on earth I should do, Otis drove into the driveway.

I opened the front door and stepped out on the porch even as Otis was getting out of the car. "Is your brother at the McPherson party?" he asked.

"Yes," I said. "How did you know?"

"I guessed," said Otis. "All the jocks and jock wannabes are there. I've just driven by the house and there are three police cars outside."

"I've just had a weird call from someone about him," I said. "Can you take me?"

"Sure. Should we tell your parents? Where's their car?" said Otis, looking around.

"My dad's out of town," I said, "and my mom's at a friend's."

"Grab your coat," said Otis. "We'll boot on over." So I grabbed my coat, raced out of the house and, as Edith wasn't with Otis, piled into the front seat.

★

There were four police cars and two ambulances at the McPherson home by the time we arrived, and there were many more cars parked in the driveway and along Highway 6. (The house was on Highway 6 which, despite its name, was nothing more than a two lane road leading out of Queensville and south towards Tweed.) The nearest neighbour to the McPhersons' was a couple of hundred yards away, and we pulled over between the two homes and watched as police led about eleven boys towards their cruisers, opened the doors, and shoved them in. Conrad wasn't among them.

"You want to see if we can find him now?" asked Otis as two of the cruisers drove away.

"Yeah. Might as well," I said, and we got out, walked along the verge of the highway, and began crossing the lawn towards the McPherson home.

As we drew near the front door it opened, and a police officer stepped out. "Hey! Where do you think you're going?" he asked.

"I think my younger brother's inside," I said. "We've come to get him. I got a phone call."

The police officer looked at us speculatively for a moment. "Have you been drinking?" he asked.

"No, sir," I said. "Well, nothing stronger than a soft drink."

"What about you?" said the officer, turning his attention to Otis.

"I don't drink," said Otis.

The policeman grunted skeptically, then looked again at me. "What's your brother's name?"

"Conrad," I said. "Conrad Ellis."

"Where are your parents?" he asked.

"Out of town," I replied. It seemed easier.

"Okay," he said. "Come in. We'll see if he's here."

The house was now relatively quiet, though I knew it must have been filled with noise and action half an hour before. A chair in the hall was lying on its side, smashed—a huge framed print and its glass damaged beyond repair beside it. There were two large holes in the wall of the staircase leading to the upstairs. But if the damage here was bad, the state of the living room almost beggared belief: it was wrecked, ruined, devastated. The curtains had been torn down. The walls were covered in booze and, like the stairway, had large holes in several places. The chairs and sofas were turned over, their fabric torn. A crystal chandelier lay on the floor, and the place reeked of alcohol and vomit. Paramedics were attending to three boys and one girl among the ruins—but none of them was Conrad.

"Anyone of these your brother?" asked the officer.

"No," I said. "Are these kids okay?"

"Alcohol poisoning, concussion, who knows?" he said. "But, yeah, they'll make it." He addressed himself to one of the paramedics. "Any other kids getting attention, Ross?"

"There are four in the downstairs bedrooms," said the paramedic, not even looking up. "We haven't been able to get to them yet. Haven't checked upstairs."

The officer led us through another hall and then down a flight of stairs, and we found ourselves in an area where, I guessed, Tom McPherson and his brother spent much of their time. There was a sort of family room filled with sports posters (now ripped) and a large television (smashed), and there were doors leading to a couple of bedrooms. But we didn't venture into either of them because, huddling in a corner of the family room, a splash of sick beside him, was my brother Conrad. "Conrad!" I cried, and Otis and I went towards him.

"Oh, Jesus," said Conrad, his eyes rolling and apparently unable to focus. "Oh, Jesus, am I ever fucked up."

★

The fact Conrad was conscious and apparently uninjured persuaded the police to let Otis and me take him home. We got him to the car by propping him up between us, stopping once to let him vomit, and we nearly made it back to our house before he vomited again. ("I'm so sorry," I said to Otis. "I'll deal with it later," he replied.) When we got him inside we removed his shirt and jeans and put him into a warm shower—which he did not appreciate. We then wrapped him in towels and took him to his bedroom and put him on the bed. "There are cows," he proclaimed.

"What?" I replied, a little distracted by the need to put the shower curtain back up, if I could, and get his clothes into the washer.

"There are cows in the fields . . . and beetles," said Conrad. "And I can fly like, like Superman."

"He's high," said Otis.

"He's drunk," I said.

"He's drunk and high," said Otis. "You've had quite a night, haven't you, Con?"

"You're an Indian, Odis," said Conrad. "Columbus discovered you . . . scalping people." And he tried, without success, to pat his hand against his mouth while making a sustained war whoop—an attempt arrested by his needing to vomit again. Fortunately, this time we had a bowl to hand.

"Con," said Otis. "What did you have tonight beside the rye?"

"Coke," said Conrad. "I had coke in the rye. I wanna read Catcher in the Coke, but I can't read right now."

"That's fine," said Otis. "But what else did you have beside the rye and coke?"

"Little blue paper," said Conrad. "I licked it. Jesus, it's hot in here."

"Okay," said Otis. And then to me: "It's going to be a long night."

★

It was a long night. My mom returned around two in the morning, first outraged to find the bathroom a disaster area, then overwhelmed with concern for Conrad. She insisted on sitting with him for the next several hours, leaving Otis and me free to clean up the bathroom and his mother's car. And it was only later, days later, that I wondered why my mom had come home so late from a bridge game.

Chapter Twenty-One:
An Appointment with the Skulls

In the late fall, the local motorcycle gang, the Skulls, had estab-lished a business selling drugs in the parking lot at the back of QDSS. Every Thursday afternoon two of their members would arrive at the school on their motorbikes and spend about fifteen minutes dealing with anyone who had cash. I've no idea why the school never did anything about it or why the police weren't called. I guess it's possible they *were* called, but that they failed to respond within the fifteen minutes the bikers were there.

What was available? Mostly grass and hash—but there was also LSD, which we usually called *acid* (but also *blotter* or *dots*). Someone at the party had given Conrad a piece of blue paper impregnated with the stuff and, like a fool, he'd licked it. "Didn't it taste awful?" I asked him later. "It didn't taste like anything," he said.

So the school didn't do anything, and the police didn't do anything, and I don't blame the student government for not doing anything either—what sort of fool would want to tangle with bikers? But on a Thursday afternoon in early January, someone did just that.

It was the last period of the day and Otis and I had a spare; we were outside talking with friends when a biker pulled into the parking lot. Usually, as I've said, there were two of them, but on this occasion there was just the one: maybe his partner was sick, or maybe the club had decided no extra muscle was needed. Anyway, the one who showed up was about five-foot-eleven—four inches taller than Otis—tattooed and muscular, but with a big gut. He dismounted from his bike, walked into the centre of the smoking area, and unzipped his leather jacket. Two grade ten students, both male, immediately approached him.

"What have you got there?" asked Otis. He was carrying his walking stick, as always, and I noticed the fingers of the hand holding it were white, as though he were gripping it hard.

"Wait your turn," said the biker. "I deal with my regulars first." One of the boys fished a ten-dollar bill out of his pocket and extended it, palm down.

"What are you selling them?" asked Otis.

"Whatever they want," said the biker. "Now shut the fuck up while I'm counting."

"They're too young to be buying that shit," said Otis, taking a step towards the trio. It was the first time I'd heard him use a profanity, and I realized, in that instant, that he wasn't going to back away from whatever came. The thought scared me. Bad enough to tangle with a Ted Staunton or Jake O'Leary—but to go head to head with a biker was crazy.

The biker looked at him directly for the first time. "What did you say, nigger?" he said.

"If you think I'm a black man, you're even stupider than I thought," said Otis mildly, and he tapped his walking stick on the ground twice. He was smiling, just a little.

Sensing danger, the two grade tens stepped away from the biker. "Hey, man," said one of them, addressing Otis, "we know what we're doing."

"I don't think you do," said Otis. He raised the tip of his stick and pointed it at the biker's throat. "Get out," he said.

"You point that fucking thing at me and I'll shove it up your nigger ass," said the biker. His right hand reached towards the back of his belt.

Otis had become adept at wielding his walking stick. Before the biker could produce what he was reaching for, my friend flicked his wrist in such a way that the tip of the stick hit his adversary in the testicles. The biker dropped to his knees, clutching at himself. An ugly little knife clattered on the concrete.

Otis put his stick under the larger man's chin and forced him to raise his head. "Go now," he said, "and leave your shit behind . . . so I can flush it." The biker made to move sideways, but Otis's stick was at his throat in an instant. "Do as I say," he said.

Slowly, clumsily, the biker pulled several baggies of dope from pockets inside his leather jacket. He had weed, hash and, yes, little pieces of blue paper. He put them in a sullen little pile on the concrete floor of the smoking area, then scrambled to his feet. "Good-bye," said Otis.

The biker turned and headed back towards his bike. When he was about five yards from it, however, he turned again and pointed at Otis. "You don't know what you've started," he snarled. "You have no fucking idea."

"Nice to meet you, guy," said Otis, smiling. Then he gathered up the biker's wares and, true to his word, took them into the school to flush them.

★

Of course, this event was soon the talk of the school. Everyone knew of it. And of course, too, people understood that things would not end there. Bikers did not back away from a fight—particularly if the enemy was a single grade twelve student who had, as they'd see it, ripped off some of their product. There would be repercussions—and those repercussions would come quickly.

At recess the next day a number of Otis's friends assembled in a library seminar room. For whatever reason—maybe because it was recess, or maybe because she liked a number of us—Miss Leggat looked the other way when we took possession of the space. It could even be that she'd heard news of the smoking area confrontation, and that this was her way of showing moral support for Otis. In any event, we were left unmolested for fifteen minutes. Bruce was there, along with Big Andy and Janet and John and Megan; Otis himself was there, and Edith, and I was, too, though my guts were roiling; and to my surprise, we were joined, after a couple of minutes, by Stephen and Dent.

"You've got a big problem," said Stephen, coming into the glass-enclosed room with Dent hard on his heels.

"I've got a problem," Otis agreed. "But I've got friends, too."

"Are you here to help?" John asked.

"Yeah," said Stephen, sitting down. "But I think the Indian is crazy."

"People say you're a little crazy, too," said Big Andy.

"I hope you've got some kind of plan," said Stephen. "Because those bikers are gonna do something, and do it soon. They'll know where you live," he said, addressing himself to Otis, "and they'll be planning a visit."

"I don't have a plan yet," said Otis.

"I have," said Bruce.

We turned towards Bruce with some surprise. No one would ever have mistaken Bruce for a lightweight, but that he should take the lead in a situation like this was unexpected. But our friend's eyes were gleaming behind his spectacles. "Have you ever heard of a *son et lumiere*?" he asked.

No one had. "Is that some sort of Chinese thing?" asked Stephen skeptically.

"French," said Bruce. "It's French for *sound and light* show. It's where you put on a big show with all kinds of different lights and sounds and voices, but usually not with people."

"How do you get the voices, then?" asked Dent shrewdly.

"They're recorded," said Bruce. "Or people can speak over microphones. Or you can do both. Whatever. It can be a really big deal."

"So what's the plan, Mr. Sound and Light?" asked Janet. She was chewing nervously on a wad of gum.

Bruce leaned forward, his hands clasped together on the table. "I agree that the bikers will come to Otis's house," he said. "So the thing we need to do is to be ready for them. I think they'll come at night, because that's when they figure it'll be easier to scare him."

"They don't get up 'til the afternoon anyway," said Stephen.

"Okay," said Bruce. "So what we do is, we rig up the trees and the house with speakers and lights and fireworks, and we keep watch, and when they arrive—boom! We hit them with the biggest freaking sound and light show anyone has ever seen!"

There was silence for a moment. "And how do we do that?" asked Dent.

"*I* can do that," said Bruce. "I need money for fireworks and chemicals, but I've got pretty well everything else. I know what I'm doing."

I thought about the light show Bruce had created in his bedroom a couple of years before to accompany the music of Pink Floyd and Supertramp. If he had continued to work at his skills in the interim, and if he had the equipment, or access to it, I could well believe he'd be able to put on a pretty impressive sound and light show. But would it be enough to scare a gang of bikers?

"Does anyone have any other suggestion?" asked Otis. He looked around the table, but no one spoke. "So let's try this," he said.

Chapter Twenty-Two: Sturm und Drang

Otis booked off sick from the convenience store that afternoon and drove his mother out of town to stay with Mr. James's sister—a widow like herself. Meanwhile, Bruce, John, Big Andy, Stephen, Dent and I used Stephen's hearse and Bruce's father's van to transport eight large speakers, four amplifiers, two spotlights, three huge buckets of liquid detergent, and hundreds of yards of cable and god-knows-what-else to Otis's home. As soon as we arrived, Bruce put us to work hoisting the speakers into trees or placing them behind bushes. Janet and Edith, meanwhile, had taken our pooled funds to spend at a store that sold fireworks, and as the shadows lengthened they arrived with what Bruce had directed them to buy—hundreds of sparklers and thousands of fire-crackers. "I hope you know what you're doing, Bruce," said Janet as she dropped the sparklers beside him.

"I know exactly what I'm doing," said Bruce. "Now go help the others run the cables."

My role in this was simple but, I liked to think, important. Bruce had set me up in the Jameses' living room with a reel-to-reel tape recorder, a stereo system, and a sound-effects album called "General Mayhem." He showed me how to record a series of sound effects on one channel, then start the disc in a different place, record again, and lay the second recording aurally on top of the first. "Do that four times," he said. It took me a while to line things up, but laying down the tracks was surprisingly easy once I understood the technique, and I soon had a fifteen-minute tape made up of sirens, whirring helicopter blades, police whistles, and machinegun fire.

Once Bruce was sure the speakers were in place and hooked up to outlets in the garage and the front hall, he took over the recording equipment and reconfigured the stereo and tape systems.

He then brought us all inside briefly and, with a large microphone, taped all of the males shouting hoarsely. "Go ahead and swear," he said: "Fuck this, and screw that! Up against the wall, assholes! I've got the bastards!" If we'd been doing this for any other reason, it might have been fun, but the gathering dusk lent a real sense of urgency to our task.

Otis returned at six, bringing a shopping bag filled with submarine sandwiches. While the rest of us ate, Bruce worked with the sparklers, some duct tape, a coil of what looked like silver, three highway flares, and a plastic pipe he said he'd borrowed from his father's workshop.

"What's the silver stuff?" asked John.

"Magnesium ribbon," said Bruce.

"What are you doing with all that?" asked Big Andy.

"Don't ask," said Bruce. "The less you know about this, the better. Just make sure you stay right away from this thing when I've set it up."

Otis was talking quietly to Edith and Janet off to one side of the house. "No way!" said Janet, her voice rising suddenly.

"I think you should," said Otis.

"We're not going anywhere, Otis," said Edith. "The more witnesses, the less chance they'll do anything really violent."

Bruce overheard this, and I saw him give a half-smirk. "Why are you smiling?" I asked.

"Otis needn't worry about the girls," said Bruce. "I got us all covered."

At seven-thirty, Bruce conducted an inspection. He set the volume controls very low on his amps, and went from speaker to speaker making sure they were working. He then tested the spotlights. Finally he produced a package of fuses from his pocket, sought out the Jameses' electrical panel, and replaced the fuses that were there with a set of his own. "This is the weak spot," he said. "We're taking a bit of a risk here, but I think it'll be fine."

"What have you guys told your parents?" asked Otis. We had each told our various moms and dads a cock-and-bull story of one kind or another. John's parents thought he was at a bible study. Big Andy's thought he was at a wrestling practice. I'd told mine I was working on a big geography project. "My parents did-n't ask," said Janet. "I just told mom I was here," said Edith. Stephen and Dent weren't part of this conversation; they were watching Bruce's work with unfeigned fascination.

"Okay," said Bruce. "Battle stations. Edith, you and Janet need to go to the upstairs bedrooms so you can give us an early warn-ing when the bikers are coming. Big Andy and John, you need to go to the spotlights in the front yard and get ready to shine them at people when I fire them up."

"That'll pretty well blind them," said John.

"That's the idea," said Bruce. "Peter, you come and help me with the sound equipment. Stephen, you've got the siren on your car. Dent," he paused. "You sure you're up for this?"

"Yup," said Dent, grinning from ear to ear.

"Okay," said Bruce. "Otis, I left you out when I was planning this. What do you want to do?"

"I'll just wait for them on the front porch," said Otis. "They'll expect me to be hiding somewhere."

"Okay, then," said Bruce. "Let's do this."

And so the wait began.

★

I'd read that much of war is waiting, and we did a lot of wait-ing that night—and it was, of course, dark and cold. Eight o'clock. Nine. Nine-thirty. Ten. Ten-thirty. Eleven. Eleven-thirty. We waited, and we talked back and forth, and every now and then someone slipped away to the bathroom in the house or, in the case of the males, peed in the bushes.

"My pecker's freezing," called Big Andy at one point.

"Get John to rub it for you!" Janet yelled from the upstairs bedroom.

At twenty to twelve, the phone rang. "Should I answer it?" I asked Bruce.

He hesitated a moment, then called out to Otis. "Should Pete answer the phone?"

"Yeah. In case it's my mom!" Otis called back.

I picked up the phone. "Hello?" I said. There was silence at the other end, then whoever it was hung up. "They hung up," I reported.

"It was the bikers, then," said Bruce. "Making sure Otis is home. They'll be here soon." We shared the news with the others, and a little wave of apprehension passed among us.

At five to twelve a figure emerged out of the darkness at the back of the house, briefly surprising everyone. It was Conrad. "Is Peter here?" he asked. Otis sent him inside where I was. "What are you guys doing?" Conrad said, surveying the amplifiers and cables with astonishment.

"We're waiting for the bikers," I said.

"Mom and Dad are freaking out," he said. "Dad's about a half hour away from calling the police. I said I'd see if you were here."

"Why didn't you just phone?"

"The number's not in the directory," he said. "What's with all the equipment?"

At that moment, Bruce and I heard scuffling footsteps on the second floor, then Edith came to the head of the stairs and called down: "Motorcycles! About ten of them."

"Got you," said Bruce. He raised the volume level on his speakers just a little, and breathed into them, "Show time. Stand by." A moment later we could hear the bikes, and they swiftly grew louder and louder until they were a roar in the driveway. Then, ominously, the bikers switched their engines off at the same time. Bruce put a finger to his lips, jacked up the volume levels on his amps, flicked the turntable on, then gently placed the needle on a record. Immediately the area surrounding the house was filled with a bass rumbling. It was at once threatening and beautiful—clearly human, but somehow otherworldly as well. It built for a moment, then there was a kind of swelling and a single tenor voice soared above the others, singing in a language other than English—and at that instant Bruce flicked a switch on a little box and the spotlights outside came brilliantly alive. The bikers, who were standing next to their motorcycles, raised their hands to shield their faces.

"Holy shit," said Conrad.

But Bruce was just getting started, and the music was building in intensity. Just as the tenor hit a particularly high note, Bruce started the reel-to-reel tape-recorder, and a moment later we heard whistles, then helicopter noises—the bikers turned from side to side in bewilderment, at which point the recorded sirens began—and Stephen turned on the siren he had on his hearse, parked just behind some trees.

"Are there cops out there?" said Conrad. "I didn't see—"

But at that moment our taped voices emerged from a couple of hitherto unused speakers, and we discovered that Bruce had done something to distort the sound: our voices sounded much deeper and harsher and weirder than they really were. Several of the bikers, I saw, had climbed back on their motorcycles, and one of them was shouting at the others—though his shouts were immediately drowned out by several thousand firecrackers exploding over the course of about one minute, set off, I realized, by Dent, who must have been lurking somewhere close to the culvert at the end of the driveway. As soon as this cacophony began, the remaining bikers remounted and began kicking their machines back to life.

Every *son et lumiere* must have a climax, however, and Bruce had prepared a doozy: just as the firecracker barrage was coming to an end and the motorcycles began to fishtail out of the driveway, a highway flare came soaring through the air and landed right in the middle of the pack. There followed the most enormous explosion I had seen outside the movies, and seven of the bikers were thrown off their bikes, while the three who had reached the road raced off like the proverbial bats out of hell . . . only to find that several gallons of liquid detergent gave their wheels no purchase on the asphalt, and they slid spectacularly into the ditch. And at that instant two real police cars came tearing up the road from Highway 6.

"Aces," said Bruce. "Now, let's hide the amps in the basement."

CHAPTER TWENTY-THREE: NOOR

If the bikers who came for Otis had been members of a major club like Satan's Choice or the Hell's Angels (who weren't active in Ontario in the 1970s) we would have been in serious trouble, but the Skulls were lone wolves—a group of criminals, yes, but a group united only by a fondness for motorcycles, intoxicants and intimidation, and not affiliated with anything larger than themselves. And like a surprising number of bikers I've met over the years, these guys were formidably superstitious: while they had a powerful thirst for revenge, I suspect they felt Otis had some kind of weird power at his fingertips—a suspicion that gained strength when he was the only one to come forward and show his face that night. The rest of us slipped out the back door and struck out across the fields as soon as the amps were stowed away in the basement. The speakers would have been easy to find if the police had looked for them, but the local detachment had their hands full with ten agitated bikers, and by the next morning when they came back to ask Otis some pointed questions, Bruce had made sure everything but the concentrated liquid detergent and firecracker debris was cleared away.

"So you don't know anything about this detergent?" asked the investigating officer, a greying fellow in his early forties, as he stooped to run his fingers across the road.

"I think it's Joy," said Otis. "It smells like it."

"But you don't know where this Joy came from?"

"I believe it's the sort of thing you find in big kitchens—industrial kitchens," said Otis.

"But *you* didn't bring it here?"

"No, sir," said Otis, honestly enough.

"And what about all these exploded firecrackers?"

"I think you're right, officer."

"What do you mean, you think I'm right?"

"I think they *are* firecrackers. And maybe some road flares as well."

"I don't like bikers." The officer—a man no taller than Otis himself—looked directly at my friend. "But that doesn't mean citizens can take the law into their own hands. Do you understand me?"

"Yes, sir," said Otis.

"Let's not have a repetition of this," said the officer. "If you feel threatened—call us."

"I will," said Otis.

"So maybe you and your friends can pick up the garbage. And you can tell the boy who *found* the magnesium ribbon that that stuff's too dangerous to screw around with."

"Yes, sir."

"All right, then. Do you play Monopoly?"

"I have played it," said Otis.

"You've just used your get-out-of-jail-free card. But there's only one."

"Thank you, sir," said Otis.

"Make sure you clean up really well."

So we got away with it. Or we thought we did.

★

It's not that the next seven or eight months passed without incident. When you're in high school, things happen every day: teachers get angry or have nervous breakdowns, grades rise and fall, classmates self-destruct or achieve remarkable things, friendships evolve . . . but in the months that followed our confrontation with the bikers nothing of remotely comparable scale presented itself. My close friends and I went to class, played sports, spent time in each other's homes, and came to know Queensville a little better. My family rubbed along; the distance between my parents did not narrow, but it didn't seem to grow either. I began to see, too, that many families were not as close as I once imagined mine to be. I did find, though, that Conrad and I had more in common, and he seemed quietly grateful that Otis and I had come to collect him from the McPherson party—and that I hadn't told our father. And clearly our mother hadn't told him either.

When spring rolled around, Mr. Spurr telephoned me one evening and asked if Otis and I could come into the museum on the next Saturday afternoon. "Some interesting historical artifacts have come to light," he said, "and I'd like to get them catalogued and into the cases before the museum reopens." We agreed, and we showed up to find Mr. Spurr already hard at work. "It's good to see you boys," he rumbled at us, and he shook us both formally by the hand.

Mr. Spurr's new artifacts were curious things. They consisted mostly of even more letters from nineteenth- and early-twentieth-century scientists and politicians, but Otis and I swiftly noticed something odd. Most of these letters were dated at roughly the same time as the letters we had already had on display, and said many of the same kinds of things ("copious thanks for your truly extraordinary contribution," "I can't thank you enough for your incisive commentary," "the suggestion you made about beak size was more helpful than you could possibly imagine"), and what distinguished them from their predecessors was largely that they were a little more effusive, the stationery a little more varied, and the penmanship more conspicuously old-fashioned. Mr. Spurr didn't seem troubled by this; he had already packed the older letters away somewhere, and our challenge was simply to make notes about the new letters in the catalogue, frame them in good quality frames, then arrange them attractively on the walls or, as the spirit moved us, in display cases. Apart from these letters, the only new items were James Alfred Spurr's pocket watch, a pair of the great man's spectacles, and a small jade statue of the Buddha that, Mr. Spurr told us, his grandfather had kept on his desk.

"Was he a Buddhist?" Otis asked.

"No, Otis," said Mr. Spurr. "He was a man of wide and diverse interests, and he sought wisdom in unconventional places. He taught himself Sanskrit and other ancient languages—and he was enormously helpful with Hendrik Kern's famous translation of the *Lotus Sutra*."

"Do we have a letter from Hendrik?" I asked.

"Not yet," said Mr. Spurr, pensively. "But I shouldn't be surprised if one eventually came to light." And, remarkably, one *did* appear, at the beginning of June, and found its way into a new case with a brass plaque announcing, boldly: SPURR CORRESPONDENCE WITH RELIGIOUS FIGURES & SCHOLARS.

"It's quite remarkable that one should have come up at auction so soon after our conversation," Mr. Spurr said. Otis and I nodded gravely, but, shortly after Mr. Spurr left later that day, Otis, staring intently at the letter, made the observation that it would have been even more remarkable if one hadn't. And I saw his point.

So the James Alfred Spurr Memorial Museum reopened at the end of June, its operating hours once again Tuesdays through Saturdays from ten to five—though Mr. Spurr warned us we might have to open on at least one Sunday that summer, in the event any visiting scholars wished to have a private viewing of the letters and other objects. "My grandfather is beginning to attract the attention of professional historians," he told us.

This summer, the summer of 1975, as with the one previous, we saw stunningly few visitors, and Otis and I worried anew that this might lead to one or the other of us being laid off, but our concern was assuaged somewhat when my father told me that Mr. Spurr had a significant private fortune, and that the museum was probably something of a vanity project. In any event, our wages were always paid in full and on time.

Sometime towards the middle of July we began to receive regular visits from a little Indian girl who lived in a subsidized housing project several blocks away. Now, when I say *Indian*, in this instance I mean Asian Indian. Noor was very thin: we initially thought she was only eight or nine, but on her third or fourth visit she told us she was eleven. By this time she had got over the tongue-tied shyness that afflicted her on her first couple of visits, and the quality of her conversation would have indicated she was older even if she hadn't explicitly told us. At first I thought she was simply bored, but I eventually realized that she enjoyed our company, and, perhaps, felt safe when she was with us. And she was desperate to make herself useful: she seized any opportunity to clean the cases and the glass faces of the framed letters and photographs, and she liked to sweep the floors as well, and would have cleaned the bathroom if we had let her. "No, no," Otis told her. "That's dirty work. *We're* being paid to do that."

"I don't mind dirty work," she said, her large dark eyes fixed reproachfully on my friend.

"You shouldn't be exposed to the cleaning chemicals," said Otis. "You're still growing."

"I don't care," she said. "And I may never get taller than this."

"Well, we do care," said Otis. So while one of us cleaned the bathroom, and the other kept a lookout for visitors, Noor would polish James Alfred Spurr's brass letter opener, or do a bit of dusting, or empty the waste paper baskets—anything, indeed, to justify her being there, although, truth to tell, we didn't mind her company. She would readily answer questions if they were put to her, but she seemed most happy drawing pictures of characters from Charles Schulz's Peanuts comics while Otis and I talked about school and music and books.

Somewhat to our surprise, Mr. Spurr seemed taken with Noor, too, and did not question her presence in the museum. We'd grown accustomed to him visiting towards the end of the day, shortly before we closed, and he soon adopted the practice of collecting the day's modest proceeds, and handing most of it back to Otis or me. "Take the little girl to McDonald's and buy her a milkshake," he'd say, "she's too thin. And get one yourselves, too. My grandfather was instrumental in speeding the process of milk pasteurization in Canada." And so that became our routine: three or four times a week we'd lock up and walk a couple of blocks to McDonald's where Edith now had a job, and sometimes she'd time her break so she could join the three of us for a milkshake. It was, in many ways, an idyllic time—but like all earthly idylls it was not destined to last.

Chapter Twenty-Four: Another Birthday

But I've not told the story of my seventeenth birthday, which fell before we met Noor, and there's a reason for this violation of sequence that will become clear. Once again I opted to see a movie with friends, and the guest list was once again a little different, and a little bigger. Otis and Edith were a given, of course, as were Bruce and Big Andy and Janet Brightman, but this year, after much deliberation, I also invited Conrad—and he accepted. My mother was so pleased with this evidence of brotherly love that she offered to expand the guest list still further. "Why don't you invite that funny boy you met at the movies last year?" she asked. "The one who knew all the bus schedules."

"He's not really a friend, Mom," I said. "He's just someone I run into sometimes."

"Maybe you should expand your circle a little," she said brightly. "It's good to meet new people."

As it happened, Otis was present when she made the suggestion, and he liked the idea. "It would mean a lot to him, Pete," he said.

"All right," I said, shrugging. "You can pass on the invitation."

"Okay," said Otis. "And I'll pick him up."

So that's what happened. My dad drove Bruce, Conrad and me (I still hadn't secured my driver's license), and Otis drove himself and Edith and Big Andy and Janet, and they made a fairly significant detour to collect Chris the Bayridge Bus Guy—who was, in his own strange way, delighted. "Otis picked me up!" he said, running up to me as soon as he'd exited Otis's car. "He came along Maple to Earl, then to Crosbie. Then he took Hunter to Jessop—and he could have taken Glenn Pitt, but he took McGowan to Power. I live on Power. Number 42."

"I'm glad you could come, Chris," I said.

"It's your birthday. We're going to see a movie," said Chris. "Is this your brother?" He looked sideways at Conrad.

"Yes, this is my brother, Conrad," I said. I worried, briefly, that Conrad might say something rude, but he was on his best behaviour. "Hi, Chris," he said.

"Hi," said Chris. "I've memorized pi to three hundred and thirty-three decimal places."

"Good," said Conrad, taking this in his stride rather well.

"This guy's a riot," said Janet Brightman, coming up behind Chris and giving him a friendly punch on the shoulder. "Where have you been hiding him, Pete?"

"My mother says I'm just a charity invite, but I should take what I can get," said Chris. He blinked several times.

"You're not a charity invite, Chris," I said, appalled that he would say something of this kind, and even more appalled that his mother should have said it to him. (And, yes, there was a degree of self-reproach there, too.)

"No, man, we want you here," said Otis. "You're Chris the Bayridge Bus Guy! You're a character! You're larger than life! We're *honoured* you're here with us. Aren't we, Edith?"

"Really honoured," said Edith, rising wonderfully to the occasion. "I like your shirt, Chris."

"Yeah, okay," said Chris. "Do you want it?" He began to unbutton it.

"No, no," said Edith. "It looks great on *you*."

"Edith has boobs, Chris," said Janet. "It wouldn't look right on her."

"I don't look at boobs," said Chris. "They make my willy stiff. I have to do the decimals in my head to make it soft again."

None of us knew quite what to say to this, so I reached into my pocket and pulled out the money my father had given me. "Let's go and get our tickets," I said, and I turned to lead the way to the line that had already begun to form a block away.

"Could he possibly be more wonderful?" Janet said to Big Andy as we all walked along together. And I knew the reference was to Chris.

★

The movie was *Dog Day Afternoon*, starring the young Al Pacino—and my guests and I enjoyed it uncritically. "Attica! Attica! Attica!" Big Andy chanted cheerfully as we left the theatre and passed people queuing up to go into the next showing. They looked a bit bemused by this, but his good humour and enthusiasm were infectious.

"Stop it—you're embarrassing me," said Janet, just as cheerfully. "God, I'd do Al Pacino in a moment," she added. "All the decimals in the world couldn't dry me up."

"Janet!" said Edith. "God, you're so crude sometimes!" But her crossness was short-lived.

"Are we going back to your house for pizza and cake?" asked Chris hopefully.

"No," I said. "My dad's given me money to take us to Gino's." Gino's was a pizzeria about four blocks from the theatre.

"That's gonna be pretty expensive, Pete," said Otis. He'd slipped his right arm around Edith and was hugging her close as they walked along. "There are eight of us."

"I know," I said. "I was surprised." And I had been. My dad was a generous guy, but he wasn't usually given to extravagant gestures.

Conrad kicked viciously at a rock on the sidewalk, and it rocketed off the concrete and into the road. "I don't think they want us there," he said.

"Why not?" I said—but Conrad didn't volunteer anything else. He hunched his shoulders and just kept moving, his enjoyment of the movie replaced by sulkiness.

"Maybe we could all chip in a couple of dollars," said Bruce. "Just to help."

"No. No need," I said. "My dad knows what he's doing." But I wondered: What was it I wasn't picking up on? What wasn't I seeing that Conrad was seeing?

★

Gino's was an Italian restaurant, but not a particularly nice one. Many of the kids at school said the mob owned it, but my father scoffed at the idea. "It's just anti-Italian prejudice," he said. He may well have been right, but whenever I went in, there always seemed to be a number of middle-aged men with slicked-back hair just hanging around drinking beer and eyeing the customers suspiciously. On this occasion there were five of them: they looked up when we came in, and one of them gave Otis a hard stare, but they returned to their conversation after we took a couple of tables and pulled them together.

A young but tired-looking waitress came up to us. "Hey guys, do youse want to see some menus?"

"Sure," I said. "Please." And we spent some time negotiating what we'd like on two large pizzas, and agreeing on two jugs of soft drinks.

"Is this a birthday party, or something?" asked the waitress after she'd taken our order.

"Yeah, it's Pete's birthday," said Janet Brightman. "He's eighteen. How about a beer on the house for the birthday boy?"

"I'm not eighteen," I said hurriedly. "I'm seventeen. A year to go." I didn't want any attention. In those days I had a huge fear of being centred out in any way.

"Oh, I knew youse wasn't eighteen," said the waitress, and she gave a grim laugh before heading back towards the kitchen.

"You're such a wimp, Petey," said Janet—but she said it affectionately. "Man. That Al Pacino. He's no wimp, I'm telling ya . . ."

"Don't start up again, Janet," said Edith. "You'll hurt Big Andy's feelings."

"Yeah," said Big Andy. "You'll hurt my feelings." He pouted dramatically.

"Bus 22 goes all the way to the Caesar Island Ferry," said Chris. "It has to wait for the ferry. If the ferry is late, the whole schedule is thrown off. Mrs. Nye doesn't like it."

And so the meal passed. Shortly after we finished, and just as we were debating the merits of ice cream alone versus ice cream with some sort of fruit pie, the front door opened and an older gentleman wearing a Sikh turban entered. (I didn't know it was

Sikh then—none of us did.) He was dressed in a tailored suit, and carried himself very upright. He advanced to the counter and spoke to our waitress, who was reading the comics section of a newspaper. "Excuse me," he said, his voice sounding just slightly English. "I am wondering if you can tell me where—"

But he didn't get any further than that. Two of the five middle-aged men were suddenly on their feet, and one of them moved towards him. "Get along," he said.

"I beg your pardon?" said the Indian gentleman.

"I said *get along*," said the man with the slicked-back hair. "We don't serve your kind in here. And we don't want you talking to our women." He was wearing a leather coat, and he slid his hand into the left breast and kept it there, all the while staring at the older man.

There was a pause. The Sikh gentleman looked at the middle-aged Italian. The Italian looked at him. The girl behind the counter turned the page of her newspaper. "I am sorry to have disturbed you," said the Sikh gentleman, and he turned and, with some dignity, walked back to the front door, opened it and walked out.

"The dirt that comes in sometimes," said the oldest of the five men. The two who had risen returned to their seats and sat down. We breathed for the first time in a couple of minutes.

"Why don't you just ask for the bill, Pete?" said Otis quietly.

★

Later that night, at home, with Conrad and my parents in bed, I found I couldn't sleep. I left my bed and went into the kitchen to make myself a bowl of cereal. My fingers were a little clumsy, and when I opened the door below the sink to put the top of the milk bag into the garbage, I accidentally dropped the scissors in, too. Swearing, I reached in and retrieved the scissors, but brought up with them a slip of torn paper with some writing on it. "Yowsers," said the note. "When I think of your breasts—" but the end of the line was ripped off, and I was disinclined to go rooting among the banana peels and tea bags to find the rest of it. The handwriting was not my father's.

Chapter Twenty-Five: Departures & Arrivals

The end of the summer brought another great sadness for Otis. In the second week of August, Edith's dad learned that the factory where he worked was transferring its operations to Georgia in the United States, and that if he wanted to keep his job he'd have to transfer with it. He didn't particularly want to go, and his family certainly didn't, but he was the chief breadwinner, and he felt he had little choice. He had to report by August twenty-third, and Edith and her younger sister and her mother had to join him by the beginning of September, which left very little time for good-byes. And maybe, on balance, that was a good thing, because extended good-byes can simply prolong the pain.

Otis grieved. The loss of his father had hit him hard, but he'd had Edith to lean on. The loss of Edith was, in some ways, harder, because his mother wasn't emotionally equipped to help him. On the morning after he learned the news, his mother put a bible beside his breakfast cereal bowl with a number of passages highlighted. But while she meant well, her selections—which focused on Jesus coming again in glory—were not as relevant and comforting to him as she hoped.

"How's Otis?" my dad asked the day after Edith left for the American south.

"I haven't spoken with him," I said. "He didn't call last night."

"Maybe you should call *him*," said my father. "The phone rings both ways." He looked at me meaningfully over the glasses he'd recently begun wearing.

I was briefly stung, but I saw that he was right, and in the days that followed I tried to be as present to Otis as I knew how. In many ways, I now realize, I was a stunningly slow learner.

But the world wasn't finished creating distress for Otis. Towards the end of September he received a strange letter in the mail. It arrived on a Friday, and by chance I was there when he opened it. He hadn't resumed working at Becker's yet, and we had come straight back to his home after school. His mother was waiting in the front hall, in the dark, when we came in.

"There's a letter for you, son," she said.

"Is it from Edith?" he asked eagerly. They'd been writing letters to each other pretty well every day.

"There's a couple of postcards from her, but the letter is from Toronto," Mrs. James said heavily. Since moving from Toronto, she'd come to see the city as a modern-day Babylon—except, of course, for its evangelical churches, which were, in her eyes, wavering beacons in the growing dark.

"Thanks, Mom," said Otis, and he kissed her forehead as he took the letters and postcard. "Is it okay if Pete and I get a drink?

"There's milk in the fridge," said Mrs. James. Every morning, I knew, she mixed up a jug of milk made half from bagged dairy milk and half from powdered milk and water. I found it awful, but I drank it when I was there. It was one of the economies Mrs. James had adopted since her husband had died—and, for all I know, it was necessary.

Otis and I went into the kitchen together while his mother retired to her room, where she listened, for hours on end, to a Christian radio station beaming its message from south of the border. We sat down at the table to drink our milk, and Otis read and pored over the postcards. "She's settling in," he volunteered. "She likes her classes." Georgia, of course, didn't have a grade thirteen as we then had in Ontario, but Edith had been accepted right into a local college. "She says the professors are nice, but everyone's crazy about football." He laughed; we both knew Edith couldn't care less about football. But at last he tore his attention away from the postcards and opened the envelope, which was addressed, awkwardly, to *Odis* James.

I studied Otis as he read the letter. Outwardly, he didn't change much, but it was as though a tiny shadow crossed his face, a shadow whose depth I could not then gauge.

"What is it?" I asked. "Is something wrong?"

He was silent for a moment, and he continued to look at the letter—a single smudged sheet of foolscap, its message scrawled out in pencil. "It's from my aunt," he said evenly. "Or someone who says she's my aunt."

"Your dad's sister?" I asked, stupidly.

"No," he replied. "My real mom's sister."

"What does it say?" I asked, but he didn't answer. He just sat there looking at the sheet of paper, seeing something I could not see, hearing something I could not hear. And eventually, realizing he needed to be alone, I got up and let myself out.

★

I didn't hear from Otis the next day, and when I called on Sunday evening Mrs. James's voice sounded hysterical. "He's gone," she said. "Otis is gone! I don't know where he is."

"Did he say where he was going, Mrs. James?" I asked.

"He didn't say anything," she said, crying. "It had something to do with that letter. He's taken it with him. My sister-in-law is coming down. I don't know what to do." Then she hung up, a great gust of tears hitting her just as she was placing the phone on its cradle.

My first instinct was to tell my dad and ask his advice, but he was in the bedroom having a nap, and my mom was at a friend's house. Conrad came into the room as I was thinking. "What's up?" he said, my face telling him something was wrong.

"Otis has gone," I replied.

"What do you mean, gone?"

"I mean *gone*—left for Toronto. *Gone* gone," I said impatiently. "He got a letter from someone who said she was his aunt, and now he's left home."

"No way," said Conrad. "What about school?"

"I don't know," I said. And then, hopefully: "Maybe he'll come back."

But he didn't come back. Days stretched into weeks, and there was no sign of him and no word from him. Mrs. James was summoned to the school for a consultation, and my mom said she'd heard a social worker had visited her at home, but it was as though Otis himself had vanished into a black hole. He'd apparently told no one what the letter had said, or where he was going in Toronto—or if indeed he was going to Toronto. The fact the letter had come from there didn't necessarily mean that was where he was headed.

The group of which Otis was a part did not disintegrate. Big Andy and Janet Brightman and Bruce and John and I continued to eat lunch and play euchre together—but we felt his absence (and Edith's) keenly. When you're young, friends are a huge part of your life, and Otis, I realized, had been my best friend, the one, after Mary-Lynne, who was closest to my heart. And if our passive acceptance of his departure seems strange, I can only say that now, at this remove, it seems strange to me, too. The past is indeed a foreign country.

*

The school was large, and there were many people I hadn't met or hadn't come to know well, and the opportunities to make new friends increased as time passed. John's mild-mannered kindness had attracted Patti, the gentle and soft-spoken young woman who attended Mary-Lynne's church, and she soon began to join us regularly at lunch, her shyness and piety providing a stark contrast to Janet Brightman's cheerful vulgarity. And every now and then Stephen and Dent would sit with us for a few minutes; wearing their trademark sunglasses and ironed shirts atop their blue jeans they projected an attitude that suggested they were dropping in from another planet altogether—a planet where it was quite natural to drive around in a hearse, speak a weird sort of code on their CB radios, and occasionally sound the siren Stephen could stick on his car roof in about ten seconds.

"Jesus, Stephen," said Janet Brightman one lunch hour. "Why do you wear sunglasses inside? I mean, you're not doing drugs, are you?"

"No, ma'am," said Stephen. "Never touch the stuff."

"So how come?" said Janet. "They make you look really weird. I keep expecting you to pull out a submachine gun or something. And don't call me *ma'am*."

"We don't bring our guns to school," said Stephen enigmatically.

"What do you want us to call you?" said Dent.

"Call me freaking *Janet*," said Janet. "That's my name, retard."

"Don't call me *retard*," said Dent, leaning towards her just a little, and baring his teeth. He was a little guy, but he could look threatening when he wanted to.

"Okay, okay—geez," said Janet. "I mean it nicely, for God's sake. What do you think I call Andy here?"

"She calls me *Pacino*," said Big Andy, his mouth full of fries.

"No, I don't, asshole," said Janet. "I call you *Big Dick*. And that's a—whatdycallit?—an endearment."

"It's a fact," said Big Andy proudly.

Patti blushed and looked over towards the soft drink machines. John took his cue and said, quietly, "Come on, guys. Keep it clean."

"Oh for God's sake," said Janet, "this isn't a freaking Sunday School. I'm not saying Andy *has* a big dick, I'm saying he *is* a Big Dick. But I love him anyway."

"Aw, that's sweet," said Big Andy. "But I *have* a big—

"Gotta go," said Stephen, and he and Dent stood up immediately, nodded at us, then headed out of the cafeteria and towards the parking lot.

"They're really weird," said Janet. "Don't you think they're weird, Pete?"

"Yeah. But I like 'em," I said. I hadn't forgotten Stephen's kind words to me—or the fact they'd both helped Otis when he needed it. Friends come in strange shapes and packages.

"You're such a wimp, Petey," said Janet. "Honestly, if I didn't love you, I'd step on you."

★

In early November, another young woman began to impress herself on my heart. Maureen was a good three inches shorter than Mary-Lynne—just five feet and change, as she said herself—but she made up for her small stature with a fierce embrace of life and all its possibilities. She was one of the very few among my contemporaries who took an interest in politics. She was forever reading—*Silent Spring, Small is Beautiful, The Limits of Growth, Soul on Ice, The Feminine Mystique*—and she styled herself a feminist and a socialist at a time when most of us were still trying to figure out our shoe sizes.

Mo (as she preferred to be called) was in my History class, and for the first month or two I admired her energy, her passion, but wasn't attracted to her—she seemed a little boyish, particularly after Mary-Lynne's softness. As time passed, however, I found myself thinking about her more and more, and seeking opportunities to chat with her after class. When, one day, our teacher, Mr. Goodridge, gave us an assignment that required collaboration, I took the initiative and leaned across the aisle. "Would you mind working with me, Mo?" I asked, and to my delight she smiled and nodded, "Sure." And immediately I imagined that she would become my girl.

That didn't happen as fast as I hoped. It's not that Mo was indifferent to me, but she confessed she wasn't sure about dating. "I'm worried about the planet, Peter," she told me. "It just seems so *bourgeois* to be going out—you know? I mean, I really like you, but going steady, or whatever you want to call it, it just feels a little *trivial*. I really don't mean to hurt your feelings."

I wasn't hurt so much as puzzled, but I decided to try a campaign of gentle persuasion: I didn't press her to declare herself in any way, but I made sure I regularly asked her to the movies, or arrived at her home with a couple of submarine sandwiches, or proposed going for a coffee and a donut after school, and eventually, by early December, we were seen as a couple, and she came to accept the idea, too. "You got around me, Pete," she told me on December fourth. "You snuck into my heart when I wasn't looking." I was pleased—but I was scared, too. I could not forget how my first romance had ended.

Chapter Twenty-Six: Challenges

On a bitterly cold Sunday afternoon in late January of 1976, I was reading in my bedroom when I heard the doorbell ring—followed by the sound of my mother's high heels clicking in the hall as she went to answer it. A moment later, and she called for me, her voice pitched at a level that suggested irritation.

There, just inside the door, stood Noor, whom I hadn't seen since the end of the previous August. She was wearing a winter jacket, but even so she was shivering, her arms wrapped around her body as if to husband what little heat she could generate. "Hallo, Noor!" I said, surprised to see her, but pleased, too.

To my astonishment, Noor stepped forward and wrapped her arms around me, burying her head in my chest. She began to sob, quietly at first, but then in real earnest. My mother, still hovering in the hall, looked a little disturbed, but I nodded to her, saying, "It's all right, Mom," and she left. After a bit I was able to loosen Noor's grip enough to help her shed her coat and boots and we went back to my room. I sat her on my bed, closed the door, and pulled my desk chair up to face her. "Noor," I said, "what on earth's the matter?"

And the story came tumbling out. I knew already that she lived, with her mother, in a subsidized housing development in the downtown core. Queensville didn't have much of this kind of housing, and the projects were tiny by Toronto standards, but even so they had a whiff of notoriety around them. In any event, on the previous evening she'd been returning to her apartment when she was stopped by an older man—he was about forty, she said— and told to give him a blow job.

"Was he physical with you?" I asked, my gorge rising at the thought of a grown man waylaying this small eleven-year-old girl.

"No, no," she shook her head. "He was very drunk. But I'm scared he'll try again when he's sober."

"Where's your mother?" I asked.

Noor's mother had apparently been visiting her own father in Kitchener, leaving Noor in the nominal charge of the woman next door—but she too had been out Saturday night, and she hadn't returned this morning. So Noor had spent the night alone in her apartment, traumatized and cowering in a closet.

"Well," I said, "it's simple—we have to go to the police—" but this prompted a fresh burst of tears from Noor. When the police came for someone in public housing, she said, they took him away for a day or two, but then released him. And as soon as he was released he made sure that whoever had made the complaint paid.

"Okay," I said. "What would you like me to do? How can I help?" Noor cried a little more, possibly recognizing that any help I could offer was limited, but asked me if I would come back to her home with her and wait until her mother returned that evening. I said I would.

I had, just two months before, secured my driver's license, the last among my friends to do so—my desire to squire Mo around prompting me to accelerate the process. With some difficulty I now persuaded my mother to lend me her car, a red Gremlin, and Noor and I set off for downtown, my homework in a knapsack between us. Noor had stopped crying by now, and she sat staring out the front window, saying nothing at all. It occurred to me that riding in a car was probably a novelty for her.

The public housing complex was, as I've said, relatively small—perhaps forty units in two three-storey buildings. But my overwhelming impression as I drove up was of bleakness: the building itself was light brown, with a dark brown roof; its nearer side stood close to the curb, the contents of several garbage bags ripped apart by dogs or raccoons littering the front lawn; the only trees newly-planted saplings, just traceries of twigs in the dirty brown and yellow snow. Beside this landscape, my own detached home with its sixty foot frontage and mature trees looked like a nobleman's estate.

Noor fumbled with the key for a moment as she opened the front door: her apartment was on the first floor of the second building, on the side away from the street and backing on a tall wooden fence. There were lights back there, but I guessed then, and verified later, that many of them didn't work. We went inside, finding ourselves immediately in a small living room, equipped with an ancient sofa, two dining room chairs, and a twelve-inch black and white television on a rickety stand. The room's one concession to luxury was a fine multicoloured rug on the floor. There were baby and toddler photographs of Noor on the walls, but they were unframed. The room was clean, however, as was the kitchen and dinette behind it, and, as I eventually discovered, the bathroom. I'd guess the bedrooms were, too, but I didn't see them.

I sat down in the living room, and Noor offered to make tea, an offer I gladly accepted. She busied herself in the kitchen for a while, eventually returning with two small cups on a tray with a Woolworth's tea pot, milk jug, sugar bowl, and two spoons. My heart bled a little as she poured the liquids, this tiny Asian girl pushing back against the darkness with the small ritual of tea-making—my presence in her home not a happy occasion, but prompted by the fact that a man four times her age had badgered her for sexual favours.

After we'd drunk our tea, and talked a little, Noor fetched a drawing pad and some colouring pencils, and she sat, a stuffed Snoopy beside her, drawing Charlie Brown and Lucy and Snoopy himself, while I read Margaret Laurence's *Stone Angel*. And that's how Noor's mother, Aisha, found us, when she returned, a couple of hours later, from Kitchener.

*

My mother was not happy with my involvement in Noor's difficulties, but then my mother, it seems, was unhappy generally, though I could not then see any cause. I'd occasionally heard raised voices in the bedroom, and I'd certainly seen my parents' failure to connect at the dinner table, but I'd assumed their estrangement was something they could live with—that their difficulties were no more severe than many another couple's.

Exactly a week after I'd taken Noor home, my mother came into my bedroom, where I was, again, reading. "I'm leaving, Peter," she said.

"Where are you going?" I asked reflexively, but something in her tone and appearance revealed this was no ordinary run to the grocery store or to see a friend. She was dressed in an outfit I considered a bit revealing for her age, and there was a look of strain on her face.

"I'm leaving your father," she said. "I've packed a suitcase, and I'm going. I'll be back for you and Conrad in about two weeks."

"You're leaving Dad?" I said. "But where are you going? Where will you be?"

"I'm staying with a friend," she said. "Your father and I haven't been getting along for some time."

"What friend?" I asked, getting to my feet. "Please, Mom, don't go!"

Conrad was playing street hockey somewhere, I knew, and the door to my parents' bedroom was closed, suggesting my father was taking another of the naps that had become a regular part of his routine in the last couple of years. My mother slipped into her boots, grasped the small suitcase she'd placed by the door, and turned to me. "Your dad is going to say horrible things about me, Peter. Remember there are always two sides to every story. You'll be welcome where I'm going, but I have to set things up for you and Conrad. I'll see you in two weeks." And she was gone.

I stood staring at the door, remaining there even after the red Gremlin had pulled out of the garage and disappeared down the street. Then I made my way down the hall to the master bedroom and knocked on the door. "Come in," said my father. He sounded tired.

I opened the door and stood there. The curtains were closed, and my dad was lying on his side on the bed with the jacket he wore while teaching covering his top like a blanket. "Dad," I said. "Where is Mom going?"

My dad rolled over and stared at the ceiling. I could not see his eyes in the dark, but I could hear the tears in his voice. "Your mother has gone to her boyfriend's house," he said quietly.

"Her boyfriend's!" I said. "Mom doesn't have a boyfriend!"

"I'm afraid she has, Peter," he replied. "Now, I'll make us some supper in a little while, but I think I need to be alone for an hour or so. Can you give me that, son?"

So I left him, and I went to my own room to stare at my own ceiling, and though I felt I should be too old to do so, I soon found that I was crying, too.

Chapter Twenty-Seven: Coping

Mo was wonderful. What she lacked in sentimentality she more than made up in emotional strength and resourcefulness. I called her after I'd wept for a while, and she came over immediately; we went for a long walk in the cold afternoon air, she mostly listening but, in a gesture that wasn't typical for her, holding my hand. When we returned to the house we found that my father had prepared a rudimentary meal of macaroni and cheese, and, at his invitation, she stayed and ate dinner with the three Ellis males, keeping us company on one of the most difficult nights of our lives. My father did his best to keep some semblance of conversation going, and Mo helped by talking about something she had been reading; I was mostly talked out by this stage, and Conrad was apparently in shock.

After the meal Con went directly to his room, while Mo and I did the dishes. My father hung around for a bit in the kitchen, checking the calendar, going through the receipts in a jar, and getting out the tea mugs. Mo eventually shooed him into the living room, telling him she'd bring him a cup of tea when the dishes were done. To my surprise, he went. Conrad, in his bedroom, put on a *Black Sabbath* album and turned it up very loud. Normally, Mom or Dad would have told him to turn it down, but my dad said nothing.

Mo left around ten, giving me a fierce hug at the door, and calling out a warm farewell to both my dad and Conrad. And when I arrived at school the next morning, my father having insisted that both my brother and I should go, she was waiting at my locker, and walked with me to my first class. "Who can Conrad talk to?" she asked me.

"About Mom?" I asked. I thought hard for a moment. Most of Con's friends were his fellow jocks, decent enough boys, most of them, but probably not equipped to be helpful with emotional distress. "Me," I said at length. I saw that I had a responsibility to break through my own distress and reach out to my brother.

"Will you?" she asked.

"Yes," I said. "If he *wants* to talk."

"He'll *need* to," she said, and she kissed me on the cheek and went off to her own first class.

I had dreaded telling my other friends about what had happened, but I discovered, at lunch, that Mo had taken this on for me. John gripped my shoulder when he arrived at our table, and Patti shot me a look so full of sympathy I almost burst into tears.

Fortunately, Janet Brightman arrived a moment later. "Fuck, Petey," she said, "you need to get drunk, or something. Go on a real bender."

"I don't think that would help," said John mildly.

"Sure, it would help," said Janet, "and if you had any balls, John, you'd steal some of your dad's communion wine to help a friend out."

"We don't use wine in our church," said John. "You're thinking of the Catholics. Or the Anglicans."

"What the fuck use is a church without any wine?" asked Janet rhetorically. "Is there any wine in your church, Patti?"

"No," said Patti. "I'm afraid we're useless, too." She reached across the table and held my hand for a moment.

"Well, *that's* not going to help," said Janet. "You're just going to confuse the poor bastard. "Hey, Asshole!" (Big Andy had just arrived.) "How about scoring some booze for Peter?"

"I'll steal some from my dad," said Big Andy wryly—and that silenced Janet, briefly, as she was reminded that her boyfriend was no great fan of alcohol. Mo arrived a couple of minutes later, bringing a tray of coffees for everyone, and that happy surprise distracted us for a little while.

Just as we were finishing our sandwiches and fries, Stephen showed up—Dentless on this occasion. "Howdy," he said, the Americanism sounding perfectly natural from him.

"You're too late for free coffee," said Janet. "Where's your sidekick?"

"He's got the flu," said Stephen. He opened a Coke and guzzled the whole thing, bringing the can down hard on the table when he'd finished.

"What a man!" said Janet. "Hey, Steve, what could you do to cheer Petey up?"

"What's wrong with Pete?" asked Stephen. Mo clearly hadn't spoken with him. He looked at me appraisingly.

"His mom took off," said Janet. "She's got a fancy-man stowed away somewhere."

"*Janet*," said Mo, remonstrating. I was a little surprised she'd imparted that detail, though a moment's reflection told me Janet would have pushed for as much information as she could get.

"I could take you to a titty-bar," said Stephen. "That always cheers me up."

"I don't think so," said Mo, and she draped her arm around my waist, and hugged me to her small frame.

★

I did try to speak with Conrad. That very evening, as he sat watching television in the basement, I came and sat beside him on the couch. He was watching *Monty Python's Flying Circus* and he wasn't laughing—a sure sign things were not right. "How are you doing?" I asked.

"Great," said Conrad flatly, not taking his eyes off the television. "Just peachy."

"Do you want to talk about it?" I said.

"Is Dr. Peter in, then?" said Conrad.

"Come on, Con," I said. "This isn't a picnic for me either. But we're brothers. We should talk."

"I don't think there's anything to say. Mom's gone. She says she's coming back for us, but who knows? Have you heard from her?"

"No," I said.

"Well, you've got Mo. And Mom's got this new guy, maybe. And I don't have anyone."

"You've got me," I said. "And you've got Dad. And he doesn't have anyone except us."

Conrad was silent for a moment, but he continued looking at the television: John Cleese was doing a silly walk, and usually we'd both have found it very funny. "I feel my whole life is fucked up," Con said at last. "And it's like everyone knows. They're all looking at me with pity—there's the guy whose mom's a tramp. And she isn't! She's just . . . I don't know." And with that he got up and went upstairs, taking the steps two at a time. But just as he was getting up I saw that he too had tears in his eyes.

Chapter Twenty-Eight: Choices

Our mother kept her word. A week and a half after she'd left, she called the house right after school and before our dad arrived home. Conrad answered, and while he didn't say much, I could tell from his face and posture who was on the other end. "Okay," he said. "Okay. Sunday. Yeah." A long pause, then: "I love you, too." He hung up.

"Mom?" I said. "Didn't she want to speak to me?" I was stung. I wasn't sure I wanted to speak to her, but it hurt that she didn't want to hear my voice.

"She was crying," Conrad said. He didn't look at me. "She said we should be ready for her this Sunday. We should pack up our clothes and books and anything we really need, and she'll be here at three."

"Where is she staying?" I asked.

"At this house on Middle Road. She says it's a big place, and Jeff doesn't have any kids."

"Jeff?" I said.

"I guess that's her guy."

"Are you going?" I asked.

Conrad kicked the carpet a couple of times. "Yeah. I guess. Aren't you?"

I had a moment of unexpected clarity. My father, God knows, was not the most effectual of men. His response to conflict was, I saw, to withdraw, to retreat—to take a nap. But he didn't *stay* away, and he hadn't *gone* away, either. He'd gone to ground and licked his wounds for a while, then he'd picked himself up and got back to work. He couldn't cook, certainly, but he'd put food on the table for the past week and a half—scrambled eggs on toast, baked beans on toast, macaroni and cheese, tuna and apple sandwiches, soup and grilled cheese—and he'd continued to help with homework, and to chivvy us along in the morning, and do the laundry and put out the garbage and wash the dishes. And he was affectionate, too, in his way: not the sort of man who often gave out big man-hugs or slapped us on the back, but I knew he loved us. He told us he loved us. He *showed* us he loved us.

"No," I said. "I'm staying with Dad."

"Really?" said Conrad.

"Yeah," I said. "But it's fine that you're going with Mom. I'm sure he'll understand."

"Yeah," said Conrad. "Okay." He kicked the carpet another couple of times, then went to his room.

*

At three on Sunday afternoon, the red Gremlin pulled into the driveway, and our mother came to the front door. We were in a bit of a mild spell, and she was dressed in a new, lightweight winter coat that went with the shade of lipstick she was wearing. Her scarf, too, was new and fashionable. Conrad had piled everything he wanted to take in the front hall: a cardboard box filled with clothes, his hockey bag and equipment, his school bag with his texts and binders, and the desk lamp he'd received for Christmas. He opened the door for her. I stood in the living room, a few steps back, and my dad stood in the door to the kitchen.

My mother kissed Con on both cheeks and threw her arms around him. "My baby boy," she said. "Oh, my baby boy!" She rocked him back and forth for a moment, then stood back and looked at me. "Do you have a hug for your mom?" she said.

God knows, I too wanted to have her arms wrapped around me and to be rocked back and forth. God knows, I too wanted to be called her *baby boy*. But something held me back. It probably had something to do with my father, whose face was a portrait of sadness and pain, but it also had a lot to do with an angry flame that was burning in my own heart. "Hi, Mom," I said.

"Aren't you coming, then?" she asked. Her face fell.

"No," I said. "I'm staying with my dad."

"I think that's a mistake," she said. "He doesn't know how to look after you like I do."

"He knows enough," I said. "And maybe he needs someone to look after *him*."

"That's not your job," she said sharply.

"I know," I said. "It used to be yours."

"No woman should have to look after a man!" she said angrily.

"He looked after you, too," I said quietly.

"Well, I see he's poisoned you against me," she said, pursing her lips. She bent down and picked up Conrad's schoolbag. "Let's take your things to the car, sweetheart," she said to my younger brother. Wordlessly, Conrad collected his gear and, in two trips, stowed it away in the trunk. He then came back inside and faced my father.

"Are you mad at me, Dad?" he asked.

"Of course not, Con," said my father. "Come here." Conrad stepped forward, and my father hugged him. "You're always welcome home. You know that? I love you, son." His voice was husky with emotion. Conrad nodded, not trusting his own voice. My dad let him go, and Con wavered for a moment, then turned and sort of waved at me. "See you, Petey," he said.

"See you at school, Con," I replied, digging my fingernails into my palms. And so Con left, and my mother's red Gremlin pulled out and drove away.

My father gave me a tight smile. "I'll just have a bit of a nap, Pete," he said, "and then we'll see about some dinner." He turned and went to his room, closing the door behind him. But three minutes later, staring uncomprehending at my history book, I heard him bawling in his room, and though I did not go to him, I knew I had made the right choice.

★

Life's dramas were not restricted to my home. Our action against the Skulls had kept the bikers from the smoking area for a few months, but they'd returned in November, though now there were always at least two at a time, and sometimes three. Fortunately, they had no idea who else had been involved in their troubles, but they knew, certainly, that Otis was no longer at the school. One day, in a gesture of contempt for the administration, they arranged for several lackeys to open doors for them, and then roared through the first floor of the building on their motorcycles. The principal and vice-principals were clearly angry, but nothing came of it—or nothing we knew about anyway.

And the diminution of their authority had other consequences. In early February there was a fight out in the parking lot between two grade-eleven boys. The fight itself wasn't terribly consequential, and it ended without either of them seriously hurt. What was significant, however, was that when several teachers came out and tried to break it up, the crowd around the fighters wouldn't let them through. *Get back inside the building*, they were told. And they went.

★

Of course I saw Conrad regularly at school, and we now went out of our way, both of us, to speak to each other. We didn't eat lunch together, but we would sometimes take a few minutes at the end of the hour to sit off by ourselves. On two or three occasions I bought a couple of coffees and we'd drink them—double cream and triple sugar—sitting near the entrance to the grade-thirteen common room, which I very rarely visited. Mo would remain with Janet and Big Andy and John and Patti and Bruce: she clearly felt it was important that Con and I had some time alone.

Conrad didn't say too much about life in his new home. I gathered he had a room of his own, and that it was larger than the one he'd had with us. He let it slip too that Jeff was a great fan of barbecue, and liked to fire up his gas grill even on very cold days, and that he spent hours on end working on vintage cars. "Mom said he liked to do that even when he was a teenager," he said.

"Did Mom know him when he was a teenager?" I asked.

"They used to go out in high school, or something," Conrad said vaguely.

Two weeks after he left us, Conrad came home for a weekend visit. He had a basketball practice after school, so my dad went to pick him up. While I was waiting, I set the table and started heating up a casserole someone had made for us: it had mysteriously materialized in our fridge, carefully wrapped in silver foil. I had no idea who had prepared it, but it smelled good.

When Con and my dad came through the door I exited the kitchen to greet them—even though I'd seen both of them already that day, Con at school and dad at home. "Hey, guys," I said. "There's a casserole in the oven."

"Are *you* cooking now?" asked Conrad. "Jesus, Dad, let's get take-out!" It was a weak joke, but it was a joke, and the laugh it elicited had a healing effect. We all relaxed a little. When we sat together at table that evening, the conversation flowed more easily than I had expected, Con entertaining us with stories about some of the guys on his team. But he said nothing about our mom, and my father asked nothing. I'd already decided to spare him the detail about Jeff being an old boyfriend of Mom's—assuming he didn't know it already.

CHAPTER TWENTY-NINE: A VISIT

I grew closer to Mo. In some ways we were an odd match: Mo's awareness of politics was much greater than mine, and she thought about it and talked about it so much that it sometimes made me tired. She dressed like a boy, in jeans and plaid shirts, and, in the abstract at least, I much preferred girls to wear skirts or dresses. And, as I've said before, she wasn't soft: she wasn't the sort of girl who liked to cuddle. No, if I had been asked for a laundry list of the perfect girlfriend's attributes, I suspect that list would have pointed to Mary-Lynne rather than to the girl I now found myself with.

And yet, and yet—I loved her. I found myself absurdly happy in her presence and surprisingly lonely for her when she wasn't there. I looked forward to telling her things, and to hearing what she'd done and what she thought about the people and situations we'd both experienced.

What did she see in me? Ultimately, I don't know. But one day—and it came early in my parents' separation—I was driving her somewhere in my dad's car, and she suddenly grabbed my free hand, brought it to her lips, and said, "You're a sweet boy, Petey. I think I'll keep ya." Maybe we can never fully know the mystery of another person's heart, but I chose to believe that what she said that day came from her heart, and that it was true. And I was glad Janet wasn't in the back seat, because I can guess what she might have said.

Janet and Big Andy, meanwhile, had a bit of a rough spot. It began when Janet went away on a school field trip to the Quebec Winter Carnival; Andy had moved up into the more academic stream, but he wasn't taking any languages, and like most of the boys at QDSS he had a special disdain for French. When the school trip returned, a rumour quickly circulated that Janet had got drunk one night and made out with another boy, creeping into his room and into his bed while three other boys who were also sharing the room lay awake and listened.

Andy refused to speak to her for two days, and it took Patti's intervention to engineer a conversation.

"I got drunk, Andy," Janet said tearfully, "but I didn't make out with the guy. He invited me to his room, and I told him, 'in your dreams, asshole,' and that was that. Come on, you can't really believe that I'd get into bed with some strange guy when there were three other guys in the room! I'm not crazy."

"But why does everyone say it happened?" asked Big Andy. He couldn't look Janet in the eyes.

"Because they've got nothing better to do than make up shit!" said Janet. "You know some of those people. They live to make trouble! It gets them hard. Come on, you big lug, I wouldn't cheat on you! Not even with Al Pacino." It didn't happen overnight, but Andy was eventually persuaded, and peace was restored.

And John and Patti? They were practically engaged. They sat beside each other at lunch, and in the library, and in the school bus on the way home. They alternated eating with each other's family. They did their homework together, and they read the bible together. "It's sickening," said Janet, making faces at them across the table. "They probably poop together!"

"Why do you say things like that?" asked Bruce, giving her an appalled look over his fries and gravy. "I mean, seriously, Janet—what happens in your head that you need to put that image out in the world?"

Janet appeared to consider the matter seriously for a moment. "I don't know Bruce," she said at length. "I guess it's that I feel so sad—"

"Wait for it," said Bruce. "Somehow this is going to be shoved on to me. Somehow the issue won't be Janet's grossness; it will be something *I'm* doing wrong."

"I guess," repeated Janet, entirely unfazed, "I guess it's that I feel so sad you don't have a chickie in your life, that I talk about poo to make you feel better."

"That doesn't even make sense," said Bruce crossly. "And you've ruined my lunch."

"Listen up, everyone," said Janet, clapping her hands. "We've got to find a chickie for Bruce. Let's all be on the lookout for a Mrs. Grumpy!"

★

A week after Conrad's visit, and after a couple of agitated calls from my mom to my dad, it was arranged that I should visit the house on Middle Road. Again, Friday was the day of transition, but not having a sporting commitment I took Conrad's new bus to Jeff's place. I knew several people on the bus, and chatted with a couple of them, and I saw them looking back at me after I'd disembarked, their faces a mixture of curiosity and sympathy. The high school rumour mill may have got some things wrong, but the juicy details of my parents' separation were certainly well known.

I found myself at the end of a long driveway leading to an old stone farmhouse. Much as I was dreading the visit, in some ways I had to admit Jeff's house looked handsome enough. It was a large building, just to begin with, and surrounded by trees; in the snow it looked like the kind of place that might be featured on a Christmas card. The driveway had been recently plowed, so walking along it wasn't difficult, but even so it took me a good four minutes to reach the house, and just as I approached the door my mother opened it and smiled at me.

"Have you got a hug for your mother this time?" she asked, drawing me to her before I could reply. I allowed the embrace, and let her pull me into the house, which smelled of shepherd's pie (then my favourite dinner) and wood smoke.

"That's better," she said. "Now, take off your coat and boots, and come into the kitchen and talk with me." She turned and went back down the hall. I did as I was bid, and followed her.

The kitchen was a long, galley-style affair, and very well equipped: every imaginable cooking implement and device was on display, and there was a shelf completely given over to recipe books. My mother was standing behind the front counter holding a glass of wine, with another in front of her. "Come and have a glass of wine, Petey," she said.

"Wine?" I said. "Well, this is a first." But I took the glass.

"Jeff spent a couple of years in France," she said gaily, "and he admires their attitude towards alcohol. Over there, families regularly share a bottle of wine over dinner."

"Do they?" I said. Much as I wanted it, I replaced the glass of wine on the counter. "Jeff and I aren't family," I said.

"Oh, Petey," said my mother. "Please don't be like this."

"Be like what, Mom?" I said. "I'm here. I'm here to see you and Con. But that doesn't mean I like Jeff or approve of you shacking up with him."

"Shacking up?" said my mother, half-smiling at me. "That's an old-fashioned phrase. Did you get that from your father?"

"No," I said. "Dad doesn't say anything about you. But you've hurt him a lot."

"Well, he hurt me a lot, too," said my mother, her smile fading.

"How?" I said. "How did Dad hurt you?"

"Oh, Peter, it's too adult for you to understand," she said. She put her own glass down and looked at her hand on the counter. She was no longer wearing her wedding ring.

"I'm adult enough to be served wine," I pointed out. "Try me."

She took a breath. "Your father behaves so much older than he is," she said. "He's very stuck in his ways. He was holding me back."

"Holding you back from what?" I asked.

"From being who I want to be," she said. "From growing in the way I want to grow. From trying new things. I suppose in a way it's not your dad's fault. He's who he is. But we aren't a good fit now, Petey—if we ever were. His whole life is in his books and his classes and his little routines."

"And in his family," I said.

"Well, I know he loves you boys," she said. "I've never suggested otherwise."

"And where does Jeff come into this?" I asked.

My mother took a swig of wine and struck a pose that I recognized as soulful. "Jeff is helping me to become a more fulfilled
person," she said. "He believes in me. He's teaching me to fly."

"He's teaching you to fly!" I said, astonished at the thought.

"Oh, Petey, I don't mean literally! I mean—what's that other
word?"

"Metaphorically?"

"Metaphorically. He's teaching me to fly metaphorically. And
it's exciting."

At that moment we heard a car in the driveway, and my
mother's face brightened. "That will be Jeff and Conrad," she said.
"Please be nice, Petey. Please, please, give Jeff a chance."

And I was nice. I did give him a chance. Not so much as a
favour to my mother, but because being nice seems to be written
into my genetic code, because my dad is the kind of man he is
and, perhaps, because Otis had taught me something about
behaving decently even when other people don't. And also,
because I was a guest in Jeff's house, and would be a guest at his
table, and I didn't want him to stand in the way of me seeing my
brother in the future.

Jeff himself was a tall man—six foot two or three. He had red
hair and the rugged complexion of a man who had spent a lot of
time outdoors. His handshake was firm and his voice was friendly. "Nice to meet you, Pete," he said. "Glad you could come over
at last." Conrad, in the background, waved at me.

"Conrad, why don't you show your brother his room," my
mother said.

"My room?" I said. "I can bunk down anywhere."

"Don't be silly, sweetie," said my mother. "Of course you have
a room. Go upstairs with Con and he'll show you."

So I went upstairs, and Con showed me my room, and it was
pretty impressive. The bed was a double, when I only had a single at home, and there was a really nice desk and chair, a sturdy
chest of drawers, and what I guessed to be a new bookcase. "Nice
room," I said, keeping my voice flat. "Is yours like this?"

"Yup," said Conrad, and he took me a little farther down the
hall to show me his own room. It was a slightly bigger version of

mine with a double bed, an identical desk and chair, and a few other pieces of furniture. In addition, of course, his books were on the shelves, his gear was scattered around the room, and he'd put some sports posters on the walls. He'd marked his territory. "They gave me first choice," said Con.

"Makes sense," I said.

We went back to my room and I unpacked the few items I'd brought for the weekend—a couple of pairs of underwear, shirts and socks, pajamas, some toiletries and my school books. When I opened the cupboard to hang up my shirts I discovered there were already a couple of nice, new shirts hanging there—and a pair of jeans. "Whose are these?" I asked.

"I guess they're yours," said Con. "Mom's been doing a bit of shopping."

I didn't say anything.

About half an hour later my mom's voice summoned us to dinner, and we went downstairs and into the dining room. The table was nicely set, and the food smelled very good. Jeff, Con and I sat down, and my mother served us—so that much, at least, had not changed.

Jeff raised his glass of wine before we began eating. "To the beautiful chef," he said.

My mother, who had just joined us at the table, laughed in a slightly flirtatious way—which was disturbing—and said, "Tuck in, boys. And there's lots more if you're hungry." So we ate.

We ate our salad and we ate our shepherd's pie and we talked. I didn't say a great deal myself, but my mom talked about her half day at the real estate office—I soon gathered she'd dropped down to half-time—and Jeff talked about an old Buick he was restoring, and my brother talked basketball. My mother and Jeff laughed about an agent who kept losing his pager, and Conrad's frustration with a member of his team who hogged the ball held our attention for a while. Halfway through the meal I found myself sipping the glass of wine that someone had placed by my plate.

Dessert was ice cream, and plenty of it. I helped myself to a second glass of wine.

"No more after that one, Peter," said my mother, smiling.

"Oh, let a young fella indulge," said Jeff, also smiling. "It's Friday!" And he winked at me. I put the glass down ... but picked it up again a few minutes later.

At the end of the dinner my mom rose and began to clear the table. Immediately, Jeff and Con rose too, and started to help. I got to my own feet a moment later. "Don't worry, boys," said my mother. "I'll do it. This is a special occasion, having Peter back with us." So we sat down again, and Jeff thoughtfully topped up my wine glass and, after lighting a cigarette, talked about his own high school days, and how he'd always loved my mother, and how he'd kicked himself for ever letting her go. And a sort of glow settled on the table, and things got pleasantly misty around the edges, and after a while I began to feel more tired than I would have expected so early in the evening.

"Has Peter had *three* glasses of wine?" asked my mother, returning to the dining room.

"Maybe," said Jeff, raising his glass at me.

"Maybe," I echoed, raising my own glass. I laughed. Jeff laughed. My mother laughed.

A few minutes later, Con escorted me to my room. "I like wine," I said.

"No kidding," he said.

I changed into my pajamas, sought out the bathroom, brushed my teeth, made some interesting faces at myself in the mirror, sang a little song while I peed, flushed the toilet, and headed back to my bedroom. Lying down on the bed, it occurred to me that I should say good-night before I went to sleep, and I resolved to do so after shutting my eyes for just a moment or two.

CHAPTER THIRTY: A TRIP TO TORONTO

But I was not seduced into a lasting acceptance of my mother's new living circumstances. The wine certainly defused tensions that first night, but my discomfort with my mom's decision to leave my dad for Jeff did not disappear, and whenever I saw them kissing or embracing—and they weren't shy about doing either—my anger reappeared (though I contained it). In any event, the weekend passed: Mo was out of town visiting her grandparents so there was no possibility of seeing her, and I spent as much time as I decently could in my bedroom, telling my mother I had to start preparing for my final exams.

We ate two more meals at the dining room table, but I declined further offers of wine. This seemed to amuse Jeff, who attributed my refusal to a hangover. "You need a hair of the dog that bit you!" he said, pushing a glass towards me. My mother, however, intercepted it and, laughing, drank it herself—though I think she intuited that I had other reasons for abstaining, even if she could not articulate what they were. When I left on Monday morning, hugging my mom and shaking Jeff's hand on the way out the door, I was looking forward both to school and to returning to what I saw as my real home.

"So?" asked Conrad as we walked down the drive.

I shrugged. "I don't like it, Con. I don't like the way they're always kissing and pawing at each other. And I really hate the fact that it began behind Dad's back."

"Yeah," said Conrad, his shoulders slouching a little. "Maybe Dad will be happier, though. At least they don't have to argue anymore."

"Do Mom and Jeff ever argue?" I asked.

"No," said Conrad. "Not that I've heard. But it's early yet. They're still obsessed with each other." I looked sideways at my brother, struck by his astuteness. He was looking straight ahead and did not meet my eyes.

That Monday was mostly unremarkable at school, but a surprise awaited me when I got home. My dad hadn't yet returned from work, but he'd left a message for me, written in his neat cursive: "Welcome home, Peter! Could you give Mrs. James a call, please? She badly wants to speak with you."

I dialed Otis's old number immediately, and Mrs. James answered on the third ring. "Mrs. James?" I said. "It's Peter Ellis."

"Oh, Peter," she said, sounding flustered. "I've had such a sad letter from Otis. He's in Toronto, as I expected. He says, he says"—I could hear her rustling a sheet of paper—"well, I don't want to read it over the phone. Can you come over here?"

I went after dinner, by car, the fields being too slushy for easy navigation on foot. When I pulled into the Jameses' driveway and climbed out of my father's compact Toyota, I conjured a surprisingly vivid image of Otis standing at the front door—but the image disappeared as swiftly as it had come. Mrs. James had clearly heard the car and she came out onto the porch—a dramatic break from her usual custom of waiting in the dark of the front hallway.

"Peter," she said, gesturing to me urgently. "Come inside where it's warm." She turned and went back into the house, closing the door behind her to conserve the heat. I climbed out of the car and made my way to the front door, noting that someone had cleared snow from both the driveway and the steps fairly recently. I knocked, and Mrs. James reopened the door and let me in.

Once inside the house, Mrs. James took me to the kitchen and thrust Otis's letter into my hands. In truth, she could easily have read it to me over the phone:

Dear Mom,

I'm really sorry I left so quickly. The truth is that I felt I had no choice, but I hate the thought that I hurt you.

I'm here in Toronto, staying with my aunt. You'll find the address on the front of the envelope. You'll be pleased to know that I'm enrolled in classes at an alternative high school up here.

Please don't worry about me: I'm fine. I hope you are, too.
I know that the good people at the church will help you out in
any way they can.

I'll come and visit as soon as I can. Please give my best to
my friends, if you see them, and especially to Pete.

Your loving son,
Otis.

I read this twice, looking up to discover that Mrs. James had taken the opportunity to pour me a glass of her special milk. "So he says he's safe," she said.

"Yes," I said. "I'm really glad. But I knew he'd be safe, Mrs. James. I mean, I didn't *know* know, but I was pretty sure he would be." I didn't add that I did not find the letter at all sad.

Mrs. James nodded. "Yes, but he's in Toronto, and Toronto's a very dangerous city. Will you go and visit him, Peter?" She looked me square in the face.

"Me?" I said, a little surprised. "I hadn't thought . . . Do you think I should?"

"Yes!" said Mrs. James. "Yes, because you're his closest friend. Of course, you'll need a little help . . ." And before I could ward her off she was tucking two twenty-dollar bills into my shirt pocket. "That should cover the bus and get you both a meal or two," she said. "And pay for Otis's ticket home, too."

"You mean you want me to bring him home?" I said, catching on fully. "Mrs. James, he says he'll visit when he can, but that doesn't mean—"

"The reason he can't is that he doesn't have any money," said Mrs. James. "I'm sure that's it. Will you take it to him, Peter? Will you take him the money?" I found that I could not say no to her.

★

In truth, my desire to see Otis again was just as strong as my desire to avoid disappointing Mrs. James. I missed my friend. But that didn't mean I was excited about visiting Toronto on my own. I was very much a small town boy in those days, and while

I didn't feel the horror of Toronto that Mrs. James clearly felt, I saw it as a very large and unfamiliar place, filled with all sorts of unpredictable challenges.

My father didn't discourage me from going, but he clearly wasn't keen. "Why don't you write to him and ask directly if he'd like to come home?" he said. "If he's registered at a high school there, that surely tells us something." I told him what Mrs. James had told me, that his mail was probably being monitored. "Hmm," my father said skeptically. "It doesn't seem very likely to me."

It didn't seem very likely to me either, but I'd told Mrs. James I would go. Mo offered to go with me, and for a while that changed my whole view of the trip—but her parents vetoed the idea. We were both disappointed. So, on the following Saturday, with Conrad in the backseat, my father drove me to the Voyageur bus station in downtown Queensville, and at eleven-thirty I found myself on a coach bound for Toronto, with a short stop in Peterborough en route. The whole trip, including the stop, was scheduled to take just over two and a half hours.

I had a seat by myself for the Queensville to Peterborough leg of the trip, but for the final ninety minutes I had to share with a tall, rake-thin young man. "Hey man," he said, on his way down the aisle. "Are you saving this for someone?" He gestured to the seat beside me.

"No," I said. "It's open. Help yourself."

"Cheers," he said, and he folded himself in it, then offered me his hand. "Jack," he said.

Jack was about twenty-one, I guessed, and certainly Caucasian—he was exceptionally pale—but his hair was a wild afro. "Are you a Trent student?" I asked.

"To be sure. Trent," said Jack. He pushed the seat back the extra couple of inches it would go and sighed deeply. "Going up to Toronto to see some friends. Maybe score some hash."

"Oh," I said. "Can't you get that sort of thing in Peterborough?"

"You gotta know the right people," said Jack, which didn't really answer the question. He squinted at me. "You don't smoke, do you? Weed? Hash?"

"No," I admitted.

"That's cool," said Jack. "Still in high school?"

"Grade thirteen," I said. "I hope to come to Trent next year." Mo and I had just completed our applications in February, right as my family was breaking up. I'd applied to Trent, Queen's and Carleton. Mo had applied to Trent, Western and Carleton.

"Cool," said Jack again. He rummaged through the upper pockets of his jean jacket, eventually producing a pack of Gitanes and a book of matches.

"What are you studying?" I asked.

"Philosophy," said Jack. "Nietzsche. Philosophize with a hammer." He made a gesture suggesting the wielding of a sledgehammer, then lit a cigarette and inhaled deeply, holding the smoke in his lungs for a moment.

"Cool," I said, but if Jack caught the gentle dig he was unfazed by it. He expelled the pungent smoke and tried to push the seat back a bit further. It would not go.

"These seats are built for pygmies," he said. "Pygmies. They probably got blowpipes tucked underneath them."

"I think I might take a philosophy course in the fall," I said. "I don't think it will be my major, but I'd like to try it."

"Try and get Gilchrist," said Jack, who I'd decided to christen Hairy Jack, in honour of his afro. "Gilchrist is great. Gilchrist has a mind. Most of the rest of them are just shit."

"Does he teach first year philosophy?" I asked.

"Nah, he teaches History," said Hairy Jack, confounding me for a moment. "Take some History. Take some Sociology—but stay away from the Maoists. Yeah. Philosophy, History, Sociology, that should do you."

"I think I'm supposed to take five," I said.

"Fuck it," said Hairy Jack. "Don't do what they tell you to do. Read. Think. Talk with people. Read some more. Five courses is bullshit."

"Oh," I said.

"Trent," said my friend, and he snorted derisively. "Trent, Trent, Trent, Trent, Trent—the Personal Touch. Have you seen the posters? Fucking public relations nightmare. It's all meant to bring

in the private school boys and girls from Toronto. Heh? The dad-
dies with their bucks. Daddy Warbucks. That's what it's all about.
Don't fall for it."

"So you don't think I should come to Trent?" I asked.

"Oh no, come. What the hell?" said Hairy Jack. "You can read
anywhere. The apartments are cheap. There's a nice river through
the campus. Fucking Otonabee, or something. Some Indian
name. The whole place is full of Indian names. Natives. That's
what we're supposed to call them. Not Indians. Don't call them
Indians. Not unless you want to get scalped."

"Okay," I said. I wondered what Otis would make of this dis-
course.

"So how come you're going to Toronto?" asked Hairy Jack.

"I'm looking for a friend," I said.

"Can't find any back home?" said Hairy Jack. "Hah!
Kidding. Just kidding. Has she run away?"

"He," I said. "Not exactly. He's looking for his biological
mother. He's adopted."

"Whoa," said Hairy Jack. "That's heavy. That's heavy shit. Has
he got any leads?"

"I don't know," I said. "He's staying with his aunt. He's just
met her recently."

"Heavy, heavy shit," said Hairy Jack. He stubbed out his cigarette on the underside of his boot and shook his head a few times
solemnly. "Man, I'm going to try to get some sleep," he said. "If I
shout while I'm sleeping, don't worry about it. It happens. I may
thrash around a bit, too. Don't worry. It's not a seizure. It looks
like one, but it isn't. Some sort of weird sleep disorder shit." He
closed his eyes.

Anticipating that at any moment I'd be struck by Hairy Jack's
limbs thrashing around in his sleep, I remained wide awake the
rest of the trip.

Chapter Thirty-One: Being There

The Toronto Bus Terminal was a grim and grimy place. A quick trip to the bathroom and I was even more eager to leave. I had already decided, before coming, that I would not try to figure out the vagaries of the subway system if I could help it, and my father's gift of an additional twenty dollars meant I could take a taxi to and from Otis's address without eating into Mrs. James's meal and bus money. For the first time in my life, then, I hailed a cab, and climbed in beside the driver, a middle-aged white man with an eastern European accent.

He asked me to repeat the address, but waved away the sheet of paper when I offered it to him to read as confirmation. "You know someone there?" he asked.

"Yes. A good friend," I said.

"Not a white guy," he said.

"No," I acknowledged.

"Black guy?"

"No," I said. "Native."

He grunted. "Lot of blacks in that neighbourhood. Jamaicans. Haitians."

"I don't know Toronto," I said. "I'm from Queensville."

"Many blacks in Queensville?" he asked.

"No," I said. "Very few. It's very . . . it's mostly whites."

"Maybe I should move there," he said, and he laughed grimly. "Yeah, maybe I should move there." I didn't bother asking him why, fearing a racist diatribe, and we passed the remainder of the short journey in silence—except for regular explosions of static and address information from his two-way radio.

In just a few minutes we pulled up beside a long, three-storey, flat-roofed red brick building in a neighbourhood of identical structures. It reminded me of Noor's home in Queensville, and I wondered if social housing throughout the province was based on the same model. Here, too, an attempt had been made at planting trees, though, to be fair, the trees were a little further along than the ones outside Noor's building. But my main impression was of red brick and asphalt, buildings and parking lots, stretching as far as I could see.

I handed my driver one of my twenties, and tipped him after he'd given me my change. "You should be fine in the daylight," he said, by way of reward, "but don't walk outside after dark. I'm serious. White boy like you from Queensville."

"Thanks," I said. My driver took off, lifting his two-way radio mic to his mouth as he accelerated.

I referred again to the sheet of paper on which I'd carefully written Otis's address, transcribing it from the envelope in which he'd sent the letter to his mom. This was clearly the right building, and the numbering system was straightforward. I walked along the sidewalk looking for number 76, and soon found it. A concrete paving-stone path led to a screen door fronted by a concrete step, topped off by a corrugated tin roof slanting two feet out from the face of the building and supported by two wooden struts. The ground around the path was muddy from a combination of melted snow and hard use. I went up the path and knocked on the screen door. Receiving no response, I opened the screen door and knocked on the front door itself.

"Wait," I heard—a woman's voice. "Wait. Wait." A moment passed, then a middle-aged native woman opened the door, blinking in the light. "Can't a girl get some sleep?" she said.

"I'm sorry," I said. "It's after lunch, and I assumed—"

"Who are you?" she said.

"My name is Peter," I said. "Peter Ellis." The room behind her was dark, and it was difficult to make out much detail. It smelled pleasantly of stew, however.

"What do you want?" said the native woman. Her breath was tinged with alcohol and tobacco, and her face looked ravaged. It occurred to me, though, that my first impression might have been wrong, and that she might not be much older than her early thirties.

"I'm a friend of Otis," I said. "An old friend."

She was silent for a moment, and looked at me speculatively. "Who is O-tis?" she said at length.

"I think he lives here," I said. "He wrote to his mother from here. This was his return address."

"No, you got the wrong place," said the native woman. "Ain't no O-tis here. Maybe he used to live here. He's gone now." She made to withdraw back into the apartment.

But my eyes had adjusted enough to the darkness of her home that I was able to see, though not clearly, Otis's walking stick leaning against the far wall—the walking stick that had been a gift from Mr. Spurr. "I can see his walking stick," I said. "I was there when it was given to him. I'm an old friend."

The woman hesitated for a moment, then opened the door just a couple more inches. "Maybe come back in two hours," she said. "He's gone out."

"Will you tell him I came?" I asked.

"Maybe," she said. "I've gotta sleep." She closed the door and I heard her lock it.

★

So I went for a walk. The neighbourhood didn't appear particularly threatening, but it was certainly run-down, and when I reached a commercial district I was struck by how many stores had bars on the windows. The narrow range of commercial activity also told a story: convenience stores, pawn shops, the odd ethnic grocery, laundries, and cheque-cashing services. Here and there I passed small knots of young black men, but while they looked at me, they said nothing, and I also saw old men and women (black and Asian) carrying groceries, mothers with babies and toddlers, and the odd sexily-dressed young woman. "Looking for company, Sugar?" one of them said to me, but she said it half-heartedly, as if knowing I would decline at so early an hour. Or perhaps she knew I wasn't a likely prospect just from what I was wearing and the way I carried myself.

As I walked farther, the quality of shops gradually improved: pharmacies began cropping up, and restaurants—at first greasy spoons, but, eventually, franchises, and, a couple of blocks later, places where I might have taken Mo, under the right circumstances. And finally, and rather to my surprise, I came to a huge church, set well back from the street on an expanse of lawn that would have been green in the right season. Having nothing else to do I went up the path and tried the large front door—and it opened.

I found myself in a vestibule, on whose walls were bulletin boards covered with typed notices of church meetings and invitations to charitable events. Nothing there really caught my attention, so I pressed on, opening the doors that led to the nave of the church. Passing through, I was confronted by the most beautifully engineered space I'd ever entered: the ceilings were extraordinarily high; the paucity of artificial light made the sunshine coming through the stained glass windows all the more brilliant; and the lovely stillness and quiet made me want to sit and think. So I did.

I thought about Mo, and about how I loved her, and hoped she loved me; and inevitably I thought about Mary-Lynne, too; and I thought about my dad, and my mom, and Conrad; and about Big Andy and Janet Brightman, and John and Patti, and Bruce—and Katherine (the little girl in the hospital), and Noor, and Chris the Bayridge Bus Guy, and Mr. Spurr and Stephen and Dent . . . they all came to my mind, as if presenting themselves at a kind of mental roll call; and I thought about Otis, who I hoped I would see that afternoon. And I assembled all these people in my mind, discovering, in the process, that I loved them all, in a weird way I couldn't begin to understand or explain. And I think, when I look back on it, that what I did was a kind of prayer—a lifting up, as it were, of some of the people who had touched me and shaped me. I was glad I had come in.

And just as I was concluding that I'd had something approaching a mystical experience, however quiet, a hand appeared above the top of the pew about seven or eight rows ahead of me, and, after a dramatic pause, an aging drunk pulled himself to a sitting position, his back towards me. He let out a mighty belch, slurred "Excuse me, Father," then disappeared from view once more.

★

After spending another twenty minutes in the church, looking at the religious statuary and reading the bulletin and lighting a candle in a little side chapel, I left and began to make my way back towards Otis' neighbourhood. Just a little over an hour had passed, and I discovered I was hungry, so I stopped and bought a kind of sandwich in a restaurant whose ethnicity I could not quite place. "What kind of food is this?" I asked the young man behind the counter.

"Good food," he said, smiling.

"Yes," I said—and I laughed. "But where is it from? What country?"

"From Canada," he said, pushing the joke a little. But then he relented. "Lebanese," he said. "We are from Lebanon. You not eat Lebanese food before?"

"No," I admitted.

"*Best* food," he said. "Tell you what," he added, "I give you the sandwich *free* . . . but I have to charge you two dollars for the napkin!" He laughed uproariously, and then, I suspect, translated his witticism for the older couple in the tiny kitchen behind him. They laughed, too, and the gentleman waved at me. "He big joker!" he shouted from the kitchen. "Always kidding around." I enjoyed my meal.

Twenty-five minutes later I was back on the street again, and I arrived at the door of number 76 a bit before two hours had elapsed, but within spitting distance of the target. I knocked, and Otis answered.

Chapter Thirty-Two: Some Explanations

He stood framed in the half-opened door for a moment, looking out at me. His gaze wasn't hostile, but it wasn't welcoming either. He looked—well, *strained* is as close as I can come to the expression on his face. "Peter," he said.

"Hi, Otis," I replied. And then, as he said nothing more, "May I come in?"

Otis opened the door a little wider and stepped back to allow me inside. The front door opened into the living room, now well lit by a couple of lamps, and my first impression was of cleanliness and order. However drab and run-down the exterior of the building, this space felt like a home.

"Are you hungry?" Otis asked. "I can make some food."

He made as if to leave for the kitchen, but I stopped him. "I've just eaten," I said. "I stopped at a little Lebanese place. Nice cheap meal."

"Like a tea?" Otis asked. "Or a coffee?"

"Not right now," I said. "It's good to see you."

"Have a seat," said Otis. I sat down on an old couch. Otis seated himself in an armchair. He looked at me without speaking.

"It's been a while," I said.

He nodded slowly. "So what brings you to Toronto?"

"Well, I guess *you* do," I said. "Your mother sent me. She's worried about you, and she wants me to bring you home. She gave me the money for your ticket." I produced one of my two remaining twenty dollar bills, and put it down on the coffee table.

Otis was quiet for a moment. "I can't come back with you right now, Peter," he said at length. "Take the money back to my stepmom. I have to look after my aunt. She's not doing so well."

"Is that the lady who answered the door a couple of hours ago?" I asked.

"Yes," he said. "She's got some problems. She needs family, and most of the others are back on the reserve. I help to keep her straight. She's sleeping right now, or she'd want to make us a coffee."

I privately doubted his aunt would want to make me anything, but I didn't argue. "Well, if you can't come now," I said, "can you at least give me some news to take back to your mom?"

"What do you want to know?" he asked.

"Are you going to school? Are you working?"

"I'm working and I'm taking courses at this alternative school," he said. "It's a place for natives. We learn the usual white school things and we spend time with some elders. They're teaching us about our culture. I have a lot to learn."

"So will you graduate from high school?" I asked, fatuously.

"Yeah," said Otis. "Sometime. But the other things I'm learning are more important."

I took this in. "Well," I said, "Is there anything you'd like me to tell *you*?"

He paused. "Sure," he said. "Tell me about life in Queensville."

So I caught him up on events at the school, telling him about John and Patti, and Janet and Big Andy, and about Mo. And I told him about Noor coming to my home in distress, and about my mother and her boyfriend, and her leaving my father, and Conrad moving with her. Otis listened and asked a question every now and then, but he seemed disengaged, not fully present. When at last I ran out of news, we sat for a moment in silence. In that silence I summoned the courage to ask the question that had been uppermost in my mind. "Otis," I said. "Have you found out anything about your biological mother?"

Otis took a long time to answer. "Yes," he said at last. "She's dead. She's passed. Four years ago. Here, in the city. She was living with my aunt."

"I'm sorry," I said.

"I've asked my aunt about my father," he said, "but she hasn't told me anything. I hope she will. I can be patient." He stared at his hands. "I'd like to know who he is."

I nodded. I could not imagine not knowing who my father was.

Otis looked at me directly. "Peter," he said, "please tell my stepmom this is something I have to do for now. Give her a hug, and tell her I love her. I really do. But she has the church people, and my aunt has no one. Tell her I'll come visit sometime."

"Okay," I said. "I'll tell her."

Otis nodded. "I have to go to work in an hour. Are you staying in Toronto?"

"No," I said. "I have to get back."

"I'll come to the bus station with you," he said. And he got to his feet.

"I have money for a cab," I said, brandishing the twenty again. "My bus ticket is for a round trip."

"Save the money," said Otis.

"If I'm not using any of it, I'm giving it to you," I said. "So you can put it towards your ticket when you do come." Otis looked at me for a moment, then reached out his hand for the bill. He took it and slipped it into his pocket.

★

We parted at the bus station. At the last moment, Otis pulled me into a bear hug and gave me a thump on the back that was somewhere between affection and admonishment; it left me, briefly, breathless. He did not wave, but he remained on the platform curb, digging his hands in his pockets as the bus driver ground the gears, and I felt a tug at my heart as the bus pulled away. I was very fond of John and Big Andy and Bruce, but I had—or I'd had—a particularly strong bond with Otis: I'd trusted him in the same way I had trusted Mary-Lynne, and in the way I now trusted Mo and my father. I wondered how long it would be before I saw him again.

My seat companion on this trip was a robust Asian woman in her mid-thirties. She had said nothing when she sat beside me, simply smiling shyly, but when she saw Otis watching us off from the platform she cleared her throat. "Is he brother?" she asked.

"Well, not really," I said, a little startled. And then I added, "We don't really look alike, do we?"

"Not on outside," she said. "But I think he is like brother to you."

★

And so back along the Don Valley and up to Highway 401, and from the 401 to the 115, and from the 115 towards Peterborough. It had begun to snow as we whipped along the 401, but the driver hadn't moderated his speed at all. I found myself imagining what it would be like to spin out of control on the highway—the coach tumbling over and over until it came to rest, upside down on the shoulder, or even on the other side of the median. Thinking of highway accidents inevitably made me think of Mary-Lynne, and I spent several minutes remembering everything about her I could— from the sound of her voice to the soft touch of her lips and the scent of her perfume. I felt the old sadness rise up in my chest, and I could only push it away by letting go of her image and conjuring up one of Mo. *Am I being disloyal to Mo when I think of Mary-Lynne?* I asked myself. I had no answer. I hoped not.

When once we had turned off the main highway and onto the 115, the Asian lady fished her backpack out of the overhead compartment and took out a number of small, neatly-wrapped packages and plastic containers. I looked out the window at a landscape now shrouded in darkness, but in my peripheral vision I could see that she had brought along a whole meal—a main course, grapes, an unfamiliar canned drink, and a handful of what I guessed were candies in white wrappers. When the whole thing was arrayed on her lap she nudged me and I turned to find her offering me a plastic fork. "Eat," she said.

"Oh. No, thank you," I said. "I ate in Toronto. I had lunch."

"Eat," she said again. "Is dinner time."

"No, really," I said.

"If you not eat, I cannot eat," she said, still extending the fork.

"Okay, then," I said, accepting the implement. "Thank you. I'll have a little."

"Dumplings," she said, indicating the largest of the containers, and I speared one of the small ravioli-like squares and ate it. "Good?" she asked.

"Very good," I said, taking another. She nodded and, taking a pair of chopsticks from a long box, she began to eat, too.

After the meal we talked for a while, and I learned that Diane—"my Canadian name," she said—was a massage therapist from Guelph, and that she was visiting her sister in Peterborough. "My sister very lonely," she said. "Small apartment, two children, no husband. Very hard."

"What will you do while you're there?" I asked.

"I will cook for her," said Diane. "And I will look after the children little bit. Let sister go out and make friend."

"That's nice of you," I said. My stomach felt comfortably full, and I was now sitting back, so far as one can sit back on a bus, with a cup of green tea. "Were you a massage therapist in China, Diane?" I asked.

"I professor at Beijing University," she said. "But now is not good time to be in China. Much killing of educated people. Good to get out." And this, remarkably, was the first time I'd heard anything about the horrors of Mao's Cultural Revolution. "You go to university?" Diane asked.

"In September," I said. "I don't know which one yet. Maybe Trent. Maybe Queen's. There isn't a university in my town."

"Education very important," said Diane, and she nodded her head very slowly several times, conveying that this was a deeply held belief of hers.

★

And from Peterborough, where I bade farewell to Diane, on to Queensville, passing through the little village of Marmora en route. My new seatmate was an unemployed construction worker with several beers on his breath. "Ever been there?" he asked, as we left Marmora behind.

"No, I've only passed through," I said. "I don't think there's much there."

"There's a great big fucken hole in the ground," said the construction worker. "Quarry. Big money pit. You could lose the whole fucken town in there."

"Really?" I said.

"Great big fucken hole," he repeated. "Me and my buddies, when we're drivin', we stop there just to piss in it."

"That would be fun," I said, though I was really wondering what the point would be.

The construction worker looked at me suspiciously. "This is just a pissin' thing," he said. "It's not like some fag thing."

"No. Of course not," I said.

"I hate fags," he said. "We should put them in the hole. Then fill it up with piss."

I had no answer to this, and we spent the next twenty minutes in silence—but by this time we were passing through the suburbs of Queensville and I was nearly home.

Chapter Thirty-Three: Conrad & Noor

Mrs. James was, of course, bitterly disappointed that Otis did not return with me on the bus, but she took some comfort from the news that he seemed healthy and that he would eventually visit—and she cried when I said he'd asked me to tell her that he loved her. "He's a good boy," she said several times.

I saw Mo on Sunday and brought her up to date; we went out to a movie, and then back to her home to talk and have tea and make out, nervously, in her basement. At lunch time on Monday I was in the midst of telling Big Andy, John, Patti and Bruce how Otis was when Janet Brightman arrived at the table shaking her head. "Have you heard about Chris?" she asked. "Jeez, that guy's funny."

It turned out that Chris had spent a full period in an empty boys' changing room, just off the gym, writing Queensville's complete bus schedule out on the walls. In black felt pen. From memory. "Have they suspended him?" asked Bruce.

"I don't know. Probably," said Janet. "What would make him do something like that?"

None of us knew. And we were somewhat surprised, when we thought about it, that Chris was still at the school, as we had thought the Occupational Program only lasted three years.

As luck would have it, I had to go by the school office in the early afternoon to pick up a textbook form, and I saw Chris sitting outside one of the vice-principals' offices looking very forlorn.

"Chris," I said, going up to him. "How are you?"

"I'm not so good," he said. "I'm hungry."

"I hear you got into some trouble," I said.

"Yeah. I'm suspended. They're sending me home. But my mom hasn't come. And I haven't had anything to eat."

"Couldn't you just have gone to the cafeteria while you were waiting?" I asked.

"They said to stay here. They said, 'Stay here, Chris, until your mom comes,'" said Chris, his face a study of sadness. "And she hasn't come, and she hasn't come, and I don't know when she'll come."

"I'm sorry, Chris," I said, recognizing, perhaps for the first time, just how alone and bewildered he must feel. "I think I have some cookies in my locker. Shall I get them for you?"

"I like cookies!" said Chris, his face brightening. "My gramma used to give me cookies! Are they chocolate chip cookies?"

"I think they're oatmeal," I said. "I'll go check." I nearly said, "Stay here," but caught myself just in time.

"Thank you, Peter!" called Chris to my departing back. "Thank you for getting me cookies, Peter!"

A grade-twelve boy named Jack Dawson, his year's Ted Staunton, was lurking outside the office as Chris called out after me. "What a fucking retard," he said, smirking. I said nothing. There didn't seem to be much point.

When I returned with a four-pack of cookies, Chris tucked into them with real pleasure. "These are good," he said. "These are really good, Peter. I like cookies."

"I'm glad you like them, Chris," I said, sitting down next to him. And then, my curiosity getting the better of me: "Is it true you wrote the bus schedule on the wall?"

"Yes," said Chris, his mouth full of cookie. He looked so guilty that I almost refrained from asking the follow-up question—but I wasn't strong enough. "Why did you do it, Chris?" I asked. "I mean, I'm not angry. I still like you. I'm just curious."

Chris chewed elaborately for a moment or two, thinking, then he looked down at the floor. "They told me I didn't know it," he said. "They said they didn't believe I knew it."

"Who?" I asked.

"Jack and them," he said vaguely.

"Jack Dawson?"

"Yes. He said I was too stupid to know it." He contemplated the last of the cookies. "But I'm *not* stupid."

"I know you're not, Chris," I said. "Did you tell the vice-principal that Jack said that?"

"No," said Chris, blinking at me. "He was angry. He didn't ask."

"Okay," I said. "Thanks, Chris. You take care." I rose, and went down the hallway to talk with the principal.

★

On the Friday, my dad picked up Conrad from his after-school practice again and brought him home. There was no casserole in the fridge this time, and my dad had gone through his fairly limited meals repertoire a couple of times in succession, so he said he'd pick up a barbecued chicken and some coleslaw from the supermarket, and asked if I could heat up the loaf of garlic bread that was in the freezer. I did this gladly. Conrad hit the shower as soon as he came through the door, so we didn't really have time to talk until we all sat down at table.

"So what's new with you?" I asked him, as Dad sliced and divided the chicken.

"Nothing much," he said, shrugging. Then: "I may have a girlfriend."

"A girlfriend!" I said. "Well, that's great. Is she at QDSS?"

"No," he said, "she goes to St. Mary's. She's in grade nine. Her name's Cindy."

"Tell Pete how you met her, Con," said my dad, sliding a plate towards him. Conrad had clearly filled him in on the drive home.

"She saw me play in a tournament last weekend, and we got to talking afterwards," said Conrad.

"So she was wowed by his athletic skills," said my dad, smiling.

"Yup," said Conrad. "I guess that's the way to attract the ladies. Jeff said when he was in . . ." He stopped himself.

"Well, I'm sure Jeff would know," my dad said lightly but with a world of subtext, and he began to eat. We all ate.

Conrad and I cleared the table after supper, and we both launched into the dishes—me washing and Conrad drying. My dad, meanwhile, slipped away to do some marking, or so he said. I suspect he wanted to give us a bit of time alone together.

"So how are things with Mom and Jeff?" I asked, when I was fairly confident Dad was out of earshot.

Conrad was drying a glass when I asked this, and he took a long time making sure it was streak-free. "I guess they're okay," he said. "But they're beginning to argue a bit."

"What about?"

"Well. Money. Jeff says he thinks Dad should be paying support for me."

"He said that in front of you?" I asked, a bit taken aback.

"No. I heard them talking in the bedroom," said Conrad. "And Mom said that means she'd have to take Dad to court, and Dad would probably say *she* should pay support for you."

"I don't think Dad would say that," I said.

"No," said Conrad. "I don't think Mom wants to take Dad to court. She said it could get really messy."

"Did she say that to Jeff?" I asked.

"Yeah," said Conrad. "Speed up," he added, nodding his head towards the basin full of dishes. I had stopped washing altogether, and I now resumed. "And there's other stuff," said Conrad. "Jeff spends a lot of time in Belleville, and I think that makes Mom angry."

"What's in Belleville?" I asked.

"I dunno." Conrad shrugged. "A photography club, or something. He's really into cameras."

"Does he ever take Mom?"

"Nope," said Conrad. "He says that's his private time. He says everyone needs some time alone. He tells Mom not to cling."

I didn't say anything for a moment. Just a few days before I'd heard a couple of girls at school talking about a boy they called a *Klingon*, and I'd assumed it had something to do with his being a fan of the television show *Star Trek*. Now I wondered whether they might have meant that he was *clingy*—a *Cling*-on—and that that was a bad thing. "So is Mom okay?" I asked.

"Yeah, she's basically okay," said Conrad. "I mean, she's not crying, or anything. But I don't think she's as happy as she thought she would be." He and I looked at one another for a moment. I don't know what he was thinking, but in at least a small part of my mind I was entertaining the hope that one day, eventually, maybe, our family might be restored.

★

I still missed Otis, but Mo's presence in my life became more and more significant. For a small girl, she took up a lot of emotional room. We weren't in each other's hip pockets the way John and Patti were, but that was mainly because her parents insisted on having at least one day of the weekend alone with their daughter. It wasn't that they didn't like me—Mo told me that her mom was especially fond of me, and grieved that I didn't have my own mother around—but for them, clearly, family came first, and *becoming* family would require an engagement.

In the middle of the week following Conrad's last visit, I suggested we check up on Noor, and Mo—who hadn't met her yet—willingly agreed. On Tuesday evening I called and asked Noor's mom if Mo and I could take her daughter out for a milkshake the following day, and Aisha gave her permission. After school on Wednesday, Mo came home on the bus with me and we ate supper with my dad, then I borrowed the car and we drove to Noor's home. Mo was quiet when we arrived at the complex: a thaw had taken hold a couple of days before, and the front yard of the project looked even worse than it had the last time I was there. There was mud and litter everywhere, and we could hear a stereo blasting acid rock as soon as we stepped out of the car.

Noor had been waiting for us around the side of the building, and she came running to me when she saw us. I was touched—touched by how small she looked (even beside Mo), and touched by her obvious pleasure at seeing me.

"Hi, Noor," I said, giving her a hug. "This is my girlfriend, Mo."

"Hi!" said Noor, and she surprised me by giving Mo a hug, too. If Mo was surprised she did not show it, and the three of us walked back to the car together.

But if Noor's demonstrativeness represented a change for the better, and it was certainly sweet, she had changed in other ways that were a little more unsettling. She talked a mile a minute, telling us stories about her school friends and her teachers, and she laughed in a way I found a little forced. At McDonald's she finished her milkshake quickly, then asked if she could have a glass of water. I offered her another milkshake—or anything else she wanted—and after thinking for a bit she decided to have an order of fries and a big glass of coke, and she guzzled that down and went back for another, then, not surprisingly, slipped away to the bathroom.

"Does she seem a bit odd to you?" I asked Mo.

"She seems a little manic," said Mo, "but remember this is the first time I've met her. Does she seem to have changed?"

"Yes," I said. "She seems very different."

After Noor returned from the bathroom I decided to raise the difficult subject of the man who had accosted her a couple of months before. At the mention of the episode, Noor's manner changed swiftly. "He still lives there," she said, frowning. "I see him all the time."

"Has he said anything to you since that night?" Mo asked.

"No," said Noor. She licked a fingertip and rubbed it in the salt her fries had come wrapped in, then raised the finger to her lips. "I avoid him."

"Would you like us to do anything?" I asked. "It's not too late to speak to the police, you know. I'd go to them with you."

"No!" Noor's eyes widened, and she clutched at my hand on the table. "Promise me you won't, Peter! It will only cause trouble."

So I promised her, like a fool, and after a few moments she calmed down again and resumed talking about inconsequential things and laughing. And in a little while Mo and I drove her home and walked her to her door, in spite of her saying that we didn't need to do that. She hugged us both, then opened her front door a crack and slipped inside. If her mother was home, we had no opportunity to see her.

Chapter Thirty-Four: My Father

A couple of weeks later, and following another exchange of visits—I going to my mom's new place for a mildly awkward weekend, and Conrad coming back to us—the telephone rang while my dad and I were having dinner. "Mo?" my father said, looking at me.

"Not during dinner," I replied. Mo's parents banned all phone calls, incoming or outgoing, between six and seven o'clock.

"Maybe it's Conrad," said my dad, and he went to the phone. I knew immediately that it wasn't Conrad, however; after his initial greeting my father's voice took on an unfamiliar tone. He sounded friendly, as he usually did, but he didn't sound friendly in the way he sounded with us. "I'd very much like that," he said. "Sure. Why don't we meet there. Good-bye, then." He replaced the phone and came back to the table looking slightly bemused.

"Who was it?" I asked.

"A lady I met in the grocery store yesterday," he said. "She tracked me down somehow." He picked up his knife and fork and seemed set to resume eating.

"What did she say?" I asked—with perhaps a trace of impatience. It wasn't like my dad to be coy.

He paused. "She said, 'I'm being very bold,'" he replied. "'I liked your smile and I thought I'd ask you out for coffee.'"

"And you're going?" I asked.

"Sure," he said, with a little shrug. "It's not every day an attractive woman asks me out."

"So she's attractive?" I said.

"Yes. She's a nice-looking woman."

I felt a mixture of emotions. Part of what I felt was pleasure that my father looked happy. But there was something selfish in the mix, too—the fear that our home, which had begun to feel stable and familiar and reassuring, might be threatened. It was the fear that spoke. "How do you know she isn't crazy?" I said.

He looked at me with some surprise. "Well, I guess I don't know for sure," he said. "But does a woman have to be crazy to like your old dad's smile?" And for that I had no good rejoinder.

★

So that was how Sharon entered our life. Sharon was an attractive woman in her mid-thirties—a busty, green-eyed red-head with a loud voice and a ready laugh. She seemed to fall for my dad very quickly, and he certainly seemed enchanted with her; I'm guessing that her physicality, her habit of rubbing his shoulders or ruffling his hair, was a welcome contrast to my mother's cool detachment in the last several years they had spent together. My own feelings remained more complex: I came to enjoy the energy and good will she brought to our home, but I also resented the way she sought to dominate my father's atten-tion, and I found her ripe sexuality a little alarming.

But I'm getting ahead of myself. Sharon came to dinner about a week after that first telephone call. She and my father had apparently met for coffee a couple of times, and I think my dad wanted to see how she would take to me, and how I would take to her. The meal was scrambled eggs with cheese, which my father served up without any preliminary comment.

Sharon seemed amused. "Is it breakfast time already?" she said.

"Well, not exactly," said my dad. "No cereal for you, young lady!"

Sharon seemed to find this very funny; she cackled in a way that reminded me of Janet Brightman. "What, no bacon?" she said.

"Next time," said my father. And that set Sharon off again. My dad laughed, too. I looked sternly at both of them.

"I make scrambled eggs about once a week," said my dad, pouring each of us a glass of apple juice. "Peter likes them."

"And do you like roast beef for breakfast, Peter?" said Sharon. And she howled. It didn't seem all that funny to me. Perhaps realizing this, Sharon settled down for a while, but even so the smallest witticism from my father would make her giggle. Between the interludes of unwarranted merriment I did learn a little about her: she and a male partner worked in a furniture reupholstering business, she said, and she had a daughter, Helen, who was just a couple of months older than me, and who, like Conrad's quasi-girlfriend Cindy, attended the Catholic high school, St. Mary's.

"Are you Catholic?" I asked.

"No," said Sharon. "I just wanted Helen to go to a more disciplined school than the ones in the public system."

I knew very well how undisciplined QDSS was, but everything I'd heard about St. Mary's suggested things were no better there. Janet had once mentioned that at the previous year's graduation dance no fewer than six girls had been conspicuously pregnant. It seemed impolite to bring this up, however, so I just nodded.

After dinner my dad said that he and Sharon would do the dishes, and that I should get a head start on my homework. I left them laughing together in the kitchen and went off to my books, but found I could not concentrate. I used the downstairs telephone to call Mo.

"So how's your dad's girlfriend?" she asked. I could hear classical music playing on her parents' stereo in the background.

"She's okay," I said, "but she's pretty loud. And she laughs at *everything*."

"Maybe she's nervous," said Mo.

"About what? Meeting me?"

"Sure," said Mo. "She must realize that your dad's not going to keep her around if you don't like her."

"Do you think?" I said, taken aback.

"Yup," said Mo. "Your dad would put you and Con before his dating life. So this is a test for—what's her name?"

"Sharon," I said.

"For Sharon. It's a test for her, even if your dad hasn't said so. But I bet she knows it." We talked for a while longer, but it was this insight that I took away with me after we hung up.

After Sharon left at about ten o'clock, calling out a throaty farewell to me as I stepped out of the shower, the house seemed very much quieter. A little later in the evening my dad knocked quietly on my bedroom door. "May I come in, Pete?" he asked.

"Sure, Dad," I said, putting down the novel I knew would figure prominently on my English exam.

My father entered, and hesitated indecisively for a moment. "So, what did you think of Sharon?" he asked.

Just for a moment—the shadow of an instant—I saw in him the teenager he must see in me every day. "She seemed nice, Dad," I said. "A bit loud, but I think she really likes you." He smiled, and I knew that, for better or worse, Sharon would be around for a while.

★

Mom, meanwhile, was beginning to have real troubles in her relationship with Jeff. It wasn't that they yelled at each other, or even said anything nasty. But it was possible to sense a growing tension, a sort of subtle estrangement. On my next Friday night visit we sat down to dinner together as we had on previous Fridays, but while Jeff had at least three glasses of wine, Mom didn't have any—and she made sure the bottle was out of my reach after I'd had one. Jeff was, if anything, more voluble than ever, talking at some length about his high school days, when, I gathered, he'd been something of a basketball and track star. My mother contributed very little to the discussion, saying simply, at one point, that she'd been more interested in music than sports—at which Jeff grinned wolfishly and said, "But she sure liked athletes."

"Jeff," said my mom, just a hint of warning in her voice. He said nothing further, but took a long swallow from his glass of wine.

I felt a surge of inarticulate fury at this exchange, smelling, as it seemed, of a sort of furtive sexuality in which my mother was directly implicated. It was unsettling enough to be confronted with Sharon's desire for my dad, but to have my mother's teenage sexual preferences sniggered about by a man who had cuckolded my father set my teeth on edge. "I'm going up to my room," I said. "I've got a lot of studying to do."

"Studying! You hiding a *Penthouse* under the mattress?" said Jeff as I stood up.

"Jeff," said my mom again, her voice controlled but her face unhappy.

"All right, all right," said Jeff. "Just kidding. Do what you have to do, kid."

I looked at him for a moment, then went upstairs.

★

Mo was my rock. As my father became increasingly occupied with Sharon, and my mother's new domestic arrangements began to unravel, I spent more and more time with my girlfriend. She visited often, to the extent that having four people at the dining room table (including Sharon) came to seem almost normal. And I was often in her home, too—though her parents maintained their one-day-just-for-family rule for Saturday or Sunday.

There was a sense of calm in Mo's home that reminded me of my own home at its best: her dad, like mine, rarely raised his voice, and spent much of his spare time in his workshop making beautiful birdhouses, which he sold at bird-watching conventions three or four times a year. Mo's mother was, like her daughter, quite petite, and, like Mo, too, she was very interested in politics. Mo told me she was a member of a women's consciousness-raising group that met weekly to talk about books and gender issues and women's rights. I once made the mistake of mentioning this at lunch when Stephen and Dent were paying one of their periodic visits to our table.

"So your mom's one of those bra-burning femi-nazis, is she?" said Stephen.

"No," said Mo, bridling. "And femi-nazi is a horrible word."

"I know all about them," said Stephen, unrepentantly. "Marching around with their unshaved legs yelling about women's rights. No sane man would want to touch them with a ten-foot pole. Dykes, most of them.".

"My mother is not a dyke," said Mo, leaning across the table. "Not that there's anything wrong with dykes."

"I love lesbians," said Big Andy cheerfully. Janet's mouth was full, so she contented herself with elbowing him, hard, in the ribs.

"Not this kind," said Stephen. "They're all fat and ugly man-haters."

"Mo's mom looks like Mo and loves her husband," I observed mildly. I didn't take Stephen's periodic rants seriously. I suspected they were three-fourths theatre, and only one part conviction.

"They probably keep her around so no one can say they're *all* witches," said Stephen.

"Stephen," said Mo, stabbing her finger at his chest. "My mother and her friends don't hate men. They just think women have had a raw deal, and they're trying to make things better. Got it? You doofus."

"Okay," said Stephen, utterly unconvinced.

"I like the lesbians in pornos," said Dent, just catching up with the conversation.

"Oh, Jesus," said Mo. "This is what we're up against."

"Um, Mo," said John. "I'd sooner you didn't take the Lord's name—"

"John," said Mo, "I'll be more respectful with my language when Christians start paying more attention to human rights."

"Don't you mean *women's* rights," said Dent gleefully, clearly thinking he'd caught her out.

"Women's rights are human rights, Dent, you jerk," said Mo.

"Amen, Sister!" said Janet. And then, turning to Big Andy: "And you're not getting any for the next week."

CHAPTER THIRTY-FIVE: MO'S BIRTHDAY

Mo's birthday was in late May, just a month before mine. We'd only been going out for six months, but she had become enormously important to me, and I was determined to mark the occasion in a very special way. Her birthday fell on a Tuesday, but the plan I conceived required a full hour in the middle of the day, so, with her parents' blessing, I picked her up the previous Saturday. To lend a bit of mystery to the plan, I had her put on a blindfold—actually a sleep mask—once we had pulled away from her home.

"Where are you taking me?" she asked.

"You'll see," I said.

I deliberately took a roundabout route, but we eventually arrived at Ransome Gardens—the place Otis had taken me in the wake of Mary-Lynne's death—and I parked the car in the parking lot outside the old stone wall, now mercifully free of snow. It was, in fact, a beautiful day, and while Mo wore a sweater, I felt perfectly comfortable in my shirtsleeves.

"Can I take the blindfold off now?" she asked.

"No," I said. "I just have to get something from the back, and then we're going for a little walk." I jumped out of the car, and removed a carefully packed picnic basket—egg salad sandwiches, celery sticks, baby carrots, brie cheese, grapes, chocolate chip cookies, and soft drinks—from the trunk. I then helped Mo from the car and, taking her arm, led her through the wrought-iron gate and down the winding path that led to the circular pond. The birds were singing, and a gentle breeze played in the trees.

"Where *are* we?" she said—but she was happy. She could tell she was in a nice place, even though she didn't know where it was. She was smiling as widely as I'd ever known her to smile.

When the pond came into sight, the fountain was not on, but it sputtered into life as we came nearer. "What's that?" Mo asked. "Is it water? Is it a fountain?"

"Yes," I said, leading her to the bench and helping her to sit. I then unpacked the lunch and spread it out between us on the bench, only then telling her to remove the blindfold.

"Oh, Petey," she said, "it's beautiful. It really is. What a lovely place!"

"Haven't you been here before?" I asked, more than a little surprised. It was the kind of place that families like hers tended to visit, sometimes several times a year.

"Yes," she said. "But never in May, and never with a picnic, and never with a boy I loved." And she kissed me, long and deeply.

But I had saved the *coup de grace* for last. Just as we began to eat, a young woman came up behind us and began to play a romantic song on the violin. She was in both the school band and the Queensville Orchestra, and I'd asked her if I could hire her to play for Mo's birthday. She'd said she wouldn't charge me, and would be glad to do it if I looked after her transportation there and back—and Stephen, in spite of his views about femi-nazis, had kindly agreed to do the driving. Mo teared up when she realized the music was for her.

So my contribution to her birthday was a great success, and on the actual day of her birthday she told me her parents had told her that, in future, I could visit her at home on Saturday *and* Sunday—even though we weren't engaged.

★

Exams came—and Mo and I did well. So did John and Patti. I'm not sure how Bruce did—he rarely said anything about his school results, and he'd already decided to attend a broadcasting program at a college in Toronto rather than head off to university, so grades weren't the issue with him that they were with those of us who were university-bound. John and Patti had decided they would attend the same bible college in Saskatchewan, so, again, their results were not hugely important. Upon hearing this was their destination, my dad expressed mild disappointment, believing, as he did, that the academically-talented should go to university, if they could. Janet Brightman and Big Andy would be attending the college in town where my dad taught. Janet said she'd enroll in all his classes and flash him from the front row. "Why?" I asked, not really believing her, but wondering why the thought had even entered her head.

"It'll keep him awake," she said cheerfully. "Old guys are always in danger of falling asleep on the job. I won't wear panties."

"Oh, Janet," said Patti, hiding her eyes for a moment.

"He's forty-six!" I said. "It's not as though he needs to nap every five minutes."

"Oh, he won't want to *nap!*" said Janet. "And give me a break, Patti—we all know that old guys are always wanting to jump teenage girls. It's just the way they're built."

"Not all of them," said Patti.

"*All* of them," said Janet. "Even the Christians. *Especially* the Christians. They're the biggest horn-dogs of all. You'd just have to wiggle that cute little bum of yours, and every man at your church would be bugging his eyes out."

"You are so crude," said Bruce, shaking his head. "So, so crude."

"Aw, poor repressed Brucie-Woosie," said Janet. "We really need to find you a chickie-poo, don't we?"

Mo and I had a difficult decision to make. We both wanted to stay together, but her parents, and my dad, urged us to put school first, saying that if we were meant to be together, attending different universities would only make this more clear. Looking back now, I'm a bit skeptical of this advice, but we took it. I opted for Trent, with its small size and liberal arts orientation, and Mo chose Western for its journalism program.

I had already decided I would return to the museum for one last summer. God knows, the work wasn't exciting, and I had some profound doubts about the historical integrity of many of the exhibits, but my dad, with whom I had not shared my reservations, quietly made the point that future employers would look favourably on evidence of job stability. The matter was clinched for me when Mr. Spurr accepted Mo's application to replace Otis as the second staff member.

★

But the big event of early summer had nothing to do with school or employment or, for that matter, my own birthday. The big event was a car accident—though not one that involved loss of life or even serious injury. On a warm, sunny late afternoon in early July my mother's boyfriend, Jeff, was returning from one of his regular expeditions to Belleville, when the rear of his car was sideswiped by one of the drunk drivers who plagued our roads at that time. Jeff was apparently crossing a secondary highway, and a car came whipping around a bend just as he pulled out of a side road. Jeff was certainly shaken up, but he wasn't really hurt. The problem came when police arrived to find photographs of naked eight- and nine-year old children blowing all over the highway, having been expelled from the trunk of Jeff's car by the shock of impact, and then scattered by a nice summery breeze. And when the police investigated further, they found some sordid film in several small cans, and even more in Jeff's two cameras. So, it became clear, Jeff hadn't been going to Belleville to photograph birds.

Jeff was taken into custody and charged. By the time he was released, on bail, two days later, my mother had moved herself and Conrad into a motel on the other side of Queensville. Con called us from there while Mom was out getting a few groceries. We'd heard rumours, of course, but the full details hadn't yet filtered out. "You're welcome to come home, son," said my father, immediately.

"I don't think I can leave Mom right now. She's pretty upset," said Conrad.

"Fine," said my dad. "But you're welcome any time."

"What about Mom?" said Conrad.

My dad hesitated a moment. "Your mom made her choice some months ago," he said quietly.

★

The next day, a Saturday, I borrowed my father's car and drove to the motel, a once-attractive but now run-down establishment consisting of two long single-storey buildings with fourteen rooms each, with the office, a neon sign, and an outdoor pool between them. My mom wasn't there when I arrived, but Conrad was, and he let me in. The room had two beds, and we sat on them to talk. "How's Mom doing?" I asked.

"Not too well," said Con. "She was pretty shaken up. She still is."

"Did she have any idea?"

"No. She didn't like him going to Belleville all the time, but she thought it was just a bunch of guys getting together to talk about cameras and take pictures of, you know, sunsets and flowers and shit like that. Those were the kinds of shots he showed her."

"That was clever of him," I said. "How are you?"

He shrugged. "Cindy's parents won't let me talk to her," he said. "I keep calling, and they keep saying she's out. But I know she isn't. Not when I call after nine-thirty."

"That's lousy," I said. "It's not as though you had anything to do with it."

"Yeah, but I lived in the bastard's house," said Con. "I was part of the cover—the ready-made family: mom, dad, and kid. All happy and smiley and modern." He sobbed suddenly, but just once; he stood up and turned away from me, his fists clenched. "I should have stayed with you and Dad," he said.

"You didn't know, Con. You couldn't," I said. For my part, I didn't know whether to get up and give him a hug, or just give him some space. I opted for space. "And you can come home. Dad told me to bring you home, if I could."

At that moment, as if on cue, the door opened and our mom came in. I was taken aback by the change in her. She'd always been so conscious of dressing nicely and making herself up carefully, but on this occasion she looked almost frumpy, and her unpainted face looked years older. "Hi, Mom," I said.

"Petey," she said, and she opened her arms. I gave her the first big hug I'd given her in months, and she pulled Conrad into it, too. "Oh, my boys, my boys, my lovely boys," she said.

Eventually we disengaged and Conrad went into the bathroom to wash his face. Mom had been grocery shopping again, and she put a few items into the tiny fridge, then busied herself making some sandwiches. "So," she said, with a trace of bitterness, "is your father laughing at my troubles?"

"No, Mom," I said. "You know he's not like that."

"I bet his girlfriend is," she said. "She looks the type."

"I don't think so, Mom," I said. In truth, Sharon had gone very quiet when she'd heard the news, and I wondered if she worried that my father might take my mom back. I didn't say that, though.

"I didn't know, Petey," my mother said. "I had no idea."

"I know," I said. "You wouldn't have gone with him if you'd had any idea."

"Men can be so sick," she said. "So warped. How can any man get off on shit like that?"

"I don't know, Mom," I said.

"Some of them are just walking penises—sick little penises," she said, smearing peanut butter on bread with angry little motions of her hand. Conrad, emerging from the bathroom, was stopped in his tracks by this, but our mother didn't notice. "Are you hungry, sweetie?" she asked him.

"Mom," I said. "What will you do?"

"I'll just carry on, I suppose," she said. "I have a job, and I don't think Bill will fire me over this. He knows it isn't my fault."

"But where will you live?" I asked.

"I'll rent a place somewhere," she said. "A little apartment. I'm going to go and stay with my sister for a week." This surprised me. My mother and her sister had never been close, in spite of the fact that Darlene lived only half an hour away. They exchanged Christmas cards, but that was about the extent of it. I hadn't seen my aunt since I was about eleven, and had trouble even remembering what she looked like. She was married, but she had no children, so we had no cousins.

"So can Conrad come home with me?" I asked, having no idea how she would respond.

"Yes," she said. "Yes, that's probably a good idea. You might as well let your dad take care of you for a while, Conrad," she added. "It would be better for you to have your own room. You can come back with me when I'm settled."

"Okay, Mom," said Conrad quietly. He sat down on the bed beside me, and I put my arm around his shoulders. He didn't pull away.

We ate the peanut butter sandwiches our mother had prepared, washing them down with small cartons of milk, then we gathered Conrad's belongings, which filled two large suitcases (my mom had made several trips from Jeff's house), and packed the car. "I'll just go and say good-bye to Mom," said Conrad as we slid the second suitcase into the backseat. He disappeared for a moment while I stood and stared at the cars whipping along the secondary highway.

And then I drove Conrad home.

Chapter Thirty-Six: A Visit

Sometime during that summer of 1976, Mo and I were intimate for the first time—lending a greater sweetness to a love that was already deep and rich. We were relatively late in taking that final step, but we were by no means the last among our peers. And when we did, ultimately, make love, there was nothing rushed or furtive about it: my dad had accompanied Conrad to a lacrosse tournament in Kingston one Monday, so Mo and I had a stretch of eight hours alone together. Among the many things I felt that day, the lasting one was a huge tenderness for my small, fiery partner. I'm sure I was a lousy Lothario that first time, and on many occasions subsequent to that, but our love for each other made my clumsiness seem unimportant. In the middle of the afternoon we fell asleep in each other's arms, waking to the sound of two neighbours across the street talking about moles. "I'll be your mole," I said, and gently bumped her right breast with my nose.

The job at the museum was no more exciting than it had been the two previous summers, though on a couple of occasions we enlivened things, when the place was empty, by taking turns reading aloud from an erotic novel. But on each of these occasions someone came in during the reading, and I had to stay seated behind the desk, pretending to be occupied with paperwork, while Mo surged forward to take money and give the brief spiel that Mr. Spurr had written for us. Mo thought it was very funny, but I soon realized that getting worked up at work was not a good idea.

This year, too, Noor visited regularly, though she didn't stay as long as she had the previous summer. She had made friends with a couple of girls in her housing complex, and their mothers had signed them up for a half-day arts and crafts camp at the local museum which ended, most days, with a swim at the nearby municipal pool. She would come by after her swim, her hair still damp, and tell us what she had done that day, and then she would rush off again to play with Trudy and Charice back at the complex. We felt almost parental during these visits—as if our growing child was checking in with us before venturing out again, having received a shot of love and the reassurance that we were there. She always hugged us before she left, her large dark eyes staring solemnly at us the moment before we embraced her, and she no longer talked in the manic way she had during our spring visit with her. It was as though she was calmed by knowing she could see us whenever she wished.

★

At noon on a Sunday in mid-August the telephone rang at my home—and to my delight it was Otis calling. "Peter," he said quietly. "It's been too long, man."

"Otis!" I said, recognizing his voice immediately. "Where are you? Are you in Queensville? How long are you here for?"

"Whoa—slow down," he said. "Yeah, I'm at my stepmom's house, and I'm here for a week. Listen, I've got some stuff to do for her around the place this afternoon, but can you come over for dinner?"

I showed up at six, as suggested, bringing with me a frozen apple pie I'd picked up from the corner store. It soon became clear that Mrs. James had been cooking and baking all day, however, and the meal she put on the table outshone any meal I'd ever eaten there—a huge homemade beef stew, a loaf of fresh bread, and a cherry pie. It was simple fare, but it had been prepared with a generous heart: I'd never seen her so happy. Otis, for his part, had clearly been working outside all day: the grass had been mowed, the front flower bed weeded and watered, and the bird feeder washed and refilled. The three of us ate together, and Mrs. James's grace was simple and touching: "Thank you, God, for bringing my son home safe and sound." She meant to go on, I think, but she choked up after this, and Otis had to get up and give her a hug.

Otis and I cleared and washed the dishes after the meal, and in the kitchen I was able to catch up, to some degree, with his life in Toronto. "I do my best to help my aunt," he said, "but she has a lot of problems. She's done a lot of drugs and she has trouble thinking straight." He seemed subdued.

"Have you met any other family?" I asked.

"She says my grandparents are dead," he replied. "My grandpa died of diabetes. My grandma died of cancer. They were both pretty young. My aunt won't tell me what my mother died of."

"And your father?" I asked. "Has she told you anything about him?"

"She says she doesn't know who he was," said Otis. He paused. "And maybe my mom didn't know either."

"I'm sorry, Otis," I said. I didn't know what else to say.

Otis shrugged. "I guess that's life," he said. "I can't complain. I was raised by people who loved me. Maybe that's the best any of us can ask for." Mrs. James came into the kitchen at that moment and busied herself putting away some of the dishes I'd dried. But I think she really came to make sure Otis was still there, and she touched him a couple of times as she bustled around before heading off to her bedroom to listen to her radio programs.

"It was nice seeing you, Peter," she said, pausing in the doorway.

"It was nice seeing you, too, Mrs. James," I said.

"My son is back," she said. "I knew he'd come home. Say goodnight before you go to bed, Otis."

"I will, Mom," he said. "And I'll be here when you wake up. I promise." Mrs. James nodded, and made her exit. We soon heard her snuffling and blowing her nose in the bedroom.

We resumed our dish-washing and drying in silence for a moment, and then I asked, "So what will you do now?"

"I'm here for six more days," said Otis, "then I'll go back to look after my aunt for a while. She doesn't have anyone else. While I'm here I'll do as much as I can for my stepmom, and I'll come back again around Thanksgiving."

"And you'll go back to school in the fall?" I said.

"I'll be spending more time with the elders," he said. "But I'll do some school, too."

"Okay," I said. "Great." We talked then about my own family, about my hopes and plans for the fall, and about Mo: just saying her name filled me with a quiet joy, and I wanted Otis to know how important she was to me. He listened carefully, and he smiled at my obvious passion.

"So you're happy, Peter?" he said.

"I am," I said. "I never thought I would be after Mary-Lynne died . . . but I am."

"I'm glad," he said. "Really glad."

"Would you like to meet her?" I asked. "I could maybe arrange for her to slip out for a coffee . . ."

"Not tonight," said Otis. "I don't want my stepmom to call out and find I'm not here. But I'd like to meet her later this week." So we made some tentative plans, and a little while later I slipped away.

★

Otis stayed another six days, fixing things around the house and garden, visiting with friends, but mostly keeping his mom company. On the Tuesday he drove into town to meet Mo and me at the museum for lunch. He stopped by a local submarine sandwich shop and bought three large hoagies, and we ate them together at the front desk, exchanging stories about some of the stranger visitors we'd had over the years. Otis examined the latest exhibits, including a letter, thoughtfully written in English, by Carl Jung, in which he thanked James Alfred Spurr for his "immense assistance" with the ideas of "intro- and extroversion," and a page from the diary of Charlie Chaplin acknowledging receipt of a "perspicacious letter from the eminent Canadian, J. A. Spurr," who had recommended he develop "a character who looks and behaves like a good-hearted tramp."

"Quite a guy," said Otis, arching an eyebrow.

"Remarkable," I said, doing my best to match Otis's archness.

"What *are* we exactly?" said Mo, jumping to her feet. "I mean, this isn't really a museum, is it? It's more like a piece of, I don't know . . ."

"Performance art," said Otis. "They have these installations in Toronto sometimes, and they could be real, but you don't really know at first."

"I mean, it's sort of sad *and* it's sort of funny," said Mo. "But really—what are we? Are we museum guides or actors? And if we're actors, shouldn't we, I don't know, *wink* at people as they're leaving? Or bow? Shouldn't we do *something* to tell them it's all a kind of elaborate hoax?"

"I don't think Mr. Spurr would take too kindly to that," I said.

"Yes, but Petey, some people actually *believe* this," said Mo. "Shouldn't we feel just a tiny bit *guilty*?"

"Maybe we should play circus music in the background," I said. "Just softly—not so that it takes over. You know—*bum pum bumma-pum bum pum bum pum*. Very subtle."

"Does it do any real harm?" asked Otis. "Is anyone hurt by it? I don't think so. It's a kind of harmless mythology. There are worse things. And it gives you guys a job. And it makes Mr. Spurr very happy."

"James Alfred Spurr?" said Mo.

"*David* Spurr," said Otis. "I don't suppose good old J. A. could care less."

We talked easily and comfortably together. It meant a great deal to me that my two best friends in the world seemed to like each other. And the afternoon was crowned when Noor arrived. She did a little dance of joy at seeing Otis and at having all of us in the same room. Then she insisted on trying to braid Otis's hair, which he was now wearing quite long, into a single ponytail.

★

Sunday rolled around all too quickly, with Otis's departure scheduled for the late afternoon. I picked him up just after lunch and we drove together to Ransome Gardens. I parked the car and we passed through the wrought-iron gate and along the winding path to the circular pool with the fountain.

"It's beautiful in the summer," said Otis, staring into the water from the edge of the pool.

"And in the spring," I said. "I brought Mo here on her birthday. We had a picnic."

"Old man Ransome did a good thing all those years ago," said Otis reflectively. "Pete," he added, "I have a favour to ask. Could you look in on my stepmom every couple of weeks—just to check on her? The people at the church are good about getting her to and from services and special events, and some of the older men clear the driveway and mow the lawn, but I think it would really mean something if a friend of mine came to see her every now and then."

"Otis," I said. "I can't every couple of weeks. I won't be able to. I'll be at university. But I can check on her whenever I come home."

"I'm sorry—I'd forgotten," said Otis. "I'd forgotten that the whole world changes—not just me. Dumb." He laughed. "Dumb, dumb, dumb. Don't worry about it, Pete. Maybe I should come home more often myself. It wouldn't hurt me to hop a bus every couple of weeks."

"Can you afford it?" I asked.

"I don't know," he said. "I'll try."

"Your mom would pay in a heartbeat if she knew it would bring you home more often."

"She's on a half-pension," said Otis. "She doesn't have any money to spare. I'll find a way."

"I promise I will visit when I come home, though," I said.

"Thanks, Pete," he said. "I really appreciate that."

We sat down on the bench and talked for a while about people we both knew, and then I drove Otis back to his mother's house. He gripped my hand just before he climbed out of the car. "You're a good guy, Pete," he said. "You're all growed up, you know?"

"I'm trying," I said.

"Nah, you *are* all growed up," he said.

CHAPTER THIRTY-SEVEN: A DARK EVENT

During the third week of August, Sharon began to stay overnight at our home from time to time. Dad told Conrad and me that this would happen just before dinner on the Friday. "Boys," he said, clearing his throat, "Sharon will be sleeping here tonight."

"Is she sleeping on the pull-out downstairs?" I asked.

"Um, no," said my dad. "She'll be sleeping in my room."

Conrad and I exchanged glances, but we didn't say anything. It was, after all, a natural enough progression, even if it felt a bit odd for us. I found I didn't mind very much, though it was awkward, later that night, when I heard the bedsprings squeaking rhythmically through the walls, followed by a quickly stifled cry from Sharon. *Oh my God*, I thought, *I don't need this*. But my chagrin dissipated at breakfast when I saw how happy my dad seemed, and how comfortably he behaved not only with Sharon, but also with us. He was relaxed in a way I couldn't remember his having been for a long, long time, and, reflecting on my own recent intimacy with Mo, I understood perfectly why that should be so.

"Did you hear anything last night?" I asked Conrad just before I went to work.

"No," he said, looking blankly at me. "Like what?"

"Oh, there was a dog or a fox yapping quite late," I said. "No big deal."

"Probably Mrs. Schumacher's poodle," he said. "She lets him out sometimes and then forgets about him."

"Yeah, that was probably it," I agreed.

But the peace of Sunday was shattered in the most distressing way imaginable. Shortly after seven. the telephone rang and I stumbled out of bed and got to it first. "Hallo?" I said, trying not to sound as though I'd been fast asleep twenty seconds before.

There was a sob on the phone, and for a horrible half instant I thought Mo had been killed and that this was her mother calling to tell me—memories of Mary-Lynne's death came flooding back. But the reality was almost as distressing. My caller was Noor.

"Petey," she said, weeping: "I'm hurt. He got me. He caught me."

"Noor?" I said. "Noor! What do you mean? How are you hurt? Where are you?"

"I'm at home," she said. "Can you come, Petey?"

"Yes!" I said. "Stay there! I'll be there in twelve minutes!" I slammed down the phone and turned to see my father coming out his bedroom door. "Dad," I said, "it's Noor. She's been hurt. Can I take the car?"

"Of course," said my father. "Shall I come, too? Has someone called an ambulance?"

"I don't know," I said, "but no, it's okay. I'll go alone."

"The keys are in the kitchen," said my father. "Call us."

"I will," I said, then I threw on some clothes and drove downtown like a madman.

★

Noor's housing complex was silent when I arrived at about seven-fifteen. I parked the car and ran around the first building and to the back of the second. Arriving at the front of Noor's apartment, I threw open the screen door, tried the handle of the main door, and then gave a good, decisive knock. A moment passed, then the door opened and I could just make out Noor's slight figure in the dark.

"Noor!" I said. "Are you okay? Are you alone? What happened?"

She did not answer with words, but held out her arms like a very small child. I swept her up, pushed into the house, closed the door with my foot, and took her into the living room, where I set her down on the couch. She had begun to weep quietly, and she continued weeping for the next several minutes while I stroked her hair. "Is your mommy here, sweetheart?" I asked, and she shook her head no.

At length, the story came out. Her mother was again away visiting relatives, and Noor had been left on her own. She had played at her friend Trudy's home in the front building on Saturday night and had eaten dinner there, and had set off for home after the sun had set. The man who had harassed her those months ago had been lurking at the side of the second building, and he'd grabbed her and dragged her into the stairwell, which he must have propped open. He'd assaulted her, threatened her with death if she told anyone, kissed her—a detail which occasioned fresh sobs—then left her where he'd taken her. She'd stayed there for minutes, hours, she couldn't say . . . and found her way back to her empty apartment where she'd lain sobbing on the couch until morning.

"Noor," I said. "Have you called the police?" I knew the answer, and wasn't surprised when she shook her head vigorously again to signal no.

"Do you mind if I call Mo?" I asked.

With her permission, then, I called Mo, and though it took a moment or two to persuade her father to wake her up, I was eventually successful, and I filled her in with a few terse words. While we waited for Mo to arrive I held Noor, again stroking her hair, and she fell fitfully asleep just before Mo and her dad came through the door—at which point she came fully awake and was briefly panicked. "Darling, darling," said Mo, taking over from me, "it's only me. Come, let's go to your room." And she escorted the little girl down the hall to her bedroom, leaving her dad and me alone for a moment.

"You haven't called the police?" said Mr. Howe.

"No," I said. "I've just been holding her. She needed to be comforted."

"Okay," said Mr. Howe. "But this is a police matter, you realize. That bastard needs to be dealt with."

"I know," I said. "I know."

So we called the police, and they sent a couple of officers— a man and a woman—and they began the process of taking a

statement and getting Noor to the hospital to be examined—a
journey on which Mo accompanied her every step of the way.
And I felt, as I have so very often, of two minds: glad to have been
of help, certainly, but sick at heart for not having reported the rep-
tile months before.

★

Noor's experience at the hospital was, Mo told me, very, very
difficult, though the doctor and nurses did their best to minimize
her trauma. As it was, she had not bathed after the assault, and so
the hospital was able to retrieve samples of her assailant—but getting those samples was a fraught process: Noor came from a culture where simply being seen naked by a man was a terrible thing,
so to have been raped, and then to be examined by a male doctor, rang every alarm bell possible for her. It was, ultimately, the
female police officer who put two and two together and recommended that one of the nurses take the actual sample. Mo stayed
with her throughout.

In the meantime, Mo's dad and I did our best to locate Noor's
mother, using a telephone list we found on the fridge. But, for
whatever reason, no one we called seemed to know where she
was or with whom. After we'd gone through the whole list we sat
looking at one another for a moment.

"Well," said Mr. Howe, "she can come and stay with us, I
guess, 'til her mother comes back."

"Or I can stay here," I said. "In the living room."

"Well, you could," he said, a little skeptically. "But she may
feel more comfortable in a home away from where she was
assaulted."

"Maybe," I said. I honestly didn't know.

"But she called *you*, didn't she?" Mr. Howe said, reflectively.
"Why don't we just give her the choice?"

"Sure," I said. "That makes good sense."

Noor made her choice when the police drove her home,
with Mo, in the later afternoon. She asked me to stay with her,
but the police objected, saying that if her mother couldn't be

located they would be obliged to call the Children's Aid Society. Noor immediately began to cry again, whereupon Mo offered to stay, too, and Mr. Howe offered their home as shelter—and in the middle of this, Aisha, Noor's mother, arrived.

I did wind up spending the night in the apartment, sleeping on my own sheets on the couch with a baseball bat at my side. Sometime during the very early morning the police found the man who had raped Noor, and took him into custody. I was at once relieved, and in some dark corner of my psyche disappointed that he hadn't tried to get in. I hated him in a way I'd never hated another human being before, and I would have liked to use my baseball bat on his skull.

Chapter Thirty-Eight: Seeing

The fallout from Noor's assault was significant: it was front page news, and though Noor was not named, in a small town like Queensville her identity was an open secret. The local newspaper published a fair bit of information about her assailant—a man with a string of past offenses for auto theft, common assault and making threats. He was not able to make bail.

Small towns can be ugly places, but they can be warm communities, too. Mr. Spurr was immensely agitated when he discovered that Noor was the young victim, and he had Mo and me deliver a huge basket of chocolates, books and stuffed animals to her home. And there were many similar gestures of compassion and support from citizens both prominent and little known. When Mo and I arrived with Mr. Spurr's basket, we found Noor's apartment filled with beautiful bouquets of flowers, delivered through the good offices of the local newspaper. A little more usefully, perhaps, a local businessman and philanthropist started a fund to help move Noor and her mother out of public housing, and several weeks down the road they were able to take possession of a very nice two-bedroom apartment some distance from the scene of the crime.

But that was still in the future, and in the present Noor felt profoundly violated and vulnerable. She had recurring nightmares, and she was fearful of going outside. And her mother, who had made some very bad decisions, was guilt-stricken to the point of immobilization. Mo and I visited every day, and we were distressed by how little progress we saw; our distress was not helped by the knowledge that we were going away to university in a matter of days.

Towards the end of the first week after the assault, with the Labour Day weekend approaching, I took Conrad to meet Noor, in the hope that Noor might see in him whatever she saw in me, and might find some comfort in his being in the same town after I was gone. I was moved when, after the visit, he volunteered to visit her every Wednesday to see how she was doing.

★

A few days before I left for university my mother called me at the museum and asked if she could take me out for a cup of coffee and a talk. She collected me at home later that evening, and we drove to a Tim Hortons donut shop. She'd lost weight, I noticed, and though she was once more nicely dressed and carefully made up, she looked a little gaunt.

"Are you excited about school?" she asked me.

"Yes," I said. "But I'm really sad about saying good-bye to Mo, and I'm worried about Noor."

"You can't think about those things," my mom said. "You have to keep looking forward."

"I can't help it, Mom," I replied. It occurred to me that *look forward* was the advice she'd probably given herself when she left my dad, and the mantra she was repeating to herself even now. But it didn't work for me. "I love Mo. I'm really going to miss her. And I don't know what Noor will do when we're gone."

"Well, yes, of course," she said hastily. "I didn't mean that you shouldn't think about them at all. I meant that you should put your focus on the future. This should be an exciting time for you."

"I am excited," I said.

"Peterborough's not far away," my mom said. "You'll be able to visit often. Maybe you'll even visit me, when I'm settled."

"Of course," I said.

"Your father and I are having to go to court," she said, adding a sweetener to her coffee, "so you may find he says some very angry things about me. Please don't take everything he says as gospel."

My dad hardly mentioned my mom these days, so this seemed most unlikely to me. "Why are you going to court?" I asked.

"Oh, it has to do with division of property," she said vaguely. "There's a lot of value locked up in that house." She stared into her coffee cup. "I deserve to live somewhere nice, too, Peter," she said.

I nodded. "I don't think Dad would disagree with that," I said.

"Well, we'll see, won't we," she said. We talked for a while longer, and then she drove me home, climbing out of the car to give me a hug, and hugging Conrad, too, who came out to see her. My dad stayed in the house.

★

Mo and I went to say good-bye to Noor together. She wept. Her mother wept to see her weeping. It was very hard. We promised to write to her, and promised to come by when we returned—which we'd be doing in October, for our high school Commencement. "We'll come by the day after, Noor—we promise," I said. It helped a little, but only a little.

After we bade Noor farewell, we went by a McDonald's and ordered fries and milkshakes. We sat across from each other in a booth, holding hands. There was an old man with rheumy eyes sitting at a nearby table, reading a book. Suddenly, without any apparent prompting, he began to read aloud. "This is my commandment—that ye love one another as I have loved you," he said, his voice surprisingly loud and strong. "Greater love hath no man than this, that a man lay down his life for his friends."

"Oh, God," I whispered to Mo, "a bible-thumper. Just what we need." The old fellow continued reading for a couple more verses, but two restaurant employees descended on him suddenly and ushered him, gently but firmly, towards the door.

"Oh, well," said Mo. "He meant no harm. And he's probably somebody's grandfather." She smiled. "I can just barely remember my grandfather—my mom's dad. He was a lovely old guy."

"My grandfathers both died before I appeared on the scene," I said.

"Your dad told me," she said, lacing her fingers in mine. "Are you going to stay true to me, Petey?"

"Yes," I said. "Will you stay true to me?"

"Of course I will," she said. "And I'll send you a postcard every day."

We drove out of town to a place in the woods, and made love for the last time that summer. It was sweetly sad, sadly sweet. And this good-bye also brought tears.

★

My dad and Conrad drove me to Peterborough on a beautiful Saturday in early September, the car loaded up with clothes, books and my modest stereo system. Conrad, in the back, was uncharacteristically quiet. I felt a little queasy. "Have you heard from Otis recently?" asked my dad, briefly taking his eyes off the road.

"No," I said. "But I didn't really expect to."

"Interesting fella," said my father. "I've always liked him."

Conrad's voice, newly broken, piped up from the back. "Do you ever wonder if certain people come into your life to teach you something?" he asked.

"Another country heard from," said my dad, smiling. "Are you thinking of Otis?"

"No, I was thinking of this guy at school who really bugs me," said Conrad. "He does everything he can to get under my skin. And I want to slug him. But then he'll go and do something nice, and it doesn't make sense. Most of the time I hate him, but . . ." His voice trailed off.

"I don't know, Con," said my father. "We're all bundles of contradictions. What do you think, Pete?"

"*I* was thinking about Otis," I said.

"What about him?" Conrad asked.

"I was thinking that he's a really good guy," I said. "I think he's showed me how to be a better person."

"Heavy," said Conrad. "Saintly Otis. *Saint* Otis."

I refused to take the bait. "Yup," I said.

★

The concrete spires of Trent's Champlain College were to be my home for the first of the next four years, and as we pulled into the parking lot I felt, briefly, that odd feeling most of us get at one time or another—the feeling I'd been there before. "I've got a strong sense of déjà vu," I said, the hairs rising on the back of my neck.

"Penicillin's good," said Conrad.

"Well, you've seen photographs of the place," said my father. "It could be as simple as that." He and Conrad accompanied me to a registration desk, where we found out where my room was, then the three of us hauled my gear to the third floor of one of the staircases. Already a couple of stereos were blasting away, and we caught a whiff of marijuana as we passed the second floor.

"Just like high school," said Conrad cheerfully.

My father frowned. "I hope they don't allow that stuff here," he said. Remembering my conversation with Hairy Jack, I thought that was likely a forlorn hope.

Half an hour later I said the last of my Queensville good-byes. And this one was just as tough as the others.

CHAPTER THIRTY-NINE: A BLESSING

My first several weeks at university were filled with exotic personalities and academic challenges. I found a group of friends fairly quickly in Champlain, then slowly began to meet people in other colleges, and so my universe expanded. I saw Hairy Jack once, on the bridge between Champlain and Otonabee, and I introduced myself—but he clearly didn't remember me. "We met on the bus to Toronto," I said. "Trent, Trent, Trent, Trent, Trent—the Personal Touch. Remember?"

"You've been smoking too much weed, man," said Hairy Jack, moving on, a pretty young woman in tow. She shot me an evil look over her shoulder.

"Philosophize with a hammer!" I called after him. But he did not turn.

If my head and body were solidly at Trent, however, my heart was still very much with Mo. We hadn't the money to call each other long distance, but we wrote every day—long letters in the week before classes began, and postcards thereafter. Separation and distance could not erode our affection for each other.

On the Friday morning before our Saturday evening commencement back in Queensville, Mo caught an early bus from London, arriving in Peterborough mid-afternoon. I met her at the bus station and we went back to my single room and made love and talked for hours. It was the sweetest of reunions. The next morning we caught the Voyageur bus and headed to the place we still saw as home.

★

The QDSS Commencement was a fairly big deal, though this year the school administration had inexplicably scheduled it on Halloween. Most graduates—male and female—dressed up nicely for the occasion, however, and their families showed up in force, taking their seats in long rows facing the stage at the front of the cafeteria. The school band had been deployed to provide incidental music, and the playing of "O Canada" signaled that the ceremony had begun. We graduates were arranged alphabetically in our own section, the better to expedite the handing-out of diplomas, so I was not able to sit beside Mo or my closest friends. Still, there had been some opportunity to greet people while we were assembling, and I'd hugged Janet Brightman and Patti, and shaken hands with John and Bruce and Big Andy and Stephen and Dent, and we'd quickly exchanged news of where we were and what we were doing. Stephen had defied the unofficial dress code, and was wearing an army jacket with his blue jeans. Dent's parents had clearly vetoed his following suit, but he was wearing his sunglasses.

After the national anthem was played and people had seated themselves, the principal made a brief speech about the graduating class. He wasn't a dynamic speaker, and his opening joke fell flat, but I was impressed with how well he seemed to know us as a group. I listened with growing respect for the little man with white hair. It occurred to me that he was much better at speaking to older students and their families than he was at speaking to the whole school.

The principal then introduced the local Member of the Provincial Parliament, and he made a boilerplate speech about embracing the future but not forgetting the lessons of the past. A certain restlessness grew in the crowd when he hit the ten-minute mark, but he plowed ahead for another five minutes anyway before winding up, to polite but unenthusiastic applause. The principal then introduced the vice-principal and announced that she would be reading the names of graduates, and that we should line up in our alphabetical ranks snaking from the front of the cafeteria to the back, and cross the stage to receive our diplomas from the provincial parliamentarian when we heard our own name called. It all sounded a bit awkward, but we rose, and moved obediently into a long line. As I did so I looked around and saw that my mother had slipped into the cafeteria—and was now sitting with my father and Sharon and Conrad (with whom I'd come). Truth to tell, none of them looked comfortable, but they were all there for me, and I was grateful for that.

The vice-principal, a Mrs. Buchanan, shuffled her papers, adjusted her glasses, and began reading the names: "Michael Aben. Gaby Adams. Christine Adrienne. Baillie Allen. Ian Armstrong. Susan Ashe." As she read each name and each graduate collected his or her diploma, posing briefly with the MPP while their family took a quick photo, the line moved steadily forward until I was very near the front myself. "Avery Deeds," said Mrs. Buchanan, and Avery was just beginning her own cross when there was a sudden commotion at the back of the hall. I looked back and had my second surprise of the evening: Noor was standing at the back of the cafeteria, and had opened one of the big doors and was holding it wide open—and Otis and two other native men, all three in full feather headdresses, were filing in. The two other men looked older, and they were both carrying drums.

There was a stir in the crowd. Mrs. Buchanan, who probably had the best view from her elevated position on the stage, looked a little alarmed, and she glanced sideways at the principal as if to seek direction. The principal took a couple of steps towards her, but he was equally at a loss as to how to respond. And then the drumming began.

It's difficult to convey the power of that drumming. Even in the open air, I suspect, it would have filled our ears, but in the enclosed space of the cafeteria it filled our hearts as well. It bounced off the walls and ceiling and it shook the floor; it made the lights shimmer; it sent a breeze rippling through the room— a breeze that tasted like northern lakes and pine cones and campfires. But no—the smell of fire was not simply an illusion: Otis had turned his back to us briefly, but when he turned around again he was holding a bound tuft of long grass and it was smoking. He held it still for a moment, then raised it in the air, and then he began to dance.

The sock hop in grade ten aside, I had never seen Otis dance—but then I had never seen anyone dance like this. At first it seemed little more than a purposeful shuffle, but swiftly his limbs caught the rhythm of the drums: his head arched back and his arms moved like the wings of a bird balancing, and his legs began to pound the floor as if they were drumsticks wielded by a divine drummer. It was weird and unexpected and mesmerizing and transcendentally wonderful all at once. But it was the wonderfulness that soon trumped everything else: as Otis danced, he began to move towards the stage, and as he did so he waved his tuft of long grass over each of us, smudging us—blessing us—with the smoke. And when he came to me, now just a couple of feet from the steps to the stage, he split the tuft in two with one swift motion, passed each handful on either side of my body, then danced up on the stage, describing frenzied circles with his feet as he moved, and shrouding everyone up there—Mrs. Buchanan, the principal, the Member of Parliament—with the smoke. And to my astonishment, and to the astonishment of everyone else in the room, Mrs. Buchanan, and the principal, and the Member of Parliament began to dance too, their portly white frames taking on an unexpected dignity in the embrace of the music. And even as they danced, my feet, and the feet of many of the other graduates, began to move, too—uncertainly at first, but with growing confidence as the rhythm of the drums moved into our bloodstreams and from thence into our arms and legs and fingers and toes.

And Otis continued dancing, moving off the stage now, and wreathing the smoke around those who had already received their diplomas, then moving back through the ranks of family and friends, and back and back and back until he was once more with the other two native men; and they beat harder and harder and harder on the drums for another minute, and Otis twirled faster and faster and faster, his hands holding the sweet grass high above his head—then, suddenly, silence. A long silence, pregnant with meaning and mystery. Then Otis and his companions turned and left the room.

And everyone—everyone in that hall—burst into wild applause.

Epilogue

All these years later, and the world has changed in ways few of us could have foreseen. Mo and I never did marry—though we had a good run, and even now we exchange Christmas cards and the odd newsy email. Big Andy and Janet Brightman lived together for a while, but they too went their separate ways eventually. John and Patti married while they attended Bible College, and raised three children who are now parents themselves. Bruce found a chickie-poo, and married her, and got divorced, and married again: he and his second wife are childless, but they breed Dalmatians in Winnipeg. I haven't seen Dent for years—though I'd be glad to shake his paw again. Stephen and I stay in touch: we've both gone through a bad patch or two in our quite different lives, but our unlikely friendship has grown. I'm always pleased to hear his voice on the phone, or receive one of his long, colourful letters in the mail.

My wife and I named our daughter Mary—a gracious concession on Claire's part. "I can't call her Mary-Lynne," she said. "But because Mary-Lynne died young—not because she was your first girlfriend." I understand that completely.

And Otis? An artist? A writer? A teacher? A lawyer? A Grand Chief? It's for him to tell his later story. But if you drive north into the country some distance from Peterborough, and take a left at an emerald-green lake in the heart of a provincial park, you might, in the right season, smell sweet grass and hear a wondrous drumming in the sky.

Paul Nicholas Mason

Acknowledgements

To Rachael Mason, Nina Mason and Michelle Berry for reading the manuscript and for their helpful commentary.

To Rachael Mason, Nina Mason, Denise Adele Heaps and Michelle Berry for reading the manuscript and for their helpful commentary.

To Michael Wilt, for his proofreading services.

To Chris Needham of Now Or Never for the act of faith.